THE
SCHEHERAZADES

by

Helen S. Vandervort

PublishAmerica
Baltimore

At the specific preference of the author, PublishAmerica allowed this work to remain exactly as the author intended, verbatim, without editorial input.

ISBN: 1-4241-7984-X
PUBLISHED BY PUBLISHAMERICA, LLLP
www.publishamerica.com
Baltimore

Printed in the United States of America

Don't cross the Bridge
Until you come to it.

Proverb

Dedicated to my mother, Helen Grace Bottler Stevens
1902-2006

ACKNOWLEDGMENTS

My deepest appreciation and love to the Blue Room Writers whose honest critiques and good companionship will always be remembered. Special appreciation goes to reader Dolly Hardy.

AUTHOR'S NOTE

"Be careful what you ask for; you might get it." What child hasn't heard that warning? Perhaps the same should go for authors: Be careful what you write; it might come true.

After retiring from a long career in public relations, I spent my time caring for my elderly mother, my husband and our home. Writing was a guilty pleasure as I explored the "what ifs" of fiction. With one novel published, it was expected I write another. Write what you know, they said. I know old people.

What if four mature women living in an elegant adult community got together to share life stories and maybe a secret or two? What if the main character were a cancer survivor? Little did I know when I wrote this book my husband and I would move to a senior campus, and that I'd become a cancer survivor? Perhaps I was writing about my deepest fears: aging and having cancer. So far, I am surviving both very well.

Finally, I'd like to assure my fellow residents at Touchmark at Mount Bachelor Village in Bend, Oregon, that this manuscript was written long before I met them. The few "real" portions are taken from my mother's experience in nurses training in Glendale, California, in the 1920's, and an article I wrote in 1987 for the local newspaper about Bend's first maternity hospital.

CHAPTER ONE

I've been here for three months and am still having second thoughts. In fact, I nearly told the movers to load up and take me back the day I arrived, except there was no going back. I'd sold my condo, my car, most of my clothes, and my toys—skis, bicycle, golf clubs. Even now, half my stuff is still in boxes shoved against the wall. Books, CDs, the few doodads I couldn't bear to part with, winter clothes and God knows what else wait my attention. The two or three pieces of art I'd not given away or sold are waiting for a hammer and a nail. Deep down, I know I'm here to stay, yet…

Death is out there, waiting for me to make a mistake—forget my medication, drink too many martinis, sit staring at the walls. What came naturally before—exercise, healthy diet, and mental challenges—now seem onerous. There are times in one's life when decisions shouldn't be made, particularly major ones like moving, or hiding from friends and family. But, hell, in less than a year I'd been hit with three biggies. For a control freak like me, a corporate buyout, which triggered retirement; the Big "C", and Jesse's death were not part of my long-range plan. Instead of developing a new mission statement and adjusting my goals and objectives, I bolted.

As I recall, my life took an unexpected turn when I heard a truck pull up to the side entrance of the building. Stepping out onto my second floor balcony to see if I could catch a glimpse of the new resident, I noticed other residents were curious, too. Curtains twitched and sliding glass doors opened for a better view of the boxes, bedsprings and belongings of the Villa's newest tenant. Well, what do you expect when the high point of the day is watching someone move in?

"The Villa Voice"—our weekly activity/news sheet—noted that Mrs. Carol Foreman would be joining us today, taking Suite 2B. Although I'm curiosity-challenged by some people's standards, I'll admit that I was somewhat more interested in this resident because she'd be living across the hall from me. Rumor had it that she was rich and well traveled, but that was said about almost everyone when they first moved in. Later, after clothing, furnishings and dinner conversation had been analyzed, some form of the truth rippled throughout the retirement center.

To get my mind off escaping from the Villa, I sat on the floor and opened a box of books. I tried to place them on the shelves in some semblance of order, but the subject matter was too diverse. Next, I tried placing them by size and color, but my heart wasn't into nesting. Taking a tattered copy of The Arabian Nights I stretched out in my leather Eames chair and began to read the tale of Scheherazade and how she saved her life by telling stories. The premise that death could be stalled, that time could be bought through intellectual cleverness, appealed to me. An hour or so later, a soft knock on my door brought me back from a magical land of wizards and beautiful princesses to the reality of the Villa.

I opened the door to a woman who had been tucked, sucked, and plucked to the point that she looked like a Stepford Wife—no, make that a Stepford Grandmother. She could have been in her late sixties, like me, but it was hard to tell with her meringue hair-do, its carefully arranged tendrils snaking down the sides of her face. There was something vaguely familiar about her, but at my age, nothing looks new, sounds new, or tastes new.

"Hello," she said, a tight smile pulling at her laser-smoothed lips. "I'm Carol Foreman from 2B."

"Hi. Val Kenyon, 2A." We stared at each other, trying to decide if we liked what we saw. How would she interpret my thinness, my pallor, my simplified hairstyle? "Welcome to the Villa," I said, not caring if it were rude to keep her standing in the hall rather than inviting her in.

"Sorry to bother you, but I wondered if there's a soda machine on this floor."

"Just around the corner," I said pointing down the hall. "Ice and a couple of snack machines, too."

We talked for a few minutes more, exchanging information about the views from our balconies—mine getting the morning sun and hers the sunset. Platitudes flowed easily between us—two women sizing each other up—neither making commitments to be good neighbors nor great friends. We were, superficially at any rate, getting acquainted.

I wondered how she would handle the gossip gauntlet. I still had the self-appointed communications clique confounded. It was quite simple to keep them in that agitated state: Neither confirm nor deny anything; never apologize, never explain. Depending upon the rumor of the day, I was either a snob, a recluse, or the contemplative type. There was a glimmer of truth in all that speculation.

"I hope you'll clue me in about the other residents—who to avoid and such. You know what I mean?" Did that mean I was acceptable? Perhaps I should warn her about me. I assume I telegraphed some non-committal body language as she continues her disjointed monologue. "Coming here wasn't my idea. I imagine the food here is geared to the tasteless and toothless. Maybe I can order in." She sighed and gazed down the hall. "Well, thanks for the information. I suppose we have to lock our doors every time we leave." I didn't know if that was a question or a statement, but discussing the merits of locking or not locking wasn't a topic I cared to explore in depth at the moment. We stood awkwardly at my door, as if to make sure the other person were through speaking. The burden of meeting new people, perhaps making a new friend, had become a chore. Yet, old friends and acquaintances were disappearing faster than replacements became available. Truthfully, I don't have a lot of friends. Acquaintances and business contacts, yes. Friends and family, no. But did it really matter at this stage in the game? Carol turned without another word and walked down the hall towards the soda machine.

The dinner hour settled upon the Villa with residents drifting downstairs for the first seating. Some would stop by the cozy bar for a drink before dining. I glanced at the weekly menu sheet stuck to the refrigerator with a magnet touting some long forgotten politician. Ham and lima beans, scalloped potatoes, fried chicken, vegetarian lasagna and angel food cake with champagne sauce—whatever the hell that was. No thank you. I would dine in this evening. I thought how strange that I was managing—more or less—to make a life for myself at the Villa, not yet missing the intellectual stimulation I'd once had. With a comfortable income of my own, I have all I need—a roof over my head and solitude. I like my own company; keeping the hours filled is easy, at times even interesting.

The Villa is part of an upscale retirement complex blending privacy and independence within an active community lifestyle, or so the advertisement said. That sounded good to me when I was searching for a hiding place. Each apartment has a small kitchen, a spacious dining-living area and one or two bedrooms and baths. Sliding glass doors to either a balcony or a patio fill the compact living areas with light. In all, the units are better than a box in an alley, I thought sourly from time to time.

That's not fair. The facilities are excellent—from the communal dining room to the Great Hall which functions as the gathering place for social events. If you're looking for company, there's always someone around for conversation, a cup of tea, a game of gin. However, a cup of gin and a crossword puzzle in the solitude of my apartment is more to my liking.

Across the street is The Haven, an assisted care facility for the failing and the failed who wait in luxurious comfort to die. It seems to loom large, quietly reminding me of my next stop on life's journey. Not that I feel close to that leg of the trip, but a cancer encounter sure makes you think, no matter how young you feel in your heart and mind.

I turn on the national news. The anchors report the crisis of the day with serious faces. More of our soldiers die in Iraq; a politician has charged the President with lies about the economy; a tropical storm in Sri Lanka leaves thousands dead or homeless. The President declares war on drugs. The human-interest accounts—a kitten saved from a drain pipe, and an interview with the world's oldest cricket player—are delivered with bright smiles and repartee between the sports reporter and the weather woman. The newscast could be a tape from twenty years ago and no one would know the difference.

Taking a micro brew and a wedge of Cambazola from the refrigerator, I add crackers and grapes to my dinner plate. Settling in the Eames, I put my feet up on the hassock and turn on Jeopardy. Alex Trebek is nattily attired, as usual; his contestants could use some fashion tips. I play along, rarely missing a question because none are on the Bible or Rap Stars. I feel foolish talking aloud to the TV.

Through the sliding glass doors to the balcony, I can see the soft spring twilight. As the evening darkens and Villa diners return to their apartments, lights come on one-by-one. Within the next few minutes I know my phone will ring and one of the Bridge group will ask if I'm ill since I didn't come to dinner, and would we still play tonight. Of course we'll play. It's the one thing I truly enjoy at this time. While I don't find the other three women particularly interesting, they're excellent players, and that's what counts in my book. Little did I imagine my social life would revolve around women who are old enough to be my mother.

Dee Ryan and Marion Barnes, both in their eighties, have identical dandelion-gone-to-seed hair styles. Their quarterly tight perms spring from their heads in glorious poufs. There's a four-week period when their hair is "just right." On either side of that, the perms are too tight or too limp. The topic of hair is one of their favorites.

Grace Bonner's hair is also of great concern to her. She keeps her long, thin white hair in a loose bun at the nape of her neck. She continually fights the silky strands, wailing at the injustice of not having pretty hair like Dee and Marion. My hair is neither a topic of conversation nor a goal to achieve since I keep it so short that all I have to do is wipe it down with a wet washcloth each morning. Three years ago chemo did its number on my hair. I'd worn wigs and scarves during my illness only to make other people comfortable. I preferred to be bald, just wearing a baseball cap for warmth. With remission, my hair returned with a nice wave. Its natural silver color had appeared soon after the divorce. But that's another story.

I place my plate and glass in the dishwasher, brush my teeth, and walk down the back stairs to the card room where my Bridge buddies have staked out their favorite table. As soon as I sit down, their attention is directed towards me.

"Aren't you just thrilled at having Carol Foreman for a neighbor?" gushes Marion.

The three look at me expectantly. What could I say? Carol looked like a California candy store with her pink enameled nails, teased hair, and glitzy braid encrusted designer duds. I thought she

15

looked—as the phrase goes—like she'd been ridden hard and put away wet.

"We just said 'hello'—that's all. We've decided to wait at least a day or so before becoming joined at the hip."

"Oh, Val. You say the funniest things. I don't understand them half the time, but they are funny, aren't they?" Dee says, looking to Grace and Marion for confirmation.

Marion pats Dee on the arm, leaning towards me and whispering, "Don't you know who she is?"

"I believe the Villa Voice said she is Carol Foreman and she confirmed that fact when I met her this afternoon."

"Yes, but she's really Arden Lamont!"

"And?" I said, shuffling the cards and fanning them across the table for the draw. Each of us selected a card and turned it face up.

"She's the writer! You know, the one who wrote steamy romances back in the '60's and 70's. I read them all. Her series about the school teacher who moonlighted as a stripper and became a detective..."

"Hey, are we going to play cards or not?" I interrupt. "My ten of hearts is high so I'll deal. Everybody got their money in? Dee, you're the banker tonight; Grace, it's your turn to keep score." I may have sounded a bit abrupt, but I was used to being in charge. Would anyone be more patient with me when I was eighty or ninety, assuming I lived that long?

They keep up the speculative chatter about the newest tenant as we sort our cards and settle in for the twice-weekly game. "Any special rules tonight?" Grace asks, turning to me with a mischievous smile. She's my favorite of the group—amazingly bright for her age, with a sense of being her own woman. She must have been a "pistol" when she was young.

"Rules same as always: We're allowed one brief comment about our state of health. After that, aches, pains and remedies are off-limits."

"Oh, Val. Your rules are so silly," Dee sighed. "All right. I'll go first. I've stopped using Polident and I'm using Fixodent."

We look at her, puzzled. Grace said, "That doesn't make sense. Those products have different purposes."

"Oh, right. Well, you know what I mean. Anyway, I've changed brands and I'm happy."

Marion said, "Ah, let's see. One thing. Ah...I have terrible indigestion tonight." Marion was heavy-set and legally blind. But with her thick glasses she functioned very well. We made sure the cards we used had large print.

"Did you take anything?" Dee asks sympathetically.

"Yes. A Tagamet. It should be working soon."

"I knew I was wise to skip lima beans and ham," I say. Chuckles and murmurs of agreement ripple around the table.

We look expectantly at Grace for her physical report. She removes her glasses, breathes on the thick lenses, polishing each one with a brightly printed handkerchief. As sweet and grandmotherly as she looked, her husky voice and ribald humor telegraphed her years in Montana cattle country as the wife of a large animal veterinarian. When Grace's husband died she sold her land to some movie star for an exorbitant price and traveled the world until brittle bones got the best of her. She wielded her three-pronged cane with style and dignity. A petite woman, she had a regal carriage. There was no keeping that lady down, I thought. Compared to me she was all light and laughter.

"To hell with it," Grace says. "I know Val won't tell us about her aches and pains. Let's play Bridge. No, wait. Have I told you about The Haven's newest guest? She looks around to make sure of our attention. "Well, a few days ago, a family brings their frail, elderly mother to the Haven and leaves her, hoping she'll be well cared for."

Dee interrupted to ask who told her about the new Haven guest. With a twinkle in her eye, Grace said, "Earl. Earl Smithers." I knew then we were in for a tasteless joke. Earl was the self-appointed comedian and ladies man of the building.

"He's a dirty old man," Dee said. "I won't talk to him."

"Oh, do get on with it," Marion said, frowning and shifting her position; she dabbed at perspiration forming on her brow.

"Okay. Well, the nurses bathed her, fed her a lovely lunch, and set her in a chair at a window overlooking the garden. She seemed okay, but after a while, she slowly starts to fall over sideways."

"Oh, the poor dear," Dee said.

By now, Marion had caught on. Giving me a wink, she leaned forward and pressed a hand to her ample bosom, stifling a belch.

"Well, two attentive nurses immediately rush up to catch her and straighten her up. Again, she seems okay, but after a while she starts to tilt to the other side. The nurses rush back and once more bring her back upright. This goes on all afternoon." "Oh, that poor woman," sympathized Dee.

"Later, the family comes back to see how the old woman is adjusting to her new home. 'So, Mama, how is it here? Are they treating you all right? they ask.'"

"'It's pretty nice,' she replies, 'except they won't let you fart.'"

"Oh that's terrible! You're just joking aren't you?" Dee said.

"Gottcha," Grace laughed with Marion and me, giving Dee's hand an affectionate squeeze.

Marion wiped her damp face with a handkerchief and took a deep breath. "Let's play. I may need to get to bed early tonight," she said. "Those limas are giving me fits."

I opened with two clubs; Marion passed and Dee asked, "Do you want point count or my best suit?"

"You can't talk across the table," Grace said.

"Well then, two diamonds."

"Pass."

"Three spades."

"Pass."

"Four spades."

"Double."

Marion led the two of hearts; Dee carefully arranged her dummy hand. I grunted with satisfaction at the fit of our two hands, played a low heart from the board and covered Grace's ten with my jack. Marion must have led away from a king, something she never did.

I made my bid and smiled broadly at the extra points my partner and I garnered from the penalty double. As we shuffled and dealt the next hand, the conversation once again turned to the Villa's celebrity guest.

"I wonder why she chose the Villa? She probably could live any where she wants." Grace said.

"Why not? This is a lovely place."

"Do you think she's still writing novels?"

"I haven't seen anything about a new book from Arden Lamont."

"I wonder if she's widowed or divorced."

"Probably divorced. I read someplace that she's had two or three husbands."

I let the others speculate about Carol's motives, lifestyle, and how compatible she'd be with the other residents. I yearned for deeper conversation, yet how could I expect that when I was so distant with these women, assuming they were incapable of discussing anything worthwhile.

"That's a rubber. Change partners," Grace said in her capacity as scorekeeper. Five rubbers later, we left for our apartments. I was seventy-five cents richer.

CHAPTER TWO

Flashing lights wakened me a little after one o'clock in the morning. I got out of bed and looked out the window at the canopied front entrance where an ambulance idled, its crew moving quietly and efficiently about their business. One of "us" was ill—or dead. Tomorrow there would be a large turnout for breakfast at seven o'clock. What happened? How is she or he? There but for the Grace of God…Who could it be, I wondered? The sweet Mrs. Wolper from downstairs? She must be over one hundred. Perhaps it was the woman who always wore red and wanted to tell you how sick she was, yet seemed to have more energy that most of us. Or…had Marion's indigestion gotten the best of her? I smiled at the silly notion. She said she was fine when we stopped playing last night.

I've never been a sound sleeper and it was worse now. But rather than fussing about it, I considered the early morning hours a gift of time for reading. No knocks on the door or phone calls would interrupt my solitude. Plumping up two pillows behind my back, I settled into bed again, and continued reading my old copy of Arabian Nights. The idea of postponing one's death by telling stories for a thousand and one nights appealed to me for some strange reason.

I fell back to sleep about four o'clock, but awakened at six, as usual. A hot shower to loosen up stiff joints, a cup of coffee, and I was ready for the day. I usually skipped the communal breakfast hour, opting for fruit and cereal in my apartment after a walk around the grounds, but after missing dinner the night before, I was hungry. No, that's a lie. I wanted to know who had been ferried over the River Styx. I guess I'm just as morbid as the rest of the inmates. I sat sipping coffee, watching the Today Show hosts doing their opening schitck. The knock on my door sent a chill through me. No one ever came calling this early.

"Val! Oh, Val," Dee sobbed. "It's Marion. She's gone!' "Her heart…" Grace said in explanation.

Arms reached out to me in consolation as well as in their need to be reassured that we had survived the night. I settled them at the table with coffee, listening to speculation and disjointed facts that Grace and Dee had gathered. Not that the details mattered. Marion was dead. How did I feel about that? I didn't know her well; I only spoke with her twice a week at the Bridge table. My own mortality jumped up and said "Are you next?" I wondered if I'd remembered to take my pills this morning.

Grace was saying something about the funeral. "Marion will be buried in Roseburg; that's where her husband is buried. But we'll have a simple memorial service here…that's the usual thing. Guess there hasn't been…a loss since you came."

"Sometimes family members come and share photographs and stories about…," Dee said. "Oh, I hope someone from Marion's family will come. I'm not ready to let her go."

I didn't really know what I was talking about, but I wanted to help, so I said, "I'm sure someone who loved her will come to close her apartment. Maybe that's when the memorial service will be held." Dee and Grace murmured and nodded as if that were the normal scenario.

A week later, after the cake-and-coffee memorial gathering in the Great Hall, Grace and Dee followed me up to my apartment, still not ready to let Marion go. We had—for at least the tenth time—berated ourselves for not recognizing the seriousness of Marion's discomfort at the Bridge table.

"I should have known she wasn't well when she led away from a king," I said, inviting Dee to sit down and holding a straight-backed chair for Grace as she moved carefully to sit.

"Indigestion isn't…wasn't unusual for her," Dee said. "She did love to eat. I guess there's not much pleasure in life except eating when your eyesight goes." We sat silently, lost in thought. I'd really miss Grace and Dee. Would anyone miss me? I heard Grace clear her throat.

"I hate to be crude," Grace said tentatively, "but what are we going to do about the Bridge game? Who could take Marion's place?" Grace looked at us, her eyes sad.

"How did the group get started? I asked.

Dee said, "The four of us—Marion, Grace, Donna Mason and I—moved in about the same time. We just found each other by accident or maybe water attracts its own level. When Donna moved to San Francisco to be closer to her family, we chose you because…Why did we choose Val?" Dee said, turning to Grace.

"Because she looked like she needed a friend," Grace said with a smile. Dee nodded, then filled in the details of including me in their group.

It felt strange to be discussed while sitting only a few feet from them. Grace looked at me and said, "All the other players were too slow or just didn't play at the level we prefer. But this time it's different. We're family now…" Their tears came again. I went into the bathroom for a box of Kleenex.

Family. They considered me family…and after only a few months. Perhaps they were family to me, too. After all, I hadn't seen my family for nearly a year. The grandkids and I exchange e-mail—mostly jokes and how-are-you-I-am-fine stuff. There are monthly phone calls—duty calls from my daughter. It's funny to think that my son-in-law likes me better than my daughter does. She just won't let go of the divorce baggage and my relationship with Jesse. But that's her problem.

"Here," I said handing the tissue box to my 'family.' "Is this a decision we need to make today? Just keep your eyes open for someone else who plays good Bridge. You might consider Jim Harrison. He's a good player."

"But he's a man!" Dee said in horror. "We don't want to bother with a man, do we?" Her hand trembled in front of her mouth.

Grace blew her nose loudly, seeming to dismiss my suggestion of Jim, and said, "I wonder if Carol plays Bridge?"

Dee's face brightened at the idea. "Val, would you ask her if she plays?"

My heart sank at the suggestion. I hadn't been drawn to the woman at our first and only encounter. "Oh…uh…let's let her get settled in. I'm sure you'll see her in the game room if she plays Bridge."

Grace and Dee discussed the pros and cons of asking Carol to join our foursome. "It would be a real coup, if she joined us," Dee said, in her soft, tentative voice.

"She'd be interesting to talk to," Grace agreed.

I folded my arms on the table, my mind wandering from my guests' speculation. Was I tired of playing Bridge? What I longed for was decent, deep conversation; in lieu of that, Bridge was a good substitute.

"What do you think?" Grace said, rousing me from my musings.

"Let's sit on it awhile," I said, having missed all the conversation that preceded her query.

"You're probably right," Dee said. "You have a way of just bringing it all together."

Over the next few weeks we tried various Bridge players. It got to the point where no one would play with us. They knew what we were up to, and no one liked being auditioned for a stupid card game. One day, Grace and Dee invited themselves to my apartment for martinis. I make very good martinis, if I do say so. As usual, the mysterious Carol a.k.a. Arden worked her way into the conversation.

"What's happened to Carol? I never see her in the dining room or on the grounds," Grace said. She and Dee looked intently at me, expecting great things.

"Have you heard something?" Dee asked, her eyes sparkling at the thought of some gossip.

Now I'm no gossip, but get a couple of drinks in me and I might say or do something I wish I could retract later. This was one of those times. "The staff checks on her daily, I believe, and there seems to be a son or daughter who drops in occasionally. I get the impression that they put her here. And, she takes her meals in her room."

Dee gasped at the thought of room service. "It must cost her a least ten or fifteen dollars a day in addition to the monthly fee!"

"Famous authors probably can afford it," Grace said. "Of course her fame was years ago. Maybe she made some good investments. Say…Let's see if she's in…ask her to join us. Okay Val?"

"Sure, why not." I sighed as I got out of my chair and went across the hall to the famous author's door. I tapped lightly, hoping she wouldn't be in or wouldn't hear me. No such luck. And, yes, she'd love to join us.

Introductions made, Carol declined a martini, preferring the bottle of designer water she had brought with her. We went through the usual tentative getting-to-know-you routine. Carol let us know immediately that she was a recovering alcoholic. Suddenly our martinis took on a sinister presence. I said I'd make coffee. Then Grace plunged right in and asked if Carol played Bridge.

"No, I'm afraid I never had time for that. I guess I always preferred telling stories to playing games, even when I was young."

An uncomfortable silence descended upon us. I could tell that Grace was unprepared for that answer; she gave a small cough, a nervous habit. Carol could have said she was a Life Master duplicate player, or that she'd love to learn to play Bridge. But just plain 'no' was not what Grace wanted to hear. Usually silences don't bother me, but this one did. I felt it was up to me to say something.

"Speaking of telling stories, I've been reading Arabian Nights. You remember the stories of Aladdin, Ali Baba, and Sinbad the Sailor?"

Carol perked up and said, "Those are the most famous stories, but the full version has some thirteen or fourteen volumes in translation."

"Really?" Dee said in awe, her eyes wide, as if Carol had made a very profound statement.

Carol beamed at us and said, "The volumes include fairy tales, legends, fables, parables, and anecdotes. I suppose some of the adventures were true and passed down orally."

"Oh, my," Dee said in wonder.

"Why are you reading a children's book?" Grace asked.

"No particular reason. I found this copy years ago in a garage sale for fifty cents." I reached for the old book now atop a stack of books beside my leather chair. "Here. The illustrations are delightful. The gory parts are left out. Guess Victorians didn't like their children reading about kings who kill adulterous wives."

Grace reached for the book and said, "I'm not sure I remember this." She slowly turned the pages.

Carol leaned forward and said, "It's also called A Thousand and One nights. What's the name of the king?" she asked, turning to me.

"Shahyyar."

"Yes. When Shahyyar discovers his unfaithful wife and her lover, he has them killed. His loathing of women is so intense that he marries and kills a new wife each day. Along comes Scheherazade with a plan."

I interrupted, saying, "The king was going to marry Scheherazade's sister."

"That's right. Scheherazade takes her sister's place to save her. Each evening she tells the king a story, leaving it incomplete and promising to finish it the following night."

I felt annoyed that Carol was telling about the book. It was my book, my story. I interrupted again. "She keeps this up for a thousand and one nights until the king sees the error of his ways." I wondered if I sounded as petulant as I felt. Who cares who tells the story? What's my problem?

Carol seemed to need the last word. "The stories are so entertaining and the king so eager to hear the end, that he keeps putting off Scheherazade's execution."

Dee took the book from Grace and said, "I saw a movie about Scheherazade when I was young. I think it starred Douglas Fairbanks, Jr., or someone like that."

"That must have been "Sinbad the Sailor," Carol said.

"Oh. Well, I liked the music," Dee explained.

"I'll just bet it was the music, Dee," I said. We laughed as Dee blushed a delicate pink. Her soft wrinkled skin looked younger for a moment.

Our conversation drifted to movies we enjoyed in our younger years. Carol must have spent most of her childhood at the movies. "Greta Garbo was one of my favorites. So sophisticated. So elegant. And her leading men...well, there were no men around my hometown that looked or acted like the ones on screen! Melvyn Douglas, Gary Cooper, Leslie Howard. I still think they're great. I knew I could never be a Greta Garbo type, so I thought I'd settled for being Barbara Stanwyck. I liked her attitude towards life," Carol said.

"When I was young I wasn't allowed to see anything with Mae West or Charlie Chaplin," Dee said. "My mother said they were vulgar. But when I see their old movies on TV now, they don't seem so bad. I just laugh."

"Once I left California for the wilds of Montana, my movie-going days were over for many years. But I've made up for that the last thirty years," Grace said. "I like the musicals—the more elaborate, the better. It's too bad life isn't like that."

"Oh, I love musicals, too," said Dee.

"Movies have always had an impact on people, particularly children," Grace said. "They learn how to dress, talk, smoke, drink, do drugs, have sex. That's why today's kids are such a mess now—the violence, the...coarseness."

"My mother certainly was influenced by the movies," I said. "Rudolph Valentino had such an impact on her that she named me after him." I couldn't believe that I was telling these women how I got my name. That was one of my deepest secrets. What's gotten into me, I wondered?

"That's charming!" Carol said. "I thought your name was Valerie. Valentino—or is it Valentina?"

"Valentina."

Yes. That's so much more elegant. I supposed you hated it?"

"Of course. No ones likes their own name."

"Tell me about it," Carol laughed. "My name was Carol Crank. Crank! No one has a last name like Crank! As soon as I got out on my own, I changed my name. First, I added an "e" to Carol because it seemed more...sophisticated. Then I tried out all kinds of last names. I was Carole Lamont for a while, but it sounded like I was related to Lamont Cranston—The Shadow. Remember that old radio show? Who knows, what evil lurks in the hearts of men?" she said in a staged voice. We laughed.

Carol continued. "Then I was Carole Courtland. I really thought that sounded grand...a fine name for an author."

"Where'd the Foreman come from?" Grace asked.

"My current husband—number four," she said.

"Where did you get the name Arden Lamont?"

"My publishers said I needed a *nom de plume*. They didn't like Crank any better than I did. They said Carol Courtland was too close to romance author Barbara Cartland. So I chose Lamont as my private joke and my agent chose Arden."

As the 'getting acquainted' conversation bounced politely among Carol, Grace and me, Dee had been sitting quietly, seemingly deep in thought. When she spoke, conversational gears were abruptly shifted. "What if we could do that? Stall our deaths by telling stories. How many years is a thousand and one nights?"

My banker's mind quickly did the math. "About two years and nine months. "What would you do with that kind of time, Dee, if it could be guaranteed?"

"I'd do something unusual, maybe a bit risky," Dee said. She frowned contemplating her options, then smiled. "I've always been afraid of heights, so maybe I'd take a hot air balloon ride! What would you do Grace?"

"Hmmm. I'd really have to think about that. Maybe I'd throw myself one whing ding of a birthday party when I turn 100."

My mind shifted to what I'd do with nearly three more years of guaranteed life. That would extend my remission to the point that—perhaps—I'd be cured.

Then Grace said, "What would you do, Carol, with the extra time?"

"Oh, I'd probably have another facelift. They don't last forever!"

We laughed.

"Let's do it," Dee said.

"What?" Grace and I asked in unison, wondering if Dee were thinking about getting facelifts.

"Tell a story each night. A real story, not joke stories, but real stories about ourselves."

A palpable silence settled over the room as we stared at Dee. Was she serious, I wondered? A put-down formed on my tongue, but a movement from Carol distracted me.

"That's a wonderful idea!" Carol said, for once seeming glad that she had been invited. "Women our age have so much to share."

Grace straightened up. "I like it. Stories about ourselves. We could each take a turn telling something about ourselves...about the real person."

The skeptic came out in me. "Surely you're not thinking of a consciousness-raising group. That went out in the sixties. Don't expect me to give up Bridge for storytelling."

Grace's face was transformed. "No, not that, but we have stories that should be told. I'll bet you don't know that I started a birthing clinic in Montana."

"Really?" we exclaimed in unison.

"I'd love to hear your stories," Carol said.

"You wouldn't be allowed to write them, though," said Dee, looking Carol straight in the eye. "If we are going to tell the truth, there may be things that shouldn't go out of this room."

"Oh, Dee!" I laughed. "Don't tell me you led a wicked life?"

"No, but, well,…"

"I know what you mean," I said, thinking that sometimes women have to destroy something to rebuild a life…like breaking sacred bonds, or family trust. But, then, sometimes, if we're lucky, we become who we really are.

Carol held up her hand, gaudy bracelets jangling down her thin arm. "Imagine your own biography based on the records you leave, the memories fresh in the minds of friends and family, the letters you wrote—if anyone saved them. Tell your story as if you were writing a book."

Dee looked worried. "But there are only four of us. We don't have a thousand stories to tell, do we?

Grace and I looked at each other and then at Carol.

"Of course we do," she said. "Childhood reminiscences, love stories, how we got into our careers, hopes and dreams that did or didn't come true, the good times, the bad times."

"What are the ground rules?" I asked. "I hope we get beyond sickness and death, although that's often part of our story."

Carol said, "Oh, don't worry about rules. Just share with each other, but look deep. Tell your stories profoundly."

They looked at each other, their faces flushed with the prospect of opening themselves, finding connections…and best of all…guaranteeing a thousand and one extra days of life. I didn't feel their enthusiasm, yet, maybe it would be fun.

Grace said to me, "You haven't told us what you'd do with the extra time, Valentina."

"Oh, I'd just…live."

CHAPTER THREE

E arly the next morning, I went down the back stairs to take my daily walk along the paths that encircled the retirement compound. Gated and groomed, secure and serene, Spring Hill at Bettencourt—which included The Villa—was someone's idea of a residential community for people over fifty-five. What is so magical about the number fifty-five, I wondered, breathing in the cool April air. Fifty-five was the speed limit on many roads; did the age fifty-five have a cosmic connection? Or was it simply that most people had raised their children by the time they reached fifty-five and had the income to afford a place like this? The youngest couple living at the Villa was in their late fifties and still employed. Why were they here, I wondered? Just to be free of routine household and yard chores? The average age of Villa residents was around eighty, according to the last census taken by the Marketing director. But these were active octogenarians; the pool and the weight room, the craft and card rooms were filled with 'Villains"—as I thought of us— talking, laughing and living each day as a gift to be unwrapped and enjoyed.

Striding past the Spring Hill Golf Club parking lot, I noted the number of Beamers, Lexus' and Acuras gleaming in the sunshine. Their owners didn't live at the Villa, but enjoyed single-family dwellings clustered on the hillside or the elegant condos bordering the compound's golf course. They were the active ones, not that those of us who lived at the Villa were beyond a game of golf or a brisk walk around the trails, but we needed—or wanted—a bit of care, perhaps pampering—after years of domestic chores and demanding careers. Some of us were unloved and unwanted; many of us didn't want to be in anyone's way. And some, yes, some of us, wounded by life and disease, just wanted to crawl in a corner like a sick cat and die peacefully.

I returned the friendly greetings of other walkers, but avoided stopping for conversation. One couple about my age was jogging towards the tennis courts. Tanned and fit, they were part of the 'snowbird' group who wintered in Arizona each year, returning to Spring Hill in April. Two older women, bundled up against the morning chill, were deep in conversation about constipation. I hurried on with a smile and wave.

As much as I tried to block out everything but the exceptional April morning, my mind drifted back to last evening's suggestion to tell our life stories to each other. Was there anything I didn't already know about Grace and Dee? Perhaps. Did I care about Carol a.k.a. Arden's life? Not really. But the bottom line was this: Did I want to share my life with these women? With anyone? Would it cure my cancer or make me happier to talk about the past? Probably not. The silly idea of guaranteeing a thousand and one nights of life was absurd. There are no guarantees. Telling stories can't alter our disintegrating bodies. Yet…what if the act of sharing, the commitment to the others, could enhance the quality of life and give us an edge to living longer?

An hour later, I was back at the Villa. Suddenly I was hungry. I hadn't felt this hungry in months. Chemo and radiation had made eating nearly impossible, and by the time my health improved, I was out of the habit of eating. Food no longer was a pleasure.

The dining room was still open for breakfast, but nearly deserted. Seated at a window table, I could watch the golfers chip onto the tenth green—unless they blew it and ended up in a water hazard or sand trap. Better them than me, I thought. Oh, I'd played golf—and wasn't too bad at it. But it was a business thing, a way to break into the Good-Old-Boys Club. My aggressive game helped me land the Trust Department manager position at the Bank of Boston early in my career.

The foursome on the green replaced the pin and climbed into their electric golf carts for the short ride to the eleventh tee, which was out of sight behind huge rhododendron bushes where buds were ready to explode into brilliant pinks and reds. I glanced at the menu. Pecan pancakes. I hadn't eaten a pancake in years. They were too fattening at one period in my life and then, later, food had become so unimportant to me that eating anything was a chore. When my order arrived and I poured warm syrup over the short stack, I was transported back to my childhood.

My father often made pancakes on Sunday mornings. It was the only thing he could cook, but he was proud of them and had convinced everyone in the family that he was the master pancake maker. He'd put walnuts or pecans in them sometimes. He dumped in corn or cheese, ham or anything else he thought might be good. We finally convinced him that pecan pancakes were best.

I wanted my father's love and attention so badly that I'd eat more pancakes than I wanted—or needed—since I was a chubby child, but I didn't catch his full attention until I chose my career, and then, it still wasn't enough.

Sunday was the one morning that the five of us—my parents, brothers and I—could have breakfast together. Father was away early during the week to catch the train into the city. Saturday he played golf, and mother always had some do-good meeting or hair appointment or dress fitting. Sunday was the maid's day off, so mother, father, Robert, Donald and I were a family for an hour. But now, all were gone except me. Bobby and Donny were lost in the wars. A heart attack got father, and breast cancer took mother. Now it was trying to take me; but I wouldn't let it without a fight.

I could tell Grace, Dee and Carol about my father's pancakes. That would be easy. But would they care? Childhood pancakes were hardly a serious topic. What had Carol meant when she said we should "speak profoundly" to one another? Was that the price we had to pay for an extra two years and nine months of life?

"Well, look who's here," exclaimed Earl Smithers, sitting down without an invitation. "And stuffing your face with pancakes. I never thought I'd see the day. How are you?"

"Fine, Earl. And you?"

"Fine as frog's hair, and that's pretty fine!" he laughed. "Where are your Bridge buddies?"

"Couldn't say. We aren't a matched set, you know."

"That's pretty obvious. You're one of a kind," he said with a flirtatious smile which looked more like a leer to me. "How about coming with me on the bus to the Indian casino this afternoon?"

"I'm not much of a gambler, and I hate the paper slips the machines spit out with your win/lose record. If I gamble, I want quarters and dollars to tumble out in a great racket. In my opinion, electronic gaming is the low point of high technology."

"Well, then how about taking in the movie tomorrow? Have a drink before dinner? Or whatever you want?"

"That's very kind, Earl, but no. Ask Grace. She's fun."

"I know she is, but I'm asking you. How about sitting in with our poker group?"

"Right," I said sarcastically. "I'm sure your buddies would be wild about having a woman at the table. Besides, I'm a killer player. They'd lose their shirts."

"Strip poker! I'd never thought it of you."

"Go away, Earl." I was tired of this silly sparing that passed for conversation.

"Never take life seriously; nobody gets out alive anyway." He squeezed my shoulder and left, saying, "I'll get you yet."

When hell freezes over, I thought to myself. If you ever touch me again, I'll break your arm, you silly old goat. However, for an old goat, he's nice looking, I thought as I watched him turn on the charm for two of the Villa's more fragile residents. They beamed at him and laughed coquettishly. Earl enjoyed his food and drink; he was robust without being grossly fat. Bald with a fringe of silver hair and matching well-trimmed mustache, he exuded warmth and good health. He'd been a salesman in life and was still selling. Yes, I thought, every 'home' needed a charmer to remind the widows what they once had: the ability to attract a charming companion. But at this point in life, I was still grieving over the death of my long-time friend and lover. Now there's a story the group might like, but not one I would share. Their generation probably considered lesbians a lower life form.

Pushing away my sticky plate, I tried to imagine opening up to Grace, Dee and Carol. Grace and Dee might be okay, but Carol was an unknown. What had she volunteered yesterday? Turned sixty-seven last month. No children of her own. Was still married to

Kenneth, who had Alzheimer's and was in a care facility. His son and daughter-in-law had put her in the Villa after her third session at the Betty Ford Clinic. She was bitter about being 'put away.' Well, I don't need bitter people around me. I've enough bitter of my own to open an English pub.

"Oh, there you are!" puffed Dee. "Grace sent me to find you." She sat down heavily, catching her breath and reaching for my untouched glass of water. Taking a long, slow drink, she replaced it carefully and dabbed at her mouth with a lace-trimmed handkerchief. "She's going to spend the weekend with her grandson in Seattle and she wants to know if we'll wait until she comes back before telling our stories."

"I didn't know we'd decided to bare our souls," I said. "Did we make a Devil's bargain to share our secrets?" Had I missed something or forgotten? Was this another 'senior moment' for me? We'd just kicked the idea around, but it was silly to think that anyone was really serious about telling stories to lengthen our lives.

"Well," Dee said, "we didn't actually say for sure, but everyone seemed to think it was a good idea."

"I doubt if Carol was serious," I said, hoping to take the pressure off myself. "She was just being polite yesterday, don't you think?"

"Maybe. But she said she likes telling stories. What if she just said that so she could steal our stories and write another novel?" Dee's face crinkled in concern.

"I really doubt that she's still writing steamy novels. Let's face it, Dee, we're obsolete, especially the steamy aspect at our age. Tell Grace that I promise not to share any stories while she's gone. By the time she gets back, none of us will even remember the idea."

"Speak for yourself!" Dee said in indignation. "You're younger than Grace and me, but you act like the oldest. What do the young people say now?" she said scowling in thought. "Oh, yes. Lighten up!" We both laughed. "Oh! I'm late for my crafts group. We're making table favors for the Mother's Day luncheon. They're going to be just darling with fresh flowers and ribbons. You should join us. You spend too much time alone. You need to see more people."

"You're sweet, Dee, but crafts aren't for me. Neither is Bible study, fitness class nor aqua aerobics. I can swim and walk by myself, and I have more books on my reading list than I'll ever get through."

"Fine, but you're always welcome. Let's sit together at dinner tonight."

"Okay. It's a date."

Dee bustled off, her craft basket overflowing, leaving a trail of lace snippets, pieces of thread, a stray button and a small Styrofoam ball. She wouldn't get lost, I thought; she could find her way back just like Hansel and Gretel. What's her story, I wondered? Never married, but has a gaggle of nieces and nephews who bring their children several times a year to mark her birthday or celebrate a holiday. As I recall, her younger brothers pay Villa charges. Why do they love her so much, other than she is pleasant to be around? Yes, I guess I'd like to know her story.

Before going upstairs to my apartment, I stopped for the mail and signed up for the weekly shuttle bus to the doctor's office. It was time for my six-month check-up, which I dreaded, yet each one was better than the last. Perhaps it was time to look at the glass as half full, not half empty; I trotted up the back stairs just to see if I could do it. The two flights left me breathless but invigorated. Yes. I do feel better.

When I reached my floor, Carol was peeking out of her door, as if waiting for me. Wordlessly, she beckoned me into her apartment and shut the door quietly. "I'm so glad to have caught you. I've been watching and watching! Look at this," she said shoving a crudely printed pamphlet into my hand. A quick glance was all I needed to know what it was.

"Found it shoved under your door?" She nodded. "This is from our mutual neighbor, Mabel Bleaker, in 2C. Obviously, she has given up on saving my soul and intends to save yours."

"God, no! I hate Christers. I had enough religion when I was a child to last me a lifetime. Anyway, even the Devil won't have me now," she laughed. "What's her next step in saving me?"

"There'll be invitations to church and the weekly Bible study session which she not only organizes, but leads when there isn't a visiting man or woman of the cloth. She's harmless, just annoying, unless you feel the need of spiritual enlightenment."

"Seems to me that people who read the Bible at this age are cramming for their finals." Carol sighed. "Spiritual enlightenment is nothing I crave or understand." She seemed lost in thought for a moment, then said, "How rude of me not to ask you to sit down. Would you care for a cup of tea?"

"That would be nice," I said, surprising myself. I didn't go in for having tea with my fellow Villains. While she chattered about the variety of people one finds in a facility like the Villa, I let my gaze wander over her apartment. French Provincial. Warm woods, flowered chintz, mauves and blues, fussy doodads on the coffee table and crystal-based lamps on the end tables. Good stuff, but too ornate for my taste. But then my leather, glass and chrome furnishings probably seemed pretty out-of-place at the Villa.

I visualized Grace's apartment, which reflected her years in Montana and her world travels. An Indian blanket hung on one wall, several English bone china figurines and a leaping trout carved from wood shared an end table made from a gnarled Juniper stump. Dee's apartment was an eclectic mish mash of furniture, as if she'd never had a place of her own. Her needlepoint pillows, crewel wall hangings and cross-stitched plaques reflected her interest in crafts. Her cat, Mr. Snow, added a homey touch.

"There," Carol said, placing a tray with cups and a teapot on the coffee table. Filling two delicate cups with steaming tea, she handed me one. "It's ginseng mint; I hope that's okay." She posed herself on the sofa, cup in hand.

"This will be a first for me," I said, inhaling the alfalfa-like scent. "I like tea but never think of making it. Guess I'm a hard-core coffee drinker at heart." I took a tentative sip and found it acceptable, but not particularly wonderful. "Interesting," I said, commenting on the brew. "Tell me what you think of the Villa now that you've been here a few weeks."

With partial attention I listened to her comments about the facility, the programs and residents. Why do I ask questions about things I don't really care about, I wondered? I used to be very interested in people and events. But lately, I'd turned so far inward that my listening skills seemed inadequate. At least the habit of being polite is still in place. I pulled myself back to concentrate on her monologue.

"...and I'm finally getting used to being cramped up in a small space. The food isn't very exciting. In fact, I've complained that we need a more interesting menu. Will you sign a petition regarding the quality and variety offered?"

"Hmmm," I said, wishing I hadn't accepted her invitation for tea. I didn't want to get involved in dining room politics. How do I get out of here without being rude, I wondered? I gulped the tea to get rid of it and said, "Well, thank you for the tea. I'd better let you get back to writing or whatever you do with your time." I placed the cup on the coffee table and rose to leave.

"That's the problem. I don't know what to do with my time now. I haven't written in years because I was busy taking care of Kenneth. But then his Alzheimer's got so bad that I couldn't handle him. I hate the look and smell of illness and age." She wrinkled her nose and took a deep breath. "He began wandering around the house, opening cupboards and closets, looking for God-knows what...peeing in the corners." A slight tremor rippled across her shoulders. She sighed, then said, "That's when we put him at Carlon Manor...about ten miles from our San Francisco home; they specialize in that kind of patient." She paused, looking intently at me.

I shifted my eyes from the expectant looked on her face, uncomfortable at whatever it was she wanted from me. I'm not a callous person, but instant intimacy...well, I'd kept people at arm's length for so long that it was difficult to embrace the problems of simple acquaintances. In my world of finance, deeply personal comments were considered extraneous, almost improper. She continued her story.

"After he was out of the house, I started drinking again...well, I'd already started drinking before that. His shouts, frightened cries...There's so much paranoia and hostility in Alzheimer's sufferers. Anyway, drinking seemed the only way to bear his deterioration. I was in pretty bad shape by then and got worse after he was out of the house." Again she stopped, as if waiting for a comment from me. When none came, she went on. "I sold the house with everything in it and moved into a hotel. Ben and Sheila—his son and daughter-in-law who live here in Oregon—were really pissed at me, but that was nothing new. They've always resented me." She looked away as if searching for a misplaced item.

By now I'd drifted a few feet closer to the door, standing awkwardly in my attempt to leave. I felt as if I were trapped on a long plane flight with a seatmate who wanted to talk. But Carol wasn't a complete stranger; she was—perhaps—a new friend.

Turning back to me, she continued. "I wasn't thinking ahead. Good thing I still had my apartment in New York or I wouldn't have had any furniture for here." She gave a rueful smile. "Anyway, Ben and Sheila and Kenneth's attorney did an intervention at the hotel. I guess the management called them. I get kind of…loud…when I'm drinking." A wry smile touched her sun-leathered face.

I stood quietly, my intent to leave evaporating. But Carol's monologue kept me silent. "Ben and Sheila used my unstable…my former alcoholic state…as an excuse to put me here for their convenience, taking me away from my friends in San Francisco." Again, she scanned the room with sad eyes. "Kenneth's trust says they must take good care of me or their annual stipend and inheritance is gone. I'm like the cat that a wealthy recluse leaves money to. The relatives go out of their way to make sure they can't be accused of killing the cat that lays the golden egg."

"Goose."

"What? Oh, of course. Goose."

She leaned forward, hands covering her face. Standing there—mentally out the door—I was at a loss. What did she need? I hadn't a clue how to handle someone who was fighting alcoholism and—what? Abandonment? I had chosen my isolation. She had not. The love of my life was dead. Hers was lost to a brain malfunction.

Fumbling for the clean tissue in my pocket I walked to the sofa and sat next to her, placing my arm around her shoulders. Accepting the Kleenex, she blotted her nose and eyes, smearing mascara on her carefully made-up face. "I'm so sorry. I didn't mean to fall apart. It's just that…sometimes…"

"Hey. It's okay. We all have moments like that. More tea?"

"Please."

So there we were with tepid cups of—to my mind—foul-tasting herbal tea, and her tears. "I'm so lonesome here. It was very nice of you to invite me to meet your friends. I don't know how to meet—these kinds of people. Not that there is anything wrong with them. It's just that I've always been surrounded with interesting, vibrant people. I really hate old people, well, not hate-hate. You know what I mean? I'm not ready to die; I'm not even seventy yet! I feel as if I've been put here to…hurry up the process." She straightened up and took a deep breath. "Shit. I don't really mean that. I don't know what I mean."

"I can relate to some of that," I confessed. "The only difference is that I put myself here…to…die…without bothering anyone."

"Die? You? You don't seem like you're ready to die," Carol exclaimed. "You seem so full of life."

I had no response to her observation. It would take too much explaining, sharing. I shrugged my shoulders and said, "Are you okay now?"

"Sure. Anyway, I've got a spa appointment." She took a hard look at me, frowning. "Why don't you come with me? I'm sure I could get them to work you in for a facial or a massage."

"Oh, no. But thank you."

"No. It's not a problem. A massage. My treat. I'll call now and then we'll get a taxi, if the Villa shuttle won't take us to Indulgences—that's the spa I go to.

"No, really. I can't today; I have a doctor's appointment." A small lie, but what the hell; the appointment was later in the week.

"Are you ill?" Her eyes grew wide with concern.

"Not exactly. It's just a routine check-up."

"Well, then. We'll go together sometime when you're free. I go every week for the works. What do they say? Beauty is better than brains, because men can see better than they can think." She gave a musical laugh at her own joke. "The spa's the only thing I look forward to around here. Please come next week. My treat. I'll make all the arrangements." My body language must have telegraphed a negative reply. "Please," she said with the look of a lost child, a very old lost child.

"Fine," I said, backing out the door. "Thanks for the tea."

"Thanks for the sympathy," she smiled. 'Tea and Sympathy"…wasn't Deborah Kerr in that movie?"

I smiled and shrugged, heading across the hall to my apartment, when Mabel Bleaker burst out of her apartment, yoo-hooing to Carol, who quickly closed her door. I was in for a Gospel Moment.

Mabel didn't look like a gung-ho Evangelist. She seemed quite normal—no blazing eyes or prim hair and clothing, in fact, she looked quite motherly. Her soft, round body in its pastel knit suit made her look like an Easter marshmallow treat. Her gray hair featured short bangs, reminding me of First Lady Mamie Eisenhower; rimless glasses magnified her smiling hazel eyes. Her obviously false teeth occasionally clicked when she spoke.

"I guess she didn't hear me," Mabel said. "I was going to invite her to Bible study." She stood looking at me as if I might ask to come. "You're welcome, too, of course...anytime..."

"Thank you, but no. Have a nice day, Mabel," I said grinning, my face feeling like the yellow cycloid that went with the trite phrase.

"Jesus loves you."

Right, I thought sarcastically. He's really got time to think of me, to cure me, to help me, even if I cared enough to asked Him.

CHAPTER FOUR

That evening, just as I turned the doorknob to leave my apartment, a quiet knock startled me. It was Carol. "Carol! I was just going down to dinner."

"I thought you might be. Any chance that I could go with you…of course if you've made plans, or…"

"No problem. Dee said she'd get a table. I'm sure there'll be room. Come on. I always take the stairs."

We descended in silence, watching our footing. Not too long ago, I would have run down the stairs, but now, I was more careful about a lot of things: stepping in and out of the shower, crossing streets, lifting things. It was hell to get old, but, as they say, considering the alternative…

"I'm glad I caught you," Carol said. "I've been thinking about taking some of my meals downstairs, but the first time is so…"

"Uncomfortable?"

"Yes! But I need to get used to this place since I'm going to be here for awhile."

"You could leave if you wanted to, couldn't you?"

"Oh yes. I'm not…a prisoner. I'm just a little afraid to be out on my own until I'm sure I've got the drinking licked…not that it ever is."

"Have you thought about attending The Villa's AA meetings?" I asked.

"Not yet. I was surprised that they had a group here. I suppose I should."

"What about going back to San Francisco?"

She sighed, then said, "You see, if I went back to San Francisco and my old friends, I'd be right back into a lifestyle that isn't conducive to being 'dry.' Going home is my 'carrot.' I'll go back again. I'm just giving myself a chance to..." Her voice trailed off as we encountered other residents drifting into the dining room.

"What would your...family do, if you went back?"

"Probably make a lot of noise, threats. They don't really care. It's a power trip for them right now. If Kenneth knew who I was...or if I could do anything for him...even the doctor doesn't think he needs me. Kenneth is...has...become quite...unmanageable."

This was more than I wanted to know. I felt that I should say something sympathetically profound or comforting or helpful in some way. But nothing came to the fore. Instead, I gratefully spotted where Dee was sitting. "There's Dee over by the window. She'll be thrilled to dine with our famous author," I said with a grin that reflected the huge smile on Dee's face as she saw us walking toward the table she had staked out by the corner window. Pink clouds hinted at a sunset, the first we had seen after a week of rain.

"Carol! Sit here so you can see the sunset," Dee said, trying to rise from her chair.

"No, no. Sit. I'll be fine here," Carol said, taking the chair that put her back to the wall.

Watching her eyes skim the room, pausing at one or another diner, I found myself wondering if she were taking mental notes for characters in a new novel, or just sizing up the other residents? Did she see what I saw? Hair in various shades of gray—ash, steel, pearl, dove, platinum, mouse—with an occasional dark dye job that looks like hell on old people. Eyeglasses in pastel plastic, silver and gold-rimmed, no rhinestones. This was a classy group. Waistlines thickened or gone. Sun-weathered skin, sallow and mottled; soft, pink baby faces. Facial expressions running from blank or sad to smiling and animated.

Dee was babbling on about how happy she was to see Carol and that she hoped Carol would eat with us every day. She apologized for the food, saying that she knew Carol must be used too much fancier fare, but, with so many old people—she didn't think of us as old, of course—the others enjoyed things like mashed potatoes and gravy, and macaroni and cheese.

"Yes," Carol agreed. "It's gastronomic Musak. If I see one more dish of Jell-O, I'll scream." I nodded in agreement, but Dee just looked puzzled. Carol continued. "I've contacted a wonderful caterer I used to use in San Francisco. He said he'd send me menus and recipes that could be used here. Now whether the management will be receptive to my suggestions is another matter."

We perused the menu sheet and gave our orders to the perky waitress. The high school and college-aged staff beamed and bubbled, teased and treated us as if we were their grandparents. The cynic in me imagined a class on how to act like an ideal grandchild. Well, it was a nice touch, if that were true. Even I enjoyed seeing fresh young faces and hearing about their college plans or what they would do when they finished school.

"The lamb stew looks good," Dee said. "And lemon pie. I love lemon pie. If I do say so, I used to make good lemon pie. It was a favorite of the twins—my younger brothers," she explained to Carol. "Do you have any brothers or sisters?"

It seemed to me that Carol took a long time to answer a simple question, but finally she smiled and said, "Four younger brothers."

Dee and I waited for some type of elaboration. None came. Dee took up the conversation banner. "I have—had—an older brother who became a priest and an older sister who became a nun. Both were high in the Church, but they're gone now. I don't know how I managed to outlive them," she said with a sigh and a shrug. "I also had two other sisters, who are gone now, and another brother, but he died of pneumonia when he was twelve; then the twins came. I was eighteen when they were born; they were like my own babies. Mother was too ill to care for them. My family is so good to me, always remembering my birthday and the holidays. And their children and grandchildren are so thoughtful, too." Dee rummaged in her purse. "Here's a photograph taken last Christmas. I'm sure you'll get to meet them. They phone and write and, well, they are just wonderful to me. A favorite grand-niece—Mary Alice—often comes for a visit. She's quite a character!"

I chuckled at Dee's description of the teenager. "Every time she visits, it sets the gossip machine in motion. You'll enjoy meeting her," I said.

"Do you have siblings?" Carol asked me.

"Two brothers, both in the military. One died in Korea when he was in his twenties, and the other in Vietnam. He was an early advisor in that war."

There were murmurs of sympathy. Funny, I never thought about them any more. Even though we had been close in age, we were never close as siblings, but as adults we reconnected.

"Then you're from a military family?" Carol asked.

"Oh, no. The boys were to be bankers like father. I was to be a gracious lady like my mother. The boys rebelled and went into the military. I rebelled and became a banker. Life is funny." My dinner companions nodded, agreeing that life, indeed, is strange.

"Look, look," whispered Carol, motioning her head to one side. "That woman is pouring French Dressing on her green Jell-o. Is that her idea of green salad?"

"Well, yes," Dee said in support of the action. "Betty can't eat raw vegetables, but she likes French dressing."

"Whatever works for her," I said, wondering if the day would come when crisp salads would be a thing of my past.

The decibel level of the dining room increased as late diners— those who had stopped by the Villa lounge first—filled the remaining tables. Just as we were slicking up the last of our lemon pie, Jim Harrison came over to the table and asked if I'd be a fourth for Bridge. "Guy's gout is bothering him," Jim explained. "Bob and Marv said they'd be pleased to take your money tonight."

"Tell them to be sure they have cash; I don't take checks from hustlers," I said, pleased to have been invited to play. I needed a Bridge fix; it had been weeks since I'd played.

Introductions were made, with Carol turning on the charm as if she had a switch for it. She looked particularly lovely this evening. The afternoon at the spa must have included the works—facial, hair, nails, probably a pedicure, too. It would be fun to try the spa, I thought; it had been a long time since I'd done that. Perhaps I'd accept her invitation for an afternoon of being pampered.

Jim seemed quite taken with Carol, but what man wouldn't be. After all, she was attractive in an artificial way and an author to boot. Being a retired engineer, Jim had probably never read her books, but being published, in any form, has a certain cache to it. Ah, men, I thought. You're as easy to read as a cheap novel.

"I hope we'll see more of you around the Villa," he said, smiling at Carol, then turned to me. "As soon as you're ready, we'll see you in the card room."

The three of us watched him leave. I wondered what Carol was thinking; I didn't have long to wait.

"He's certainly charming," Carol said. "Widowed? Divorced? Still married?"

Dee had all the particulars. "He's been widowed for about two years. He was a structural engineer, traveled all over the world, but settled here to be close to his daughter. She wanted him to live with her, but he can't stand his teenage grandchildren. There are four of them I believe. At least that's what Millie told me. She had set her cap for him when he first came, but he either wasn't taken with her or just isn't interested in anyone. Val is the only woman he talks to very much."

"Do you have an interest?" Carol asked me, a knowing look in her eyes.

"Good heavens, no. He only talks to me when they need a fourth for Bridge. They're a pretty hard-core bunch, rather like our group was until Marion died." The mention of Marion seemed to bring the pleasant dinner to a sad close.

Dee said, "I miss her so much. I hate being this age, knowing new friends, as well as old, are going to leave us. You'd think we could feel differently about it."

"I know what you mean," Carol said. "There should be some molecular change that gives us the strength to deal with the loss of those we love."

Carol didn't sound sincere to me; it was as if she were trying out bad dialogue for one of her novels. We sat quietly, lost in our own thoughts. I was thinking of Jesse, dead now for over a year. I didn't know if I missed her more as my best friend or as my lover of many years. There were times when I yearned to be held, kissed. My mastectomy had made no difference to Jesse, of course. She'd even been more tender and caring. But now that she was gone, I was on my own again. Not that I wanted a new lover, just a companion for good conversation, a museum prowl, or an excursion to a new restaurant. Jesse and I loved finding new places to eat. We went through our truck-stop phase, looking for the illusive piece of pie that legend said existed on the road. I'm sure our cholesterol shot up fifty points by the time we lost interest in highway pastry and went back to ethnic foods.

"Well, if you'll excuse me, I need to separate some money from the men. Glad you joined us, Carol. See you tomorrow." What a strange thing for me to say. In the past months, I didn't want to see anyone. I wasn't even drawn to Carol at first, and here I was committing myself to more—spa trips, dining, perhaps storytelling. I wondered if the others had forgotten about telling a thousand and one stories. Probably, and that was fine with me.

It was a little after ten o'clock when I returned to my apartment, three dollars richer. It had been fun to play Bridge again; I agreed to play with them the following week. The blinking red light on the answering machine caught my attention. Pressing the Play button, Dee's breathless voice instructed me to call her, no matter how late it was. She had heard from Grace.

The long and the short of it was Grace had fallen and broken her hip while visiting at her grandson's home in Seattle. She'd been taken to the hospital and the hip was pinned. In a few days she would be transferred to the rehabilitation wing. This was a lucky move, according to Dee; usually when old ladies break a hip they are shuttled off to a nursing home and left to die, often within a week.

"The doctor must have seen something special in Grace," Dee surmised. "She can be very determined, and that's a good thing because she'll have three hours of physical therapy every day once she is admitted to rehab." Dee's animated voice while telling me all this confirmed my impression that getting people well and back on their feet was her aim in life. "Then, guess what?" Knowing I wouldn't guess, she rushed on with more details. "She'll be in rehab for about a week or ten days. They'll teach her to dress and bathe and when she's ready, she'll go to Jeff's—that's her grandson—for a week or so. They've asked me to care for her!"

"Won't that be difficult for you?" I asked. "You know...the lifting and such."

"Oh, no. They'll have home health care people for all that. I'll just be there to keep her company so she won't be home alone while Jeff and his wife are at their business, their furniture store, you know.

When she's ready to come home, back here, Jeff will drive us in his motor home."

"You sound really excited about this."

"Oh, I am. It's so nice to be needed again. Grace's youngest daughter, the one who lives in Portland, is going to drive me up to Seattle when she goes to see her mother."

"Do you want me to water your plants while you're gone?" Am I out of my mind? I hate being responsible for other people's plants.

"That would be lovely. You're so thoughtful." She paused for a moment, and then inquired, "How about feeding Mr. Snow?"

"I don't do cat boxes," I laughed.

"Oh,no. I'll have the cleaning staff do that, even feed her, if you didn't want to do that. But if you'd just pet her once each day…"

"Well…"

"I'm sure she likes you."

Dead air filled the space as I thought about it. "Okay. Water plants, feed and pet the cat."

"Oh thank you! Well, good night. It's late. Not that I'll be able to sleep thinking of Grace. I hope she's not in any pain."

"Good night, Dee."

"Yes. Good night."

The second message on my answering machine was from my daughter, Kara, saying that her father had suffered a stroke. The message went something like, "Daddy is in the hospital, not that you'll care…"

I replayed Kara's message, glanced at my watch and calculated that it would be after one o'clock in the morning in Boston. My response could wait; there was nothing I could do at the moment.

After making a cup of hot cocoa in the microwave, I stretched out in the leather chair, feet up on the hassock, and thought about Charlie and my daughter. It seemed strange that Kara—now forty-five years old—still referred to her father as "Daddy." By now, I mused, "Dad" seemed more appropriate, or even "Charlie." After all, she called me "Val" rather than Mom. But I understood why. I suppose it was her way of showing her general disapproval of me. In her mind, I had been such a poor wife that I drove Charlie into the arms of another woman, putting Kara into the broken-home group of kids. Thirty-five years ago, having divorced parents was no status symbol.

Early the next morning, I called Boston and caught Kara before she left for her job as a part-time art instructor at Fernwell, a small private school in the Welsley area. My son-in-law, Duncan Burgess, was headmaster of the school. I could never understand why he liked me, despite what Kara might have told him; he made sure the three grandchildren and Kara kept in touch.

"Daddy's stroke has affected his right side," Kara said. "For some reason, he wants to see you."

"Of course, if that's what he wants. Do you have a problem with that?"

There was a long silence before she spoke. "No."

She said 'no' but I knew her well enough that she didn't mean it. "When do you suggest I fly back?"

"As soon as possible, I suppose. Do you want to stay here or…"

"A hotel is fine."

The well-known pregnant pause filled the phone line. "No, stay here. Duncan and the children will want to see you," she said.

"Thank you. I'd like to see them, too; it's been a long time. I probably can get out sometime tomorrow; I'll let you know my flight plan later today."

We hung up without further words—no "good bye" or "I love you. Not even "It'll be good to see you." We were always cordial, never overtly hostile, but there was no spontaneous warmth. Perhaps this visit will give us the opportunity to clear the air for good; I'd tried before, many times, but she wasn't ready. Would she ever be?

After buying a ticket on line, I did my laundry and straightened up the apartment; my mind drifted back to the night Charlie told me he wanted a divorce. We were reading in bed—me, a copy of Forbes Magazine; Charlie a medical journal—when he said, as causally as asking for a cup of coffee, "I getting a divorce." I smiled at the recaptured scene, remembering how I had covered up the knot in my gut with a smile then, too.

"I beg your pardon," I responded in as a controlled voice as possible.

"A divorce. You know things haven't been good for a long time. Let's be adult and flick it in before we invest any more time and energy."

"Why?" I asked, knowing full well the answer.

"Just think about it; you know why. Anyway, I'm in love with someone else. So, let's be civilized and part on friendly terms before we damage each other."

"Damage each other. Hah! What about Kara?"

"I won't fight you for custody, but I want her weekends and holidays."

"Wait just a damn minute!" My voice escalated to a pitch I knew he hated. To hell with being civilized, I thought. "You can't divide up a ten-year-old like household goods. I'm surprised you aren't suggesting that we flip a coin for her. Or doesn't your new love want the responsibility of a child?"

"She loves children. In fact…we're expecting a baby…soon. You'd never have more children…"

"Damn straight I wouldn't until I could stop working. But no, we needed money for med school tuition, for your practice, for your partnership." I remembered how the words came out in clumps as if they by-passed my brain, forming on my tongue without benefit of intelligent thought. One child in day care, a full-time job and bearing the entire household burden was all I could handle at the time. And, whatever feelings I'd had for Charlie were long gone. I bolted from our bed and began pulling underwear, sox and shirts from his dresser drawers. "Not one more minute in this house. You're out of here, Charlie!" It was as if I welcomed the split and couldn't wait until he was out of sight.

"Now don't go off half cocked," he said, putting aside the medical journal and carefully placing his reading glasses on top of it along with a yellow marker he had been using to highlight passages in the JAMA article. "You know there's more to this than money."

"Yeah. I'm a cold bitch, as you've so often said."

Ignoring that remark, he said, "We'll do this in a civilized way. I'm using John as my attorney; why don't you use one of your father's attorneys."

"Believe me, I'll get a junkyard dog for representation," I had said. "You'll pay alimony as well as child support…and I want the house. All the years I've supported your career. You own me big time, Doctor Charles C. Kenyon the Third. You'd better get your suitcase. You're out of here as of now!"

I must have been a sight that night, make-up washed off, ratty old pajamas, hair wild, ranting and raving, throwing his clothes on the floor. Not cool. Particularly not cool when Kara was discovered crying at our bedroom door. Charlie got to her first, comforting her and establishing me, through his words and actions, as the bad guy.

I pushed the memories from my mind and packed for my flight to Boston the next day. This would be a trip for healing.

CHAPTER FIVE

The 747 climbed through the broken clouds over Portland International Airport, banked and headed east. This was the first trip I'd taken since moving to The Villa. It felt good to be swept up with the energy and hassle that cross-country travel generates. Out of habit, I booked business class; first-class seemed extravagant and coach was a royal pain. How quickly and easily the tricks of travel came to mind after the seemingly million miles I'd logged during my years as CEO of Pacific Trust International. I pushed my seat back a notch and gazed out of the window. The clouds were thinning; by the time we reached the Rockies, I could look down and see the silver of meandering rivers and the green patchwork of farms and ranches of America's heartland. In spite of the scenery, my mind drifted back to The Villa.

My months of self-imposed semi-isolation evolved from preparing for death to acquiring a new circle of acquaintances, from health concerns to continued remission. I was feeling stronger each day and my attitude towards life had changed. How could I have allowed myself to sink into self-pity, I asked myself? For an in-charge person, I'd let myself wallow in unproductive thoughts and actions for too long. It was time to get back on track. What was I waiting for? A spiritual epiphany? I'm a survivor. How strange, now, to think, "brush" with cancer, not "death sentence" as in the past. It amazed me that I was finally beginning to think of the damned disease as an encounter, not a "done deal." An understanding of what other cancer survivors tried to tell me while having chemo and radiation was finally taking hold: Attitude was as important as treatment and following the doctor's instructions. Yes. The Big C and I are face-to-face, and I'm going to win.

My mind continued to bounce from thought-to-thought like the turbulence bumps that marked the flight as we crossed the Rockies. These new friends were an unexpected twist to what I'd imagined my Villa confinement to be. I thought I knew them, but really didn't. We'd never talked of our expected destinies—flirtation, marriage, motherhood, careers. How had the rapidly changing mores of the Twentieth Century made Grace's experiences different from mine? What cultural perspective in our homes led us to make our choices? Yes, I thought; I'd like to know why Grace and Dee made certain choices. Carol, too.

I thought of my teenage grandchildren—Callie fifteen, TJ seventeen and Jordan nineteen—with lives much different when we women were that age. In fact, there was no such thing as a teenager when we were growing up. Our adulthood came quietly as we took full responsibility for ourselves. Once puberty hit, we were expected to put away childish things and take our place in the home, the community and the world, assuming responsibility for our behavior, earning our freedom, as we proved capable. Some began working at twelve or fourteen in dangerous situations-—mines, factories, and agriculture. My generation was luckier than Dee's or Grace's; by eighteen, most of us were either in college, working, or married and starting a family of our own.

Now, I was in my second adulthood, not old age, not yet. I picture Baby Boomers Kara and Duncan going through their mid-life crises when the kids are gone. Would Duncan buy a Harley? Would Kara get a facelift or have an affair? Would their avocations become their new vocations?

My reveries are interrupted when the steward asks me to lower my tray. Lunch is served. Would the food still be as bad as before, or worse, I wondered.

My seatmate expressed my thoughts as he pealed the top off some hidden delight. "I usually skip lunch, but I didn't have time for breakfast this morning," he said as if apologizing for enthusiastically digging into the chicken breast crouching in the plastic container.

"Hmmm," I nodded in understanding. "When I had early morning flights, I'd often bring a couple of big oatmeal cookies from a health food bakery near my home. With juice and coffee, they were a better breakfast than the one served."

"You traveling on business or pleasure?" he said, as he struggled to get his dessert bar out of the hermetically sealed plastic envelope.

"Both. I'm going to visit my grandchildren in Boston and then go to Denver, before I return to Portland."

We chatted a few minutes more until the trays were removed, a signal that seat mate conversation could end.

Here I am, dressed in one of my tailored suits, briefcase tucked under the seat in front of me on a 747 headed across the continent for a visit with my family and ex-husband. How strange that a sickbed request from a man I once hated—and loved—would be the impetus for this trip. After seeing Kara, family, and Charlie, I'd fly to Denver for the semi-annual meeting of the corporation where I held a seat on the Board of Directors since retiring. Even though I had read the materials for the meeting, habit compelled me to bring them out again on the plane, reviewing the documents and jotting notes in the margins. For a brief time, I was again the high-powered businesswoman I'd once been before retirement, cancer, and the death of my lover had set me on a new course.

Slanting down through the broken clouds to Logan Airport, I saw my former city spread below. If no one was there to meet me, would I still know my way around the terminal? Disembarking with the other passengers, I looked for a familiar face in the crowd. Assuming that Kara would be the one to meet me, I was surprised to see my son-in-law Duncan and granddaughter Callie. Obviously, Duncan had Callie pumped about my visit because she threw herself into my arms and began an enthusiastic recitation about all the things we'd do while I was visiting. Bless Duncan. It was a good thing he liked me better than Kara did or I'd never see my grandchildren.

Disentangling myself from her exuberant welcome, I did the cheek-kissing bit with my son-in-law. "Kara and the boys okay?"

"Oh, yes." Duncan said. "She's at the hospital with Charlie; Jordan is buried in his engineering program at MIT and TJ is doing God-knows-what."

"TJ has senioritis," Callie piped. "He's just impossible!"

I could almost hear Kara's voice and inflection. Like mother, like daughter, I thought. "You can have senioritis, too, in a couple of years," I told her.

"Now don't tell her that, Val," laughed Duncan. "Do you have a bag checked?"

"Daddy, Grandma's suitcase came to the house this afternoon."

He looked quizzically at me; I explained. "I learned long ago to FedEx my luggage ahead. That way, all I have to carry on the plane is my briefcase and I never have to wait for the luggage carousel."

Duncan laughed again and said, "You CEO's know all the ropes. Poor old academics like me still have our heads up our textbooks when it comes to travel paradigms." His eyes twinkled and he gave me a hug. "Come on, Grandma, let's go see Kara and Charlie."

The long walk to the car felt good after being cooped up in the airplane. The tang in the air brought back a flood of memories, as did the drive through the tunnel and along Beacon Street, which bordered the Back Bay area where our house—now Charlie's house—was located. Did I want to see it again? Not really. All that was so long ago. As we came to Deerfield, Duncan turned on to Brookline Avenue to Beth Israel Hospital.

Boston is magical when light filters through the coastal atmosphere, wrapping pearled mist around the buildings. As my son-in-law, granddaughter and I walked from the parking lot to the hospital, our animated conversation during the drive from the airport came to a halt. It seemed as if they were as tense as I about seeing Kara and Charlie.

Kara sat at Charlie's bedside, a book open on her lap. Charlie was pale and quiet, a thin trickle of saliva oozing from the corner of his mouth. He seemed to be asleep, but I wasn't sure. When she saw us, Kara placed a finger on her lips, leaving the room and moving us down the hall a few steps. "He's had a sedative; we can come back tomorrow. How was your trip, Val?"

"Good," I said, as we did the obligatory embrace, yet hardly touching. "You're looking fine, Kara. Tell me about Charlie."

"Daddy's stroke paralyzed his right side; his speech is a bit slurred, but I think it's clearing up. The doctor says he has a good chance to recover, but he'll need extensive rehab on his right side. Of course they're concerned about a blood clot, too." Her eyes filled with tears. "His teaching career is probably over. First to lose his operating privileges and now this."

Duncan said, "At his age, it's time to retire; it's just too bad that it had to come this way."

"But he's so brilliant!" Kara insisted. "He could have taught for many more years."

Duncan and I exchanged glances. There was no point arguing with Kara; I wondered how my son-in-law dealt with Kara's attitude towards her father. As headmaster of a small private school in the Wellesley area of Boston, Duncan's experience with hiring, firing and retiring faculty was extensive. Even I had a working knowledge of personnel matters. Surely, he could tell her how things work in the academic world.

"Give me a moment with Charlie, just in case he's awake," I said, walking back to his room. Kara reached out as if to stop me, but Duncan took her arm.

He said, "It's okay; you asked her to come."

I didn't hear Kara's response, if any, as I moved to Charlie's bedside. He did, indeed, look ill. He'd become an old man with thinning hair, wrinkles and blotchy skin. How could that have happened? How long had it been since I last saw him? Twenty years or more, probably. He was so young and handsome when we met, then becoming distinguished looking as he matured, even as short as he was. Stature isn't size; it's how one lives life. But to my mind there was no one more egotistical than a short surgeon. Yeah, he's a runt, I thought with amusement. No. He's just a sick old man, a man I'd once thought I loved. I took his hand, being careful of the intravenous drip taped securely to his thin wrist.

His eyes opened slowly, just a slit at first, then wider. "Val," he said. The left side of his mouth attempted a smile, the right side frozen by the stroke.

"Hi, Charlie. I just wanted to let you know I'm here; Kara and I will come back tomorrow for a visit. Okay?"

"Val." His eyes closed again.

Was it my imagination, or hope, that he seemed pleased? Forgiveness flooded me, forgiveness of both of us. This reaction was a surprise. What had I expected? Guess I'd come to realize that there are no villains at this stage of life. It's time to forgive each other and ourselves, I thought. If I could help Charlie have a faster recovery, I'd be happy. To be honest, I'd avoided thinking about seeing him. There are times you just play a situation by ear; this was one of them. I slipped my hand from his and returned to Kara and Duncan.

Dinner that night was chaotic, with Callie dashing off to play rehearsal at school and two of TJ's friends staying for dinner. The joyous hubbub was a contrast to the quiet dinners at The Villa; being in the midst of the disorganized dinner hour was delightful. Kara and Duncan were doing a great job of raising the kids. I was impressed with their manners, their ability to talk with a woman they rarely saw, their willingness to share a bit of their life. Even TJ's friends included me in their conversation. Grandmothers have a certain mystique of being sweet and kind; I milked it for all it was worth.

Later, the kids gone for the evening and Duncan in his study working on the school's operating budget, Kara and I sat in the living room with coffee, chatting about the children, a safe topic.

"Callie has the lead in the spring musical; she's very good," Kara said with pride. "She's taking private voice lessons. In three years, we hope she'll be ready to audition for Julliard."

"That's an ambitious goal! Where'd she get her musical talent?" I asked. "You know how unmusical Charlie and I were. Are there musicians on Duncan's side?"

"Duncan has a good voice; he sings around the house all the time. And his sister, Liz, studied and performed in local productions until she got too busy with her family."

"At least TJ comes by his artistic talent naturally from you. Are you enjoying teaching?"

"Oh, yes. Although I don't have as much time as I did for painting." Gesturing to a watercolor on the wall, she said, "That's the last good thing I've done."

"I noticed it right away. It's a lovely harbor scene. Is the sailboat Charlie's?"

"More or less," Kara said, frowning at the painting. "I didn't put the name on; it would have broken the mood."

I laughed and said, "Yes. Cardiac Arrest is such a tasteless name; he was in his bragging stage when he bought the boat. Everyone could tell where he got the money to buy it."

"Daddy's an excellent heart surgeon," Kara said defensively.

"Of course he was," I said, then changed the subject. "Did you say Jordan has a late lab at MIT tonight?" knowing full well the answer.

"Hmmm," Kara said, sipping her coffee. "He should be home soon. He's doing very well, but the engineering curriculum is extremely challenging."

After we exhausted the safe topics of the children, the weather, and Kara's art classes at Duncan's school, an uncomfortable silence filled the cozy room. This was the time I had been dreading, though that sounds a bit dramatic. Perhaps anticipating is more like it. I waited for her to choose the topic.

"How's your...health, Val?"

"You can say cancer, Kara; it's a nasty word, but one I've learned to use in the conquering process." I kicked off my shoes and curled my legs up on the sofa. "I've been in remission for nearly three years; my last check-up, which was just a week ago, was good. The doctor believes the aggressive treatment we elected was the right choice. He says if the remission lasts five years, I can stop worrying, but not stop taking good care of myself. I try to eat right and walk every day; I'm still taking Moxiphenoceptin. Of course attitude is very important. I hope you're watching yourself carefully now with breast cancer in the family."

"I do, but I worry about Callie more than myself; I suppose there'll be better detection and cures by the time she is at the age of concern."

Again there was conversational space. Finally, Kara said, "Do you like where you're living?"

"More or less. It's quite pleasant for what it is. There are times when I wonder why I'm there. I'm just now beginning to meet people, other than the Bridge group that absorbed me when I first moved in. One of the women died of a heart attack. We haven't found a replacement for her, but I often fill in for a foursome of hard-core male Bridge players."

"Hmmm," Kara said. Again there was a long pause. She finally spoke. "Perhaps Callie and I could fly out to see you this summer."

"That would be lovely! Portland has lots of things to do and see, and the Oregon coast is magnificent. We have Mt. Hood in our backyard and, well, we'd have a great time."

Again, Kara responded with, "Hmmm." A nice non-committal sound; I heard myself saying it throughout our years together, but did it serve Kara well when she was growing up? It was strange to hear an echo of myself. Do all daughters become their mothers, I wondered?

"What are you going to say to Daddy?" Kara suddenly asked.

The question brought me up sharply. I felt my eyebrows arch, but quickly composed myself, putting on what I hoped was a non-committal face. "Well, that all depends on what he says to me. I'll ask him how he's feeling and if there's anything I can do for him. How does that sound?"

"Don't be sarcastic, Val."

"I'm not." I suddenly felt defensive. "If you have a problem with me talking to your father, you should have told me to stay away. I didn't ask to come."

"Why did you come?" Now that was the real question. The obvious answer was that I was invited, but that's not what she wanted to hear. Could I share thoughts of my own death with her? She might think it maudlin or self-serving, if I did. How do adult children feel when parents talk about their own deaths? Probably the same way I felt when my mother was dying, that she just wanted some attention and that she would never die. Of course I was wrong, very wrong. Lacking the medical advances we have today, breast cancer took my mother painfully and quickly.

"I'll be as candid as I can, since I don't honestly know the reason, other than Charlie, well, you said he wanted me to come." I uncurled my legs from the sofa and folded my arms across my chest. Now there's a defensive bit of body language, I thought. In an attempt to look relaxed, I reached for my now-cold coffee, took a sip, then replaced the cup quietly on the saucer. "I thought I would die three years ago when my mammogram showed the tumor. For a very brief time, I toyed with the idea to forgo treatment of any kind and quietly die. But Jesse wouldn't hear of that." I watched her carefully at the mention of Jesse. A frown flickered across Kara's face, but she remained silent.

"Of course smart people don't do that. They work with their doctors and give it at least one good try to get well. I knew I wouldn't spend my life searching for the cure, but I'd do everything I could, just once, to meet the challenge. It was a tough year, but I made it through the treatment." I paused, trying to arrange my thoughts; Kara was watching me. I took a deep breath and continued.

"Then Jesse was killed; she was my rock, the one who pulled me through the chemo, the radiation. When she died, it felt as if I had died." I felt tears forming; my voice was less controlled than I wanted.

"Jesse was a close friend?" Kara asked, more to fill the silence I had created than to elicit an answer. She knew Jesse was my best friend, but did she know she was also my lover? Was now the time to explain that relationship?

CHAPTER SIX

I took the easy way out by staying on course, keeping it focused on Kara, Charlie and me. "Yes. Jesse and I had been close for nearly 20 years. There was nothing we didn't share. I suppose that since I faced—perhaps am still facing—death from disease, rather than old age, I can relate to what your father is going through. Life is too short, for both of us, to harbor any anger after all these years. We need to forgive each other. After all, there once was love."

Kara remained quiet, her face turned from mine. "Look at me, Kara," I softly demanded. "Your father and I are nearing seventy. We've had good lives, except for divorce, but who's to say that was wrong; that by splitting up, we didn't achieve better lives? I know it was hard on you, but for God's sake, that was over thirty years ago. When you've had a disappointment, use it to become stronger, then move on. You're a grown woman with a fine family, a career, talent, a lovely home..." I paused, anger surfacing in spite of my determination to keep it at bay. "Give it a rest!"

I stopped, afraid I'd gone too far; but what the hell, this scene had to be played out one day. Why not now? I leaned towards her, the coffee table serving as a benign barrier. "It's important to forgive, not only others, but ourselves. I've learned that in the last three years. I give you this bit of wisdom now, while you're young, so that you don't have to discover it yourself twenty or thirty years from now."

"What do you mean forgive yourself?" Kara asked in an almost inaudible voice.

I took a deep breath, searching my mind for an example. "Everyone does dumb stuff, clumsy things, in their life. Haven't you ever had a day in the classroom when the whole thing just fell apart and then you mentally kicked yourself for the next few days, thinking 'I should have said this, or done that, or if I'd only…'" I saw her nod ever so slightly.

"For years I tried to fulfill the expectations of others, to be what I wasn't. Instead of being resentful, let that kind of stuff go. Forgive every clumsy thing you've done. Then forgive others for unkind words, for shitty deals; none of it is important now; if you get the chance, talk to the ones you've hurt, make amends, if you can." Again, I saw a slight movement of agreement from her. "That's why I'm here to see Charlie. I probably wouldn't have come without his request and your blessing. There were too many bad feelings years ago, but I've put them all away; now I'm willing to dust them off and make things right between your Dad and me and, I hope, with you."

She sighed deeply, as if considering what I had said. "Any other motherly advice you've forgotten to give me?" At least she smiled when she said it.

"In fact, there is. I gave up guilt when I turned forty."

"Guilt about Daddy and the divorce?"

"Well, yes. That would be part of it. Let's see if I can explain what I mean." I drained the last of my cold coffee and began. "I'm not talking about criminal guilt, or ethical conduct involving a breach or moral law or violating an ethical precept, but failure to do what people expect you to do.

"Guilt is a feeling of culpability for imagined offenses or from a sense of inadequacy. This self-reproach, usually over some family issue, custom, or decree, can immobilize a person, crimping her style, clouding her life view based on her own standards and rights."

"What kind of crimes?" Kara asked, leaning forward, her forearms resting on her knees. I couldn't remember the last time she had paid as much attention to what I was saying.

"Well, I didn't get the laundry done on time; my house isn't tidy enough; my home décor is non-existent; dinner was late; I forgot a friend's birthday; I didn't take the time to shop for the perfect Christmas gift for so-'n-so."

"We all can't be Martha Stewart!" Kara laughed.

"Exactly. But sometimes, the perceived offence is of a more serious nature involving family members. Did you take time for yourself rather than catering to a loved one? Did you buy something less than necessary, instead of putting the money into the savings account? Did you say 'no' to a plea for your time?"

"I guess all women have chastised themselves for doing what they want, rather than caving in to the family's every whim," Kara acknowledged.

"Exactly. All women suffer from disposable guilt when we say or think, 'Why didn't I...You fill in the blank."

"How do you give up guilt? What's your process?"

"I figured out the emotional, financial and social price I'd have to pay to see if I could afford it."

"Your divorce wasn't expensive, then?" she said bitterly.

"Remember, I gave up guilt at forty. The divorce was in my thirties. Yes, I felt guilty for not being able to make the marriage work, even though there were lots of things wrong with it."

Kara seemed to consider a sharp response, but then said, "Okay. Go on."

"There's a lot of discretion between selfishness and being a doormat; finding the line that best serves us without running roughshod over others is the trick."

"That sounds hard. Are you guilt free now?"

"Afraid not. My sin at the moment is discontentment."

"What's the matter with that?"

"Nothing, but its how I deal with it. I can be a grumbling malcontent and drive everyone crazy, or I can do something about the situation. That's been my struggle ever since I moved to The Villa."

Before I could continue, Jordan burst into the room, welcoming me with a big hug, and saying, "Come into the kitchen and talk to me while I find something to eat." His invitation was divine intervention as far as I was concerned. It seemed to me that Kara needed time alone to sort things out.

Late the next morning, Kara picked me up after teaching her early class at Duncan's school; we drove to Beth Israel Hospital. To our surprise, Charlie was sitting up in bed.

"Daddy!" Kara said, a broad smile spreading over her face. "Just look at you!"

Charlie gave us his half smile, never taking his eyes off me as Kara kissed his left cheek. "I'm...I'm doing...well...this mor...ning," he said.

"Oh, yes!" Kara beamed, looking back at me while I stood in the doorway, waiting until she was through fussing over him. "Would you like a sip of water? Juice? Have you had lunch yet?"

I watched in amusement as she smoothed the sheet and moved his tray table over so slightly. There had been a time when I thought her attachment, the possessiveness of her father, was in the unhealthy range. But, she had married, was a good wife and mother, so I couldn't really fault her, especially now.

"Val," he said, extending his left hand.

I quickly went over to him, took the offered hand and kissed him on his "good" side. "Hey, Charlie. You look a hundred percent better today than you did yesterday."

"Feeling better."

"Kara said, "I'll feed you lunch, okay?"

"Fine," he said, pausing, as if he needed to gather his strength. "You look...great, Val" He spoke carefully, halting at times to carefully form his words.

"Thank you. I'm doing well; been in remission for almost three years. In less time than that, you'll be back on your sailboat. Do you still have the Cardiac Arrest?"

"Yes. But I...don't...sail as much as I used to...not since the accident." He touched his damage right arm with his left hand. "At least the stroke affected my bad side."

The boating accident had finished his career as a heart surgeon. While there wasn't any visual damage to his right hand, some of the control and feeling were gone. Fortunately, Harvard Medical School kept him on its faculty, allowing him to teach Medical Ethics, as well as selected cardiac topics.

"Ah. Here's lunch," Kara said, efficiently adjusting the tray table and uncovering the thick Melmac dishes when the attendant had gone. "Looks like you're on semi-solid. There's chicken rice soup, and tapioca pudding, and crackers and apple juice. Tea, too." Perched on the edge of the bed, she carefully fed him.

I could tell he was uncomfortable being helped, yet seemed to accept his daughter's ministrations because she needed to do something for him; he probably would have had trouble feeding himself with his left hand. As he ate, I told him about The Villa, trying to keep it amusing. "You'd love my neighbor, Mabel; she's always trying to save my soul, but how can I take anyone seriously who has a pet bird and twists her hair in pink foam rollers?" I embroidered each story about Dee and Grace with silliness; telling about Carol took no embellishment. Even Kara seemed to enjoy my description of the "home."

I told Charlie what wonderful grandchildren we had, and that I'd be flying to Denver in two days to attend a PTI Board meeting before returning to Portland. By the time Kara was finished feeding him lunch, I'd exhausted my repertoire of non-controversial topics.

"Well, we mustn't tire you, Daddy. We'll come back tomorrow."

He reached out to me again and said, "Come back …later…Val."

"Yes. Kara will check with your doctor to make sure we don't tire you, okay?"

"No. Tonight, Val."

Kara and I looked as each other, then at Charlie. "Sure," I said. "Callie and I are going shopping this afternoon at Copley Place and Quincy Market. We might even get to Antique Row, if we have time, and maybe to the cemetery."

"Mother!" Kara said, her eyes wide with a warning look that said I'd crossed the line.

Charlie chuckled softly and winked his good eye at me. I wondered if Kara realized she'd called me 'Mother' instead of Val. It had been a long time.

It was early evening when Jordan dropped me off at the hospital on his way to study with friends; Kara would pick me up after she retrieved Callie from her voice lesson. Charlie and I were alone for the first time in decades. We sat grinning at each other, holding hands like an old married couple. Finally, he spoke.

"Who would have thought things would end like this?"

"End? Who says this is the end?" I chuckled. "You'll be up and out of here in no time."

"No. Things aren't quite what they seem, but I don't want to worry Kara."

I nodded in understanding. "She loves you very much. Be honest with her. She's a big girl. Now tell me what I can do for you."

"Just coming is all. I wanted to say I'm sorry for. .

Sorry that I called you…all those names and caused you so much grief."

"I caused you a lot of grief, too," I laughed. "I was a cold bitch. There were things I didn't know then that I found out later."

"Is that why you never remarried?"

"Yes. You didn't spoil the institution of marriage for me." Again, I smiled, trying to keep things light. "For years I did what was expected of me, at least to the best of my ability. My mother was set on me marrying a man with good prospects. I certainly did that." We smiled at each other again. "You became all and more than my parents wanted for their daughter and themselves. I was in deep trouble with them for years for divorcing you."

"Kara said you have a close friend, a woman photographer?"

"Yes. Jesse Goldman. No doubt you've seen some of her work in GQ and Vanity Fair; she also has work hanging in several notable galleries. She died last year in a commuter plane crash; she was on assignment. I was to go with her, but I didn't feel well enough that week." Tears filled my eyes. There was still conflict between losing Jesse and having my life. "Our friendship was very special."

"I'm glad you had someone. What a shame it had to end that way."

"Yes. Enough of that." I smiled, stowing my emotions away. "Now, let's talk about you."

CHAPTER SEVEN

Dee had one eye on the afternoon movie and the other on her current needlepoint piece that would become a pillow for her sister-in-law's birthday. Relaxed and snug in her apartment, Dee was pleasantly settled for the afternoon. With Grace in Seattle recovering from her broken hip, Val in Boston, and Carol at her weekly spa appointment, everyone was where they were supposed to be at the moment. There were other friends and acquaintances at The Villa Dee enjoyed, but she also liked solitude at times; today was one of those.

She enjoyed the old musicals the Turner Classic Movie channel featured in the afternoon. Today's movie—Lovely To Look At starring Howard Keel, Kathryn Grayson, Ann Miller and Red Skelton—was a remake of the Broadway show Roberta. The costumes were as lush and romantic as the music. She paused in her work, giving full attention as the lovers, Keel and Grayson, sang their hearts out, reunited, after a misunderstanding had separated the couple. Just as they embraced for the chaste kiss, she heard a knock at her door.

Pressing the television mute button, Dee heaved herself with difficulty off the sofa to answer the door. Her grandniece Mary Alice Ryan stood smiling shyly, as if she might be sent away.

"Mary Alice," Dee exclaimed. "What a delightful surprise! Come in, dear."

"Hope I'm not bothering you…"

"Good heavens, no. We can have tea. Take off your…cloak," Dee said eyeing the long wine-red vintage cape that covered the teenager from neck to ankle.

"Yeah. Okay."

A visit from her grandniece was always an experience. When the teenager came calling, the whole retirement center was set a-buzz. "Did you see her clothes? Her hair? The ring in her nose?" Today's outfit topped them all.

"Well look at you!" Dee said, surveying the outfit the teenager revealed on removing the cape. The elderly woman tried to be non-judgmental at the sight of high black boots, black fish net hose with the knees torn out, a black leather mini skirt and black lace blouse over a black bra. Mary Alice's hair was shoe polish black—an improvement from the green she had once attempted. Her eyes were rimmed with Kohl.

"And what's this look called?" Dee asked, putting the teakettle on to boil.

"Goth," Mary Alice replied, admiring herself in the gilded mirror on the dining alcove wall. "Mom and Dad hate it. I think it's totally cool."

"Goth? As in Gothic?"

"Yeah."

"Well it certainly is a change from your hippie outfit," Dee said, recalling the tie-dye shirts and love beads Mary Alice had worn for a few months. At least each phase was mercifully brief.

The young girl gave her old aunt a hug and patted Dee's tight white curls. "You've got a new perm. Cool."

"Oh, yes. A bit tight right now, but in a few weeks it will be just right." Taking down plates and cups, she handed Mary Alice a package of Pepperidge Farm cookies. "Would you put these on the plate, dear." Dee measured orange-spiced tea leaves into the heated teapot, and then asked, "What brings you way out here? No school today?"

"Oh, yeah, well…there's school, but…we got out early and I…took the bus here."

This didn't quite sound like the truth to Dee, but patience was one of her greatest virtues. Her philosophy was "wait long enough and the truth will come out."

Dee was searching her mind for the name that Mary Alice had chosen for herself. Not long ago the girl informed her family that she was to be called Ginger. Dee was more agreeable to the change than the rest of the family. After all, "Mary Alice" was a rather old fashioned name.

"Tell me again your new name, dear. It was after a music group you said? The Condiments?"

"No," giggled Mary Alice nee Ginger, placing the plate of cookies on the table. "The Spice Girls! Oh, Auntie Dee, you are so funny. I love you!" Auntie Dee was a "hoot" as far as Ginger was concerned. She had great stories to tell and was never impatient with the teenager. She was the young woman's one adult confidant.

"I imagine name changes often happen. I can't remember when the family started calling me Dee instead of Dedre."

"Is that your real name? Oh, I love it. From now on, you shall be Aunt Dedre. That sounds so elegant!"

Blushing with pleasure, Dee asked, "How's school?"

"A total bummer! It's Dumpsville. I'm just a stress puppy all the time. The teachers are so lame and there's this freak magnate in Social Studies that is, like, eeuww. You know?"

Dee listened carefully, trying to figure out exactly what Ginger was attempting to communicate through short burst of inarticulate teen-speak, punctuated with "duh" and "bummer."

"You see, there's this totally cool dude, Jason, who thinks I'm the ultimate. But my folks get all, like, up tight, about any guy factor. I tell them to, like, chill out, but they are, like, clueless! Jason is soooo cool and he rides this hot motorcycle. My folks won't let me, like, ride with him. Go figure."

There was more information delivered with much animation and eye rolling. The gist of the monologue, as far as Dee could tell, was that her grandniece was in love and wanted to get a job and move away from home. Her parents didn't like Jason and disapproved of an "after school gig. Ka Ching." Dee interpreted this to be a job of some sort.

The two women sat quietly sipping tea and nibbling cookies, watching the television action. The romantic musical finished, a black and white gangster film careened across the screen.

"What movie is that?" Ginger asked.

Dee watched the car chase and the bursts of flames from the Tommy guns. "I think…there's Edward G. Robinson…in the derby hat...I think it might be Public Enemy or...the schedule is right there..."

"That's okay. It doesn't matter," Ginger said.

"When I was your age, there were lots of movies like that...gangsters and shooting and criminals with their gun molls."

"What's a gun moll?"

"I was never quite sure, but they were young women who hung around the bad men, pouring them drinks and smoking. Maybe they carried an extra gun in their purses in case their boyfriends lost theirs."

There was no response from Ginger; she seemed distracted. Dee carefully placed her empty teacup on the saucer and asked, "Are you having problems at home?"

"Oh, Aunt Dedre, is it that obvious?" Ginger ran her thumb across the black lipstick imprint on the delicate hand-painted cup rim, leaving a gray smear.

"Well, dear...er, Ginger. I always enjoy your visits, but one in the middle of the week, on a school day?" She paused, waiting for the girl to respond. When she didn't, Dee continued. "I hope you'll wait before deciding to leave school and get a job. And if Jason really loves you, he'll wait until you graduate."

The girl silently picked at the black polish on her fingernails. Her downcast expression touched Dee's heart. She knew about unrequited love, how life could be so disappointing when one was young and in love. "I had a suitor when I was your age; we lived in Chicago at the time. But it didn't work out. I suppose it was just puppy love. He lived a short distance away, but because his home was across the bridge, it was another world as far as my parents were concerned. Poor foreign trash they called him, even though my father admitted that Tito was a good worker."

Ginger looked up, raising her eyebrows in interest.

Dee continued. "Tito and I met when he came to our door one snowy day and offered to shovel our front walk for fifteen cents. Father said he'd give him a nickel. Well, you should have heard Tito talk! By the time he got through, Father paid him a dime. I think that's what Tito wanted all along to do the job." Dee's eyes crinkled up in mirth and remembrance.

Taking a more serious tone, she continued. "I watched from inside our warm house while he labored in the below-freezing air. I gave him a cup of tea from the pot that was always simmering on the back of our kitchen stove. He had curly black hair, big brown eyes and a cleft in his chin. His skin was a beautiful color, too, not pale and freckled like mine. Baldavino. Tito Baldavino. He was the most beautiful boy I had ever seen." Again, Dee's old eyes saw what Ginger could not.

"All that winter he shoveled our walks and chopped wood for us. You see, Father had a weak heart and couldn't do a lot of the heavy chores. When Mama or the babies didn't need me, I'd throw on a big old coat of Father's and stand outside, talking with Tito while he worked. We'd always be careful that no one saw us; I'd stand close to the porch or near the back door. You see, my parents didn't approve of him. He had to drop out of school to earn money to help his family. They had lots of children, just like our family. Of course the Depression was on and everyone was having a hard time.

"What's a Depression?"

"Hmmm," Dee said, struggling how to describe something that her generation knew about but the young did not, could not, conceive. "Well, in 1929, the stock market crashed and..."

"Oh, yeah. Bankers jumped out of windows and stuff; we read something about it in school. Daddy was worried about one coming again last year when his stocks dropped a lot, but they came up again really fast."

"Yes, but way back then, it took years for things to get better."

"Tell me about Tito. What a neat name!"

Dee smiled, hoping that Ginger wouldn't decide to change her name again; a niece called Tito just wouldn't do. She cleared her throat and went on with the story. "Our families went to the same church, but the Baldavinos sat in the back pews of St. Ignatius while we sat up front. It was so hard for me not to turn around and look at him. I loved his smile and the way his hair hung down over one eye." Dee paused and looked at Ginger to see if she were listening. Ginger was resting her chin in her hands, looking very young and sweet, Dee thought.

"Totally cool! Jason is the best looking guy in school, well he's not really in school any more." Ginger looked thoughtful, then said,

"Your folks wouldn't let you hang out with Tito? Bummer! What happened?"

"Spring came and Father kept hiring Tito to do odd jobs. He spaded the garden and repaired the picket fence and the gate. In the fall he raked leaves. I was sixteen that year; so was Tito, or he thought he was. With so many children in the family, not all important events were recorded in the family Bible. Even then, there could have been mistakes by a day or so, he said. Tito was born in Sicily and was about ten years old when his family immigrated to America. He could read and write English and Italian; I thought he was very smart and very…exotic.

Ginger gushed. "Totally romantic!"

Dee nodded and continued. "Working was more important to his family than going to school because he had to help feed the family since he was the oldest. His father worked in a slaughterhouse until he lost his job because of the Depression, but Tito managed to keep his job there cleaning up at the slaughterhouse. He sure had a gift of gab! Even though he worked all the time and had to help his family, we managed to see each other when he'd work for us. Sometimes on Sunday, we'd find a few moments after church to talk, but Mama and Father always were cross with me if they saw."

"I know what you mean," exclaimed Ginger. "Parents are so lame. They think I'm still a baby; I'm not going to do anything stupid. They just don't understand how things are now. They look at everything like when they were kids. They…" She sighed in exasperation. Anger spent, the girl urged her aunt to continue the story.

"Tito thought I was pretty, or at least he said he did. He asked me for a lock of my hair. It was red then and really curly, hard to comb. One night when I was alone in the bathroom, I clipped a thick curl and tied it with a blue ribbon. He had the biggest smile when I gave it to him after church. He'd bring me wild flowers and pretty stones he found near the river when he'd come to work for us."

"Jason gives me stuff sometimes, too. Well, maybe it's more like going out to McDonald's or Taco Bell." Ginger frowned, as if she were trying to think of something romantic Jason had given her.

Dee smiled, then said, "The Depression had hit our family too, but we never really went hungry like some families did. There were always vegetables and fruit we grew in our garden and canned each summer. My brother Michael raised rabbits and chickens. I didn't mind eating the hens when they were too old to lay eggs, but I sure hated to eat the rabbits. I usually gave my portion to one of the little kids."

"Oh, ick! I couldn't eat rabbit either. That's gross!"

Dee smiled at Ginger's disgust, then went on with her story. "The only thing that kept the Baldavinos from starving were the soup bones and meat scraps that Tito would steal from the slaughterhouse. They had a very difficult time. Once I sneaked a big doll blanket to Tito for his sick baby sister.

"So you see, 1932 was not the time to fall in love. Tito and I fell anyway. We kept our secret because my parents were dead-set against him, being lower class and all. But things like that don't stay secret, especially when my older sister, Agnes, knew about the relationship. She told my parents and they forbid me to ever see him again."

"My folks better not ever tell me to not see Jason again!" Ginger said, flouncing around to find another casually cool pose on the sofa. "It would be Splitsville; I'd run away from home!"

Swallowing a typical adult response to the inflammatory statement, Dee continued. "Well, to make a long story short, we had one last meeting before he left to find his fortune. Our plan was that he would return and marry me at Christmas. He said he'd write every day. Of course he didn't, but occasionally I'd get a postcard saying he was working hard and that he loved me. He didn't come back that Christmas or the next."

"Oh, that's sad," Ginger said, placing her smooth hand on Dee's gnarled hand.

"I understood that it would take a while for him to make his fortune and anyway, I was young and Mama needed me at home to help with the babies. Michael left to study for the priesthood and Agnes became a nun, so I was all the help Mama had."

"You were like a slave! I wouldn't have done that."

Ignoring Ginger's outburst, Dee continued. "Father was a bank teller in 1933 when the President closed all the banks. Father lost his job, but then he went to work for the WPA as a clerk. That made things better for our family. We even went to the Chicago World's

Fair. Nineteen thirty-four was a better year for us. Father still had his job and had gotten a raise. That helped make things easier."

Dee could see that she was losing Ginger's attention now that the story had begun to sound like a history lesson. So she took a lighter tone. "Of course I didn't really understand all of what was going on then. I was just a silly girl in love, waiting for her suitor to return. I was in such a tizzy that Christmas—1934 now—thinking that Tito would come back. I had this whole scene in my head where he would come walking up the street and ring our bell and tell Father and Mama that he had a job down town and wanted to marry me."

"My parents just don't understand things either! But you do." Ginger said. "I'll listen when my kids come to me with something important."

"I'm sure you will, dear." Dee patted the young girl's hand and continued her story. "Two days after Christmas—oh, I remember it so well. Father and Mama were in the parlor. Father was reading his paper and Mama was knitting; I was in the kitchen doing the dishes. Suddenly the little ones began making a hoorah about a car that had stopped in front of our house. Father answered the bell because we weren't expecting anyone and no one we knew had a big Packard like the one parked at our gate.

"Well, to make a long story short, it was Tito!" The old aunt could see that she had Ginger's full attention again. "He had on a brown pinstriped suit and a soft gray Fedora and his arms were filled with fancy-wrapped packages and a bag of oranges. The little kids went wild when they saw the oranges." Both women smiled at the image of an unexpected visitor bearing gifts.

"Father invited him in and asked him to sit down. This was the first time he ever allowed any odd job people in our house. I hardly recognized Tito. He was bigger and taller and—oh, yes—even more handsome! I just stood there all trembly amid the hullabaloo the boys were making.

"Father and Mama were surprised, of course, with all the gifts he brought our family. And his car, too. Father was very impressed with the Packard since we didn't even have a car. We always took the streetcar everywhere. My parents couldn't believe that Tito was interested in me. While they talked, I ran upstairs and put my hair right and put on a clean middy blouse. When I came back down,

Father and Mama shooed everyone out of the parlor and left the two of us alone. You see, while I was upstairs, Tito asked Father for my hand in marriage—all very proper, impressing him even more."

"Oh, how romantic! I wonder if Jason would do that?"

"Well, I didn't marry Tito. He had told my Father that he had his own business in transportation, but that was a lie. Later when we talked alone, he told me how he earned his money." Dee paused for effect. "He was a bootlegger!"

"Really? Just like the in the movies?" Ginger asked with a dramatic flare.

Dee nodded her head and said, "Not exactly like the movies, but...still...Anyway, with Prohibition over, now he was running numbers and playing the horses. He was a gangster!" Again she paused for effect, watching Ginger's eyes widen. "Well, he didn't really say he was a gangster. I just knew that what he was doing was illegal. Not that I had some high moral calling at eighteen, but I was afraid. The newspapers had lots of gangster stories and I'd seen moving picture shows about gangsters, so I knew how dangerous and how bad people like that could be. I was afraid...for him...and for myself."

Dee increased the tempo of her story. "Of course I couldn't tell my parents about Tito's business. I simply said that I no longer loved Tito. Mama's only concern was that I wasn't very pretty and I wouldn't get many chances to marry someone with money."

"Oh, that's so cruel! You're beautiful, Aunt Dedre!"

The old woman smiled, pleased with those words. She hadn't often heard them, whether sincere or not. "As I look back, I'm sure I made the right decision. Even though I never married, my life has still been rewarding with my extended family, especially you, Ginger."

She reached out for the young woman's hand. They sat quietly, smooth and wrinkled fingers entwined.

"You're telling me to cool it, aren't you?"

"Who am I to give you advice?" laughed the old woman. "Let's just say that, sometimes, waiting can be the best choice. I'm sure another wonderful young man will come your way. Perhaps you'll find him in college."

"Yeah. College. I took my SATs and got a high score."

"There. You see?"

Dee felt guilty about lying to her niece, but Mary Alice had lied too. Walking the young woman to the front door of the retirement center lobby, Dee watched her run down the curved driveway and meet a young man on a motorcycle. Mounting behind him, she tucked the ungainly cape around herself and put on the helmet he held out to her. Bus, my foot! Dee said a silent prayer that her beloved niece would arrive home safely.

Yes, Dee had lied. Oh, there had been a Tito and they did fall in love. When he returned with his big car and bag of oranges there had been much excitement, but he had not asked permission to marry her. He had asked Dee as they stood alone on the front porch in the cold. Whispering softly, she had said, "Yes! Yes! Yes," melting into his arms, inhaling his scent, mirroring his passion as they kissed. Her cheeks felt warm whenever she remembered how her body felt when he kissed her. They arranged to see each other the next day to make plans.

When she told her parents of Tito's proposal and her acceptance, her father said there'd be no "Wop gangster" in the family. Neither Dee nor her family had knowledge of any underworld connections, but, her father, as usual, had jumped to conclusions. Then her mother chimed in, saying, "She's not very pretty, you know; she may never have another chance to marry someone with money." That remark stung, had stuck with Dee for all the many years she had cared for her sick mother. Someday, Dee thought, she might tell Mary Alice the truth about Tito. But now, the story related in hopes that the young woman wouldn't make an unwise decision, would stay as told.

Sighing, Dee meandered through the lobby and down the east wing hall to her apartment. Mr. Snow, fresh from another extended catnap, demanded attention and dinner. Dee crooned to the cat, stroking his long white fur, explaining why she had to tell half-truths to Mary Alice. Now that Dee had been able to explain her motivation, if only to a cat, she felt justified and brightened at the thought of having Carol all to herself as a dinner companion this evening. Val was intimidating sometimes, seeming to dominate their gatherings even when she was quiet. It was as if Val knew everything already and never felt it necessary to ask questions or freely give answers. Maybe that's why Val wasn't very interested in telling stories about their lives. This evening, alone with Carol, Dee would be able to ask her all kinds of questions and not feel stupid.

However, dinner didn't turn out quite as she'd anticipated.

CHAPTER EIGHT

Dee secured a table by the window and eagerly watched for Carol's arrival; her anticipation of their dinner together made her feel a bit lightheaded. When she saw Carol leading Jim Harrison to the table, her hand on his arm, Dee's lip quivered with disappointment.

"Look who I found. You don't mind if Jim joins us," she said, smiling first at Jim, then at Dee. She didn't wait for Dee's small nod, allowing Jim to pull the chair out for her. "I told Jim it's just you and me tonight with Val off to see her family."

Dee's cheeks grew warm as she managed a smile, albeit a small one. "Of course," she said and began to study the menu. She suddenly felt awkward, as she often had when young. Glancing up from the menu, she saw how pretty Carol looked after her day at the spa—hair perfect, nails gleaming a bloody red, make-up deftly applied. Dee's imagined frumpy self emerged, replacing the happy diner she'd been a moment ago. Jim was saying something to her—or was it to Carol?—as he took the chair between them.

"Well, Dee. What looks good tonight? She felt some "ahs and ers" coming from her mouth, before she blindly settled on the first item that caught her eye. "Fish?"

"Good choice," Jim said. "Red snapper's fine eating. What about you, Carol? Have anything you want. It's my treat."

Carol laughed coquettishly at the standard dining room joke. Because meals were part of the monthly fee residents paid, there was no need to buy dinner for anyone. Dee smiled politely at the jest and wondered how she'd get through a serving of red snapper. She hated fish; she'd enough fish growing up Catholic. Once she'd drifted from the Church, fish on Friday was anathema to her.

Dinner ordered, Jim turned to Dee again, asking if she had found a weekly Bridge game to her liking. "Not really. With Grace in Seattle and our interest in..." She stopped, unsure if she should mention storytelling to Jim. "We just seem to be busy with other things," she added lamely.

"Where'd you say Val was?" he asked Carol.

"She flew to Boston to see her daughter and family," Carol said. "Then she's going to Denver for some reason."

Dee brightened, eager to tell what she knew. "Val has a seat on the Board of Directors at PTI; it's the annual meeting."

"PTI?" Jim asked.

"Pacific Trust...International," Dee stumbled, hoping she'd gotten the name of the corporation correct. "It's a banking...business...or something."

"Oh, yes," Jim said. "I remember. She was CEO until Bank Nissan bought out PTI."

Carol raised her eyebrows and looked first at Jim, then at Dee. "Really? I didn't know she was so...well placed. Val keeps a low profile, to say the least." She sounded a bit peevish at not being privy to such information. Not that it really made any difference, but she never liked to be the last one to know things.

Neither Dee nor Jim seemed to pick up on Carol's pique. Jim said, "I hear that The Professor's going to be back soon."

"Who's that?" Carol asked. Again, she felt a sense of annoyance. But what could she expect being one of the more recent residents to come to The Villa? She smiled charmingly at Dee and Jim.

Dee said, "John Gurian, your neighbor in 2D. I heard that he'll be back from his trip to Machu Picchu tomorrow. He's been gone for at least a month. He's a retired English professor from the University of Portland, I think. He's widowed with no children. It seems as if he just uses The Villa as a base for his trips."

"I saw the cleaning staff in that apartment this afternoon," Carol said. "That explains it. So he travels often?"

Jim responded this time. "Yeah. Exotic places. Interesting, but physically demanding venues. He went trekking with a group in Nepal last year; hiked for four or five days from their base camp near

Katmandu." Jim touched Carol's arm. "Guess I like my creature comforts too much now after my years of international travel." Carol laughingly murmured her agreement, her eyes flickering over Jim's face.

Dee looked down at her meal, uncomfortable with the flirtation between her dinner companions. Conversational pauses made her edgy, so she said, "John always gives a slide show and talk about his trip; everyone at The Villa is invited. The programs are very interesting; it's like being there without all the trouble." She felt pleased with herself at the moment. Situations like this often made her uncomfortable, "useless as tits on a boar' as her Mother used to say of her. However, Dee still hadn't had the opportunity to ask Carol any of the questions she had planned. As dessert was served, a gap in the animated conversation between Jim and Carol about their travel experiences gave Dee her chance. "Carol, tell us how you became an author."

"That," Carol said with a laugh, "is a long story."

"We have time," Jim said. "I'd be very interested." His engaging smile was not lost on Carol. Their eyes lingered a bit longer than Dee thought necessary.

"Let's see," Carol said, pushing her untouched desert a few inches away. "My performing career over—and that's another long story that I won't go into—I took a job as a typist for one of Hollywood's screenwriters. It was a boring job, but it kept the wolf from the door and I learned about plot lines and character development. I took the opportunity to read scripts from the dozens stacked around the office. So many were never used." She took a sip of water and continued.

"The structure of a story began to fall into place for me. Of course I'd been an avid reader for years, particularly romances. I loved love stories—boy meets girl, boy loses girl, boy gets girl. I'd often thought I could write one, but never tried."

Dee leaned forward, trying to catch every word; this was something she could share with Grace when they were together in Seattle. Jim seemed genuinely interested in Carol's story, too.

"I was walking along Sunset Boulevard one day and saw an old typewriter in a pawnshop window. The price was too high, but I managed to talk the pawnbroker down enough so—if, I gave up lunches for a week—I could afford it. I think he was just glad to get the thing out of the way; it wasn't very good.

"Anyway, I began working on my first novel at night. I wasn't a terribly dedicated writer; there were always fun things to do—dancing on the pier, nightclubbing, beach picnics, swimming." She paused, her mind sorting out what she'd tell Jim and Dee. "Well, you know what I mean…when you're young; it was a party town, as you can imagine, although not like it was in the '20s and '30s."

Jim motioned with his coffee cup and asked, "When was this?"

"Hmmm. Let's see. About 1952 or '53. Marilyn Monroe and Jane Russell were big stars then and Cinerama was changing the look of movies."

"Oh, I loved Cinerama!" Dee said. "I felt queasy when I saw the roller coaster movie."

"The one I remember was 'How The West Was Won'", Jim said.

"That one and The Robe, and Mad, Mad, Mad, Mad World came out in the mid-Fifties," Carol said, giving Dee a quick smile before turning her attention back to Jim. "It took me over a year to get my manuscript to the point where I was ready to show it to anyone. By then, I'd made some friends who were willing to look at it and tell me if they thought it had possibilities. And, I was about to be married to…well, that doesn't matter, because he was much older than I and it didn't last very long…but he had connections. That's what it took, connections. Like any artistic endeavor, it's who ya' know. He knew the right people to get it published. Fortunately, the public liked it and the publisher offered me a contract for two more."

"What was the name of your first novel?" Dee asked.

"God," Carol laughed. "I still shudder over that. It was The Prince of Passion." Dee and Jim laughed with her.

Jim said, "I get the impression it wasn't on the New York Times Bestseller List."

"Definitely not! But I did make it on the list by my sixth novel, Cold Heat; there was some talk about a movie, but a new type of film was emerging, Easy Rider and Midnight Cowboy."

"Oh, I remember Cold Heat," Dee said. "I was a bit shocked at some…at…well, anyway, I read all your novels. They were quite…educational." Dee's face flushed as Jim and Carol laughed.

Jim spoke directly to Carol, lingering over the words. "I'll bet you were quite a teacher; ya' know any new tricks for old dogs?"

The dining room was beginning to empty; the waiters—high school kids dressed in black pants or skirts, and white shirts—were eager to finish their work for the night. Jim pushed his chair away from the table and said, "May I offer you ladies a drink in the bar?"

"Oh, no, thank you," Dee said, holding her breath in anticipation of what Carol would say. Would she tell Jim she was an alcoholic? Would she lie or just offer a pretty evasion?

"I'd really rather go for a walk," Carol responded with a flirtatious smile at Jim.

"Fine," he said, then looked at Dee. "Will you join us?"

"Oh, no, thank you," Dee muttered, not wanting to be in the middle of the flirtation, which had been thrust upon her during dinner. "I need to...feed Mr. Snow...my cat."

"Well, then. Shall we?" Jim said, offering Carol his arm.

Dee scurried back to her room and Mr. Snow, not that the cat needed feeding again. The white Persian with one blue eye and one green eye was Dee's confidant, a good listener. At least talking to Mr. Snow was better than talking to herself, Dee thought, unlocking her door.

"Guess what, Mr. Snow?" she said scooping the sleeping cat off the sofa and settling him on her lap. "Carol and Jim are flirting with each other. I wish Val were here so I could tell her. I wonder how things are going in Boston? I wonder how she feels about seeing her ex-husband? It must be hard to be a patient when you're a famous surgeon."

Mr. Snow squinted sagely at Dee and kept his counsel.

CHAPTER NINE

Tired from the flight home, I wasn't much in the mood for a visitor, but Dee wouldn't be put off. Her news was too good to keep, she said. I couldn't imagine what had happened at The Villa that was so earth shaking, but Dee would tell me. As far as I was concerned, not much could possibly have happened at The Villa in five days unless a massive case of food poisoning had wiped out half the residents. See, there I was, being my old self again. This time, I couldn't blame Kara for my mood. She had been more open than I had ever seen her before. I'm sure it was because Charlie was glad to see me, rather than any motherly advice I'd imparted. At least seeing Charlie hadn't been as bad as I had expected, although I hadn't had any idea of what to expect. The tap on my door interrupted my unpacking.

"Hi, Dee. Come on in. I brought you a present."

"You didn't need to do that," she said, looking very pleased. "I'm just glad to have you back! How was your trip?"

I gave her a gaily-wrapped jar of hand cream from one of the tourist shops in Boston's historic district and said, "Fine. No lost luggage and the flights were on time. You can't ask for much more than that. It was good to see my daughter and her family. Charlie's very ill, but he's making progress; Kara wants to take him home for a while when he's through with in-patient re-hab. But that will be a couple of weeks. Now tell me your news. Did our monthly rates go up or something?"

Ignoring my remark, she tore off the tissue and gave me a beaming smile of appreciation. "You shouldn't have. Thank you. Let's try some now," she said, unscrewing the lid. We each took a dab, massaging it into our hands as if the wrinkles and age-spots would magically disappear. Blue veins like mountain ridges snaked from arthritic knuckles to bony wrists. Our hands had seen hard work— Dee's from caring for family, mine from the keyboard and calculator.

"This smells wonderful!" Carefully screwing the top back on the jar, she sat heavily at my small dining table saying, "First, Carol and Jim Anderson are seeing each other! I see them together all the time since the three of us had dinner the night you left." She paused for my reaction, which was next to nothing.

"That's nice. How's Grace?"

"Aren't you surprised about Carol and Jim?" Dee persisted. "Carol's still married and..." Here, she lowered her voice, adding, "Mabel thinks they are...sleeping together."

"Look," I said, sitting in the chair across from her. "Carol's husband is...gone, at least mentally. What's the harm in two consenting adults enjoying each other's company? Anyway, Mabel just needs to tend to her own business."

Dee frowned, and nodded, as if their friendship was okay now that I'd more or less sanctioned it, then said, "Grace gets to go home, well, to her grandson's house this weekend. Her youngest daughter, who lives in Portland, will drive me to Seattle early Sunday morning. She'll come back that evening, but I'll stay until Grace can come back here."

"That's great. You two will have a fine time," I said, standing up, giving Dee a hint I was through being social. She didn't catch on, so I sat again.

"The next thing I want to tell you is that Grace is really, really serious about sharing our stories with each other. It's as if she thinks she can't get well without them. Truly," she said, probably noting my skeptical look. "I promised her that the four of us would get together as soon as she was back. I even have a story to tell when I see her in Seattle. It's about Carol, how she wrote her first novel. Of course I'll share that with you, too."

"Great, just not tonight. I'm really tired from the flight. It may be seven o'clock here, but my body is on Boston or Denver time."

"Oh, I'm sorry; I didn't think about the time difference. Have you had dinner?"

"I'm fine. Any other news?"

"Oh, I almost forgot. The Professor's back from South America!"

"Really? Great. I enjoyed his last slide show. Machu Picchu this time?"

"I think so; his talk hasn't been scheduled yet, but we know he's back because Carol saw the staff cleaning his apartment and she asked who lived there and other people have mentioned his return."

She babbled on, happy to be the first to share a variety of Villa news with me. So-and-so had moved out and an Asian couple had moved in. The craft group had finished their Mother's Day project and was starting on Father's Day centerpieces. I hadn't seen her as happy or as animated since Marion's death. It was good to have the old Dee back, I thought. And, I felt more like my old self, too. Seeing Charlie, and hearing him say "I'm sorry" was a real lift. Kara still seemed distant, but perhaps she and Callie would visit me this summer and we could talk again. Callie and I had had a great time shopping and then I took her to the cemetery to show her where her great grandparents were buried. I'm not big on visiting graves, but it seemed appropriate for me to pay respect to my parents. Where would I rest, I wondered? Since I was planning to be cremated, guess I'll go anyplace Kara and Duncan cared to dump me.

The high point of the trip had been the board meeting with PTI in Denver. It exhausted me, confirming my suspicion that I was beyond working full-time again, but that I had the energy and mental capacity to contribute to the quarterly meetings. I was already looking forward to the fall meeting.

"Well, that's quite a bit of news for just five days," I said, as she caught her breath and sat back, seemingly satisfied with her role as messenger. "I'm dead tired. Let's get together tomorrow." We rose and I walked her to the door, opening it and stepping out into the hall to make sure she'd get my message. "Tell Grace that we'll share stories as soon as she's back. If that's what it takes to get her well, I'll cooperate."

A strange thought came to my mind that life had become a series of visits to ill people who needed to draw strength from friends and relatives. Who had I drawn upon when I had become ill? Jesse, of course, but then lovers are vitally interested in each other. Who else? Good friends Mitch and Judy; my assistant Colleen, but no kin, no family. I'd told Kara, of course, but tried not to lean on her. Did I make a mistake by not asking her into my life at a very traumatic time? Probably. I'll do better next time.

"Oh, thank you for agreeing,' Dee said squeezing my arm. "And I love the hand cream. Thank you again!"

It was then I noticed Mabel's door open a crack. Were we in for another Gospel Moment? But the door quietly clicked shut. Just normal nosiness, I thought. Poor woman. You'd think her God and fellow believers would be enough for her. The missionary zeal is one I'll never understand. If people want spiritual support, it's certainly easy to access. I guess it was the challenge to convert sinners and non-believers that kept the Jehovah's Witnesses and Mormons going. But Mabel was neither of those; she was in her own world of Christian conversion.

CHAPTER TEN

Several days later, Carol invited us to her apartment after dinner for our first story session; this surprised and concerned me. She hadn't wanted to wait for Grace, for some reason.

I hoped Carol and Dee weren't expecting some great true confession eruption. Tapping on her door, I again heard the click of Mabel's door closing. I felt the beam of her eye through the peephole set in each apartment door. Knowing that I could be seen as a tiny, far-away form was unnerving. I had the desire to peek back at her. Fortunately, Carol opened the door and bade me "Enter," which I did to a room amassed with candles, their scent enveloping me in some tropical essence. The sound of recorded wind chimes and flutes filled the room.

Carol's flowered caftan and dangling jewelry made her look like a high priestess arrayed for a ceremony. Dee was settled on the sofa in a polyester pants suit, looking as out of place as I in my jeans and sweatshirt. This is too weird for me, I thought.

"Sit, sit. Let me pour you some tea. It's Jasmine," she said, ignoring my declining response. "I know; we just had dinner, but we need to have some ritual with our story telling. Tea, music, candles are all part of it."

"Look," I said. "If incense and chanting are going to be part of this, count me out."

"Val, don't be so stuffy," Dee said, cautiously sniffing her cup of tea. "The candles and music make tonight seem very special."

"Okay. But let's not get too far out."

Carol laughed, saying, "A glass of wine would enhance our sessions, but it will have to be tea with me."

Again, I interrupted. "Sessions? You make it sound like a visit to a psychiatrist."

"No, not at all," Carol said. "I was just trying to make this more fun, to put us in a mind-frame for telling stories, not just having conversation."

I gave her my 'Hmmm' response and she continued. "Okay, you win. No chanting, drumming or blood sacrifices." We laughed, suggesting a few other rituals that we would not employ. "Can't you just see Mabel with her ear to the door, trying to figure out what we're up to?" I said. "Twice I've heard her door click shut as if she had been spying."

"Really?" Carol said. "You know, I think you're right. The other evening when Jim left, I got the feeling that she was watching." Again we laughed. But Dee stood up for Mabel.

"You're being unfair to Mabel. I've gotten to know her through the crafts group; she's really very nice."

"What's her story?" I asked.

Dee beamed in her role of messenger. "Well, she's widowed; her husband was a very successful hymnal salesman. He traveled all over the Pacific Coast. And," she said, pausing for dramatic effect, "Mabel said he had a very beautiful tenor voice. He'd often sing at churches, which bought his hymnals. He was so good, that a television ministry invited him to sing. He'd hold one of his songbooks and sing from it, inviting viewers to join him in song at home. If they didn't have a hymnal so they could sing along on whatever page, they could buy one from the program and the cost of the songbook would be used to help the heathens in Africa."

Carol and I rolled our eyes at each other.

"Now don't be that way," scolded Dee. "Anyway, Harold—that was her husband—was hit by a bus when he was crossing the street in Los Angeles."

This struck Carol and me as very funny; we couldn't help but giggle.

"Oh, you two are terrible! I'm not going to tell you anything more," Dee said in disgust.

Yet she had to hide a smile as Carol laughingly wiped tears form her eyes, saying, "Hit by a bus…" Once again we 'lost it' in laughter.

Finally recovering our composure, Carol asked Dee, "Has she ever tried to convert you?"

I chimed in. "Mabel knows better than to buck the Pope for Dee's soul."

"Oh, Val!" Dee said with exasperation. "I dropped out of the Church a long time ago. Mabel sees me at Sunday services sometimes here, at The Villa." She stopped, befuddled as to where the conversation might go.

"I'm just teasing, Dee," I said. "Don't mind me." Then I looked at Carol, who was fussing with the tea tray. She settled herself more comfortably in her chair, took a deep breath and began to speak.

"Okay. I'll tell one of my stories tonight so that Dee will have something to share with Grace this weekend. But remember, this is my story and you can't share it with anyone unless I give permission." She looked at us, seeking agreement.

"Sounds good to me," I said; Dee murmured her approval, too.

Carol used a CD remote control to turn off the background sounds of flutes and wind chimes; I leaned back on her flowered couch, kicked off my loafers and curled my feet under me. Now that the ritual and sharing ground rules were established, we settled ourselves for the first evening of extending our lives for one thousand and one nights.

"Just pour more tea whenever you're ready," Carol said. "I'm going to tell you about my days in burlesque." She paused, to see out response. There was a soft intake of breath from Dee. I felt myself relaxing; this might be fun after all.

"I ran away from home when I was fifteen. It was at the end of the War...W.W.II. A very generous woman, Kate McGinty, gave me a job in her restaurant, McGinty's Seafood Bar and Grill. It was located down on the Seattle waterfront.

"She knew I lied about my age, but took me under her wing. She said a woman had helped her out when she was young and it was payback time. She never told me about her life, but I assume she had run away from home, too. Kate helped me find a room a few blocks away from the restaurant and gave me free meals; she said she knew what it was to be hungry and she didn't want me to earn my dinner the way she had to.

"I'd been working there for about six months, first as cashier, then hostess, and finally a waitress. When I wasn't working, I stayed in my room and did a lot of reading; Kate said that it wasn't entirely safe on the streets, day or night.

"At work, I had to fend off drunk servicemen, as well as Kate's husband, Drem. He was your basic dirty old man, more talk than do, but he still made me uneasy. Kate kept him around out of habit and to serve as a bouncer. She was the brains of the business; he was the muscle. Drem was a huge man with muscular biceps and boot-shod feet big enough to intimidate any rowdy who might want to liven up the place. Down the block from the bar was the Blue Moon Theater, a sleazy place that showed 'blue' movies and hired a few local women to strip on weekends."

"Real stripteasers?" Dee queried with wide eyes.

Carol nodded, saying "The stripping done in those days—the '40's—was nothing like today. Nudity was forbidden. No one ever went farther down than the G-string; pasties or a skimpy bra were required. It depended upon the town how far down the stripper could go. Seattle was more open than, say, Portland. I'm sure there were private shows, but I was never part of that." Carol paused for a sip of tea, then continued.

"The owner of the Blue Moon was a Greek named Acrisius. Occasionally, he'd book a touring burlesque troupe with comics and professional dancers. Headliners included exotic dancers like Tempest Storm and Hot Toddy, Queen of the Quiver. The burlesque troupes traveling the West Coast circuit would play major cities and some of the large towns for a week or two, then move on. The acts included magicians, ventriloquists, comic skits, and a dance team, which would perform between the strip acts. Each stripper had her own persona and style."

Needless to say, she had our full attention. I poured Dee and myself another cup of tea.

"Drem kept telling me I should go to work at the Blue Moon, that I'd be a sensation. But I had no interest; I was quite happy working for Kate. She became the mother I should have had; she protected me. I needed some security at that time and she gave it to me. But then my family got wind of my whereabouts."

"How?" I asked.

She frowned, as if trying to find the right words or tell us at all. "I had a boyfriend in high school, Buddy Willets. When he quit school to join the Navy, that's when I ran away; there was nothing left for me in Bellingham, except more of the same miserable home life." Again she paused, her storytelling stride broken. It seemed to me that this was part of the story that she hadn't planned to include. She began her narrative again.

"He and several of his shipmates just happened to come to McGinty's Bar and Grill during my shift one night. We were both shocked to see each other. It was good to see him, yet it wasn't, but that's a story for another time. Later he told his sister where I was and she told her mother, who told my father."

"Back to burlesque," I said, more interested in that than young love.

"Where was I? Oh, yes. The Blue Moon Theater. Drem introduced me to Acrisius, the theater's owner, and he introduced me to one of the comic teams who had lost their straight man...woman, really...and they were willing to give me a try, even though there were lots of other girls in the troupe. I'll have to admit that I looked a lot better than most of them. The burlesque circuit was tough on women; it wasn't something I would have chosen, but it gave me a chance to get out of Seattle before my father found me. The two old comics were willing to give me a try before the troupe moved on; they were very sweet old guys who'd worked on the East Coast circuit in the early days when burlesque was big. They had this corny — oh, let's be charitable and call it 'classic' — skit about a doctor and a patient."

By now she had us giggling at her story. She was in her stride as storyteller, hands and arms waving about in illustration. Her use of dialect and expression must have been learned during her years in Hollywood; she could have been an actress.

"I was to be the nurse who handed rubber, soft mallets and fake surgery instruments to the 'doctor' who would tell jokes and act like he was operating. The other comic — the patient — would scream and yell, flop around, fall on the floor and do other silly stuff. Of course there was always the rubber chicken and the seltzer bottle with water going all over the stage, me, and sometimes, the audience."

Dee and I were laughing out loud now, right along with Carol. I had never been inside that kind of theater and I was reasonably sure

Dee didn't frequent them either. It was fun to have a second-hand peek into a world so-called nice young ladies knew nothing about.

"The costume was small and tight to begin with, but I had been eating well and had quite a bustline on me. I also had to wear very high-heeled shoes that were too big for me. You can imagine how nervous and uncomfortable I was—first, being on stage in front of rowdy men, and second, in a costume and shoes that weren't comfortable or conducive to moving about and doing what I was supposed to do. I kept dropping the props and had a terrible time retrieving them. I finally just bent from the waist. Well, as we used to say in grade school, 'I see London, I see France...'"

Dee and I chimed in together. "I see someone's underpants!" By now, we were laughing so hard that we had to wipe tears from our eyes.

"My nervousness and newness to the act revitalized it. They signed me to a contract for the rest of the tour—about three months—and I disappeared from Seattle and my father. After a few times on stage, the dancers and strippers convinced me to replace the panties with a G-string. That really made the act a hit."

Dee said, "Weren't you...embarrassed?"

"At first, yes, but on stage you're so busy making sure you're in the right place at the right time, doing what you're supposed to be doing, that you forget about the audience. In fact, I felt safe. It was as if the men couldn't cross that line between the darkened theater and the brightly lit stage."

"Was the money better with the act than at the bar and grill?" I asked. Typical banker, I thought to myself; always looking at the bottom line.

"It was, which surprised me. I also enjoyed my new 'family' of girlfriends. The older strippers and dancers took good care of us younger ones." Carol picked up the sound system remote control and selected a cut on the CD of Gypsy. "Ya' Gotta Have a Gimmick" filled the room. "Do it with a trumpet..." sang one of the strippers. We listened for a moment, remembering when Gypsy with Ethel Merman was the top Broadway show.

Carol lowered the volume and continued her story. "After a while, I was asked to develop my own strip persona. I didn't have a clue how to develop my own act. Basically, you had five minutes on stage to establish a mood, shed your clothes and get off stage. For example, one girl wore a bra and G-string with yellow feathers on it. She started out in a cage and danced to the old song "I'm Only A Bird In A Gilded Cage." Another girl did an Arabian Nights thing, and some just wore evening dresses and elbow-length gloves.

"But the old gals decided that I should be a cheerleader because I looked—and was—young. Besides, I couldn't dance to save my soul. By capitalizing on my youth, the cheer leader image allowed me to jump around and wave pom poms—kind of like the fan dancer."

"You had more than pom poms, didn't you," Dee asked in astonishment.

"Sure. I had a tiny white pleated skirt, bobby-sox and saddle shoes, and a letterman sweater that I'd remove, then tease the audience with the pom poms over my pasties."

"How long did you do this?" I asked.

"Only for about three or four months. The troupe had made the circuit down the coast to San Diego, then started back up to Seattle. When we got to Portland, I dropped out. I didn't want to go back to Seattle and I was..." Carol stopped, looking intently as us, then continued. "It was just time to do something else...and that will be a story for another night."

Dee said, "I'm afraid I don't have anything that interesting to tell."

"I should hope not!" I exclaimed, smiling at her, then turned to Carol. "Did you use any of your experiences in your novels?"

"Oh, yes. But much of the stuff I wrote about, I hadn't experienced. For instance, the series about the schoolteacher who was a part-time detective..."

"Oh, I read all that series," Dee gushed. "I remember how she went undercover as an exotic dancer. Now I know why your descriptions were so good."

"You don't have to experience everything to write about it," Carol said. "I was never a schoolteacher—or did much of what I wrote about—but with a little research and a wild imagination, the stories just fell in place for me."

"Dee told me of your days typing Hollywood scripts. That must have been valuable," I said.

"It was quite an education...understanding dialogue and the structure of a story were really helpful." She paused for a moment, as if thinking back. "I saw so much…manipulation…of the young people who wanted to be movie stars. Acting never appealed to me. It was true about casting couches; friends of mine—we were just kids—had to do some pretty crazy stuff to make it in show business."

She sighed and sipped her tea. "I married a young would-be actor, but we were only together about a year—Mexican marriage, Mexican divorce. Then I married an older man; well, let's save that for another time, too. Whose turn will it be next?"

"Dee? Or maybe Grace can be next," I said. "She's the one who really wants this story telling."

"Good idea," Dee said. "I'll share Carol's story with her, if that's okay, and when we come back, it will be Grace's turn."

I stifled a yawn and stood. "Great story, Carol. I'm afraid I don't have anything that exciting. Being raised a 'lady' was very dull. I dutifully went from high school, to college, to marriage to motherhood. Then, well, divorces are old hat."

Carol shook her head in disagreement. "There's always an interesting story behind a divorce. Why did we make poor choices? What was it that made us want to get out?"

"Or get thrown out," I laughed.

"Really? Sounds like you have a story to tell," Carol said, opening the door and ushering us into the hall.

We stood chatting for a few minutes, our laughter coming easily, when the stairwell door opened. The Professor hesitated for a moment before greeting us.

"Ah. Ladies. Good evening. Looks like a party," he said.

"Hi, John," I said. "Have you met our new neighbor Carol Forman? Carol, John Gurian, from 2D." They shook hands, exchanging formalities. "I think you've met Dee Ryan?"

"Oh, yes. Nice to see you again, Dee." John said, smiling at her, then glancing into Carol's open apartment with its flickering candles, their exotic scent drifting into the wall. "This looks like a gathering of…dare I say…witches?"

Dramatically, Carol said, "Double, double, toil and trouble; Fire burn and cauldron bubble."

"I see you know Macbeth," John said.

"Carol laughed, saying, "Not really; just part of a scene I had to memorize in high school. The witches were the only part that caught my fancy."

He nodded, rather sagely, I thought, as if he'd encountered many students who felt that way. "Good evening, Ladies. Please keep the chanting down," he said unlocking the door to his apartment.

Our too-loud laughter must have brought Mabel to her door. Peeking out and saying, "Is everything all right?"—just increased our mirth.

Dee recovered first, saying, "Sorry we were so noisy, Mabel. Everything is fine."

Mabel nodded, her pink foam rollers bobbing vigorously. "I'll see you in crafts tomorrow?" she asked, directing her query to Dee, yet staring wide eyed at Carol, now framed in the flickering candlelight of her doorway.

"Oh, yes. Goodnight, Mabel."

Clapping our hands over our mouths to stifle more laughter, I imagined us mounting imaginary broomsticks and flying to our lairs.

CHAPTER ELEVEN

That weekend, after Dee left for Seattle, Carol convinced me to join her at the spa for 'the works,' as she put it. The Villa's van dropped us off at Indulgences as Carol finished telling me what was planned for our day of pampering. "First, a mud bath, then we'll get steamed, have a massage and a make-over—hair, face, nails; lunch, too, of course. Why don't you invite John to have dinner with Jim and me tonight? The four of us could have a lovely evening."

"No, I don't think so," I said. For a moment, I wished I could be as outspoken about my sexual preference as Carol was about her alcoholism, not that they could be equated, I thought. Homophobia will always be with us, so I'd kept my private life quiet for career reasons, but the generational and cultural attitude towards homosexuality was something I'd never shake.

"It would be fun! At least sit with Jim and me; we'll see who we can catch for you."

"I'm not fishing," I laughed. "Those day are over for me."

"They're never over; trust me." Her simpering smile seemed unattractive for a woman her age. Yet, who says seniors can't enjoy flirtation, the chase, the down-and-dirty? Touch is critical to survival; where this tactation originates shouldn't be an issue, but Victorian ideas still haunted me. Jesse had almost purged me of my mother's teachings, but occasionally, I'd have a lapse.

After registering at the spa desk, we changed into thick, white terrycloth robes. "I know you'll love the mud bath. Come on. This way," Carol said, opening a door with a brass number '3'.

Slatted wood flooring and tiled walls, an elaborate multi-showerhead and two steamtables with coffin-like glass domes would be our space for the next hour. It had been years since I'd done this; several times, Jesse and I went to Calistoga for wine tasting and spa-ing, as we called it. My body had been whole then and smoothing the silky mud on each other was incredibly sensuous. But now, I'd have to reveal my scarred body to a woman I hardly knew.

An attendant tapped on the door and entered with a large bowl of therapeutic mud, placing it on a tall wooden stool. "Be sure that you don't put this on your face or the soles of your feet; it's very slippery," she said. "I'll be back in a few minutes to get you settled on the steam tables; would you like eucalyptus or orange aroma therapy today?"

I shrugged my shoulders at Carol, who said, "Eucalyptus?" She raised her eyebrows at me and I nodded agreement. This was her project; she could choose. When the attendant left, Carol hung her robe on a hook by the door and began smoothing the silky concoction on her sun-wrinkled body. "Come on, don't be shy," she said. When I joined her at the bowl, she gawked at me and said, "My God! You have cancer?"

"I'm in remission." My jaw felt tight, but I attempted a smile in an effort to get pass the awkward moment.

"Val, Val. You are such a mystery! You must tell us about your cancer. Here let me do your back and then you can do mine." I turned, a bit tense as I waited for her touch.

There had been a time, soon after the divorce, that I yearned for a warm touch—a touch beyond that of my child—of connecting with another human without words, without the need to explain the intimate contact, the simple joining of finger tips, lips, breath, the sexual tension that goes with exploring a zone of violation. The men who escorted me to business functions—dating me in their minds—never met those needs. And, God knows, I tried the male-female thing after the divorce, but I knew what I was. Hadn't I read everything I could find on that which was forbidden by law, history and politics? But thirty years ago, not that much had been well researched or well written. But I knew what I wanted, what I needed. Getting it was another matter. So I blocked that part of my life, channeling the sexual energy into being the best-damned banker I could. Even when I met Jesse I was afraid of being misconstrued; no, of being construed. But she saw; she knew, and patiently nurtured me to the breakthrough. She made me whole.

I felt the warm mud as Carol efficiently smoothed it over my shoulders and upper back. Scooping up a second handful, she smeared it on my lower back. "Oh my God! You've got a tattoo on your butt!" She shrieked with laughter and I had to join her. Jesse had the same reaction the first time she encountered the small Talisman rose on my left cheek. I remembered how she said in awe, "Lady, you've got balls!"

"That was a fortieth birthday gift to myself," I said. "Back in those days, tattoos weren't de rigueur. I did quite a bit of research to find a tattoo parlor that looked clean and respectable. A friend went with me; he was concerned about me dropping my drawers in a place like that."

"He?"

"I have a close friend who owns an art gallery in Portland. He looks great in a tuxedo and often was my escort to functions that called for a date. We enjoy each other's company without any pressure to be more than companions."

"You mean he was gay?"

"Was, and still is," I laughed. "We're still great friends."

By now, the attendant had settled us on the steamtables, closing the glass domes and placing cool cloths on our foreheads. The aromatic steam and the warm mud began to do its work on our bodies. Muscles and minds went limp. It was a lovely feeling, one I didn't know I needed. There are times to let go, not be in complete control, I thought. A healing visualization I'd been taught during my regimen with chemo and radiation came to mind. I pictured the tumor shrinking, the area clean and healthy, the scars fading, any foreign materials in my bloodstream dissolving and being released through sweat and breath. I'd be clear, healed.

It was late afternoon by the time we returned to The Villa, relaxed and polished from head-to-toe. I promised to have dinner with Carol and Jim, aware that they'd probably con John into sitting with us. Oh, well; what the hell, I thought. I might even wear the pale blue knit dress tonight. I hadn't realized how much I'd let myself go in the grooming department since Jesse died. She had liked our dichotomy—my crisp, tailored style in contrast to her eclectic swirl of long skirts and bright colors. Her mass of dark curly hair, loose or secured atop her head with chopsticks was a magnet to my hands. I could never get enough of the sensual silkiness, its almond-like smell. No, I won't tell the Scheherazades my love story. They can tell me theirs.

Dinner with Jim, Carol and John was pleasantly uneventful, with John excusing himself early to prepare for his eight o'clock slideshow. I've never been into looking at people's vacation slides, but John's were excellent. It was obvious he had a teaching background and knew how to show-and-tell the best of a trip in forty-five minutes. It was well received by my fellow Villains. Afterwards, several of us gathered in the bar to show John our appreciation by buying him a drink. Earl appointed himself as MC for the evening.

"This Irishman goes to the doctor and finds out that he has cancer and only a month to live," Earl Smithers said, pausing to make sure he had our attention. Carol, Jim, John and the others began laughing as Earl got into the story. I didn't find cancer humorous, but Earl could be forgiven for his ignorance of my situation. He had a knack for telling jokes; often his delivery was funnier than the story itself.

The men were enjoying a Scotch while Carol and I sipped soda and lime. I would have ordered a martini but had become more conscientious about taking care of myself. Or was it that I didn't want to put Carol in a difficult position? Since when did Val Kenyon become someone's keeper, I wondered?

"So he meets his son, Sean, to have a couple of pints at the local pub and tells him the news. Then they run into several of the Irishman's friends. He tells them—while they are drinking—that he has only a month to live because he has AIDS. Later, his son asks him why he told them he had AIDS instead of cancer."

Attempting an Irish brogue, Earl delivered the punch line. "Because I don't want any of them fellas making a move on your mother when I'm gone."

Groans and chuckles were Earl's reward. Then Jim said, "You know, Earl, you've got some competition for storytelling from the ladies."

"Really? Okay, Val, Carol, tell us one."

I shook my head; I'm the world's worst joke teller, but Carol smiled brightly and leaned forward in her chair. Placing her glass on the table, she said, "Once upon a time a beautiful, independent, self-assured princess happened upon a frog in a pond. The frog said to the princess, 'I was once a handsome prince until an evil witch cast a spell on me. But, Lovely One, just one kiss from you and I will turn back into a prince. Then we can marry, move into the castle with my mother, and you can prepare my meals, clean and mend my clothes, bear my children and for forever feel happy doing so.'" The men were nodding as if this were the perfect arrangement.

"That night, while the princess dined on frog legs..." Here Carol paused to see if her audience pictured the scene, then gave the punch line. "She laughed to herself and thought, 'I don't fucking think so.'"

I thought the story was hilarious and gave a great whoop, but the men only gave polite laughter to Carol's joke. I guess it was a gender thing, as well as a generation thing. Women our age aren't supposed to know, let alone say, the f-word.

Jim said, "Pretty good, but I'm thinking of your other storytelling—you know, with your friends."

My heart sank and I saw a flicker of a frown on Carol's face. Jim continued. "These ladies tell real stories to each other so they can live longer, like in A Thousand and One Nights, to stall the Grim Reaper."

"Jimmy," crooned Carol, "You weren't supposed to tell."

"So that's what was going on the other night. I accused them of being a coven of witches," John said. "Instead, it was the Scheherazades!"

While everyone else laughed, I felt myself shrinking into the cushions of the chair. As far as I was concerned, our storytelling wasn't something for general consumption. Now, our secret was out. And, we'd been branded with a name.

John turned his attention to me, but saw my discomfort because he started telling us about ancient literature. "It's quite common for people to tell stories as a way of protecting themselves or extending life. An early example is The Decameron, an early Renaissance story-bank of a hundred or so classic tales. It was written in Florence around 1350 during the time of the plague; hundreds of thousands of people were dying neglected in the streets. Boccaccio, the author, writes about seven young women and three young men who leave the city to avoid the plague. For diversion, they begin to tell one story a day for ten days. So telling stories to ward off death isn't unusual."

"What kind of stories did they tell?" Earl asked.

"Oh, comic, tragic, the fantastic, the pornographic and the realistic," John said. "The stories come from all parts of the Mediterranean area; they include sultans and caliphs, friars and merchants, Arabs, Jews, Christians."

"Pornographic, huh?" laughed Earl. "Give us an example!" John shook his head and laughed.

Carol said, "I doubt if any of those stories could hold a candle to the jokes you tell, Earl!" She turned to John saying, "Didn't The Canterbury Tales basically retell some of the same stories?"

"Yes. Some say that seven classic dirty stories originated in The Decameron; we just keep updating them to meet our century and culture."

Earl motioned for another drink and said, "Did you hear the one about…"

I stood, interrupting Earl as I wasn't in the mood for anymore of his tacky stories. "It's late, so if you'll excuse me." I turned to John, saying "I enjoyed your presentation, John. Thanks for sharing your travels with the 'Villains'."

"Villains?" Earl said. "That's a great name for us, Val. If you can call us Villains, we can call you and Carol The Scheherazades." Carol and I groaned. I guessed that by tomorrow night, everyone at The Villa would think of us differently.

John rose, saying, "I'll walk upstairs with you. Good night all."

Earl, Carol, Jim and the others settled back around the cocktail table calling their 'good nights' to us. I could hear Earl begin another story.

CHAPTER TWELVE

John and I climbed the back stairs in silence. I think John knew his naming us did not amuse me. As we came to my door, John said, "I meant no harm; sorry if I intruded into a private place."

"No problem; good night," I said, unlocking my door. But John didn't continue to his apartment, instead he stood awkwardly as if he were planning to come in. Earlier in the week, we'd had dinner each evening with Carol and Jim, and gone for walks in the morning, exchanging small bits of our past lives with each other. Even now, after his slide show on Machu Picchu and the drink in the bar, it seemed as if we had never met.

"Say, I've got something from my trip you might like," John said. "I'd invite you to my place but it's a mess. Let me get it and bring it over. Okay?"

Baffled, I said, "Sure, John. I'll leave the door ajar." I gave my apartment a quick glance, chiding myself for caring what he might think. As usual, my place was tidy, almost sterile with its chrome and glass-topped coffee table and end tables, my black leather chair, footstool and loveseat. My computer desk was neat, all papers filed away. No plants or craft baskets cluttered the room, only a beautifully framed Georgia O'Keefe print, several of Jesse's photos, and the stacks of books and magazines—"The Atlantic Monthly," "Smithsonian" and "Forbes"—made the room look inhabited. A soft tap on the half-open door and John entered carrying a large tissue-wrapped bundle.

"I don't know why I bought this; I have several similar things, but..."He suddenly seemed shy, ill at ease. We never grow up when it comes to the boy-girl thing, even when we're adults, I thought.

Taking the package, I invited him to sit while I unwrapped the unexpected gift. A soft alpaca throw in cream, taupe and gray spilled across my lap. "This is beautiful! I couldn't..."

"Oh, yes. Please. I'd like you to have it."

"I don't know what to say."

"Say 'Thank you' and enjoy it," John said with a smile. "No dye is used; all the colors are natural, even the reddish accents, and the black, too. Alpacas come in a wide variety of colors." His voice trailed off, as if he'd said too much.

I scrunched the throw in my fist, feeling the springy hand-woven fabric, then put it to my cheek. It was silky and warm. "Thank you. You're much too generous." Draping it over the back of my chair, I perceived a change in the room, as if the throw made it more homelike.

"Would you like coffee?"

"Yes, please."

"Decaf or regular?"

"Decaf, please; may I look at your books?"

"Of course," I laughed. "You sound like an English professor."

"I'm always interested in what other people read, although my curiosity can seem intrusive at times."

For the first time, I really looked at him. Of average height, he was tanned and wiry with a full white beard, short and neatly trimmed. His hair curled slightly over the collar of his shirt; half glasses rode low on the bridge of his nose. It was if I were seeing him for the first time, seeing beyond the "Professor" label that had been given him by residents of The Villa, as well as seeing him as a possible friend, not merely a man.

Handing him a mug of coffee, I settled myself in the recliner, feet up on the footstool, my back warming in the caress of the soft wool throw. "Do you approve of my reading tastes?"

"Eclectic, erudite; a Renaissance woman, perhaps?" he said in a teasing tone. I couldn't decide if he were making fun or complimenting me. I noticed that he held the tattered copy of A Thousand And One Nights.

I said, "Tell me more about the self-extension theme in The Decameron; I'm afraid literature got short shrift in my MBA program."

"Self-extension. Yes, that's a good way to put it. Boccaccio sees that humanity and moral law are collapsing during the time of the plague. Most, but not all of the stories are thematic: tales of man as the plaything of fate, of ingenuity overcoming fate, of love as destruction, love as pleasure, tricks played by wives on husbands, and other deceptions." He leaned back on the loveseat and gazed at the ceiling, as if searching his mind for information he'd not had to bring forth in a long time. "Boccaccio, as author, is there to remind the reader of his intention: to tell each story to an ideal reader, not a scholar, nor a priest, but a woman of leisure."

"Well, we certainly are in our leisure period here at The Villa," I laughed.

He nodded and continued. "The Decameron setting is a luscious mock-court, a perfect pastoral, devoted to the roles of teller and listener, dominated by women. The stories themselves function as a deferral of sexual consummation, a sublime tease." He reached for his coffee mug again and said, "I'm afraid I've slipped into my old lecture mode. Sorry."

"No, I'm interested. You see, intellectually, I know that telling stories won't really extend our lives, but…" I stopped, unsure how to go on.

"Tell me about your storytelling group."

I chuckled and shook my head. "Why not. It's a fair exchange." I paused, organizing my thoughts. Did he know the women involved? Did it matter?

"Grace Bonner, Dee Ryan, Marion Barnes and I played Bridge several times a week during my first months at The Villa. We were hard-core players. It was the game, not chitchat nor friendship that was important to us, well, at least to me. When Marion died, we couldn't find a suitable replacement; guess we're Bridge snobs." He smiled, as if he understood the human interaction I was attempting to convey.

"Carol moved in about that time and we invited her for a martini. She doesn't play Bridge and doesn't drink, but being an author, does know how to tell a story. I wasn't enthused about the idea of sharing our lives with each other, but Dee, and particularly Grace, think that we can extend our lives by a thousand and one days, if we share personal stories. These stories are to be more that just the usual getting-to-know-you conversation. It was my fault for showing them that book, but it was Carol's idea, no, it was Dee's idea to tell stories. Now, Grace thinks she can't get well without the process."

John was staring at a framed print on the wall opposite the loveseat. "I get the impression that you don't believe that life can be extended by any means," he said, turning from the erotic art. I shrugged and let my eyes wander to the picture, wondering if John saw what I saw in the print. A thin pewter-colored frame with a white mat held a reproduction of Georgia O'Keeffe's 1925 painting of large, labia-like red leaves—enormous, sensuous, velvety.

Turning back to John, my response was disjointed. "Logically, it won't increase life by a minute. Yet, the support-I hate that word when it comes to women: support groups, child support, support hose." He smiled. I struggled to explain. "Just the commitment to spend some serious time with each other, may make our remaining life richer."

John carefully placed the tattered book of fables on the coffee table next to his empty mug. "There are moments in life when something touches us deeply, stirs our spirituality. I believe that those moments extend our lifetime. Spirituality has nothing to do with organized religious practices. In fact, I disdain mind-numbing dogma that passes as spiritual access. Spirituality is the 'ah ha' when the mind, body and spirit come together and everything seems right. It's a connection to something bigger that opens up self-exploration, self-regulation." He paused, looking at me, then said, "It's seeing with new eyes, achieving awareness, balance and choice—unlimited choice—for your own well-being. It's being able to answer the question, 'Does my life make sense?'"

"And does yours?" I asked, not to intrude in his life, but perhaps to learn if I could achieve the 'ah ha'.

"It does now. As I told you the other day, I really wanted to be an anthropologist, but my mother insisted that I follow in her footsteps. Literature. I was a pretty wimpy kid, and as I look back, my father was never one to stand up to mother either." He smiled ruefully. "The more I travel to out-of-the-way places, the more things make sense to me. For example, we were on the train to Machu Picchu before dawn; the ride through the Urubamba Gorge is spectacular and when we arrived, we were allowed to wander on our own, to find solitude, to meditate, to absorb." He paused, then said, "That's when mind-body-spirit joined and the 'ah ha' came."

"Surely, you can't mean that a person must travel to find spirituality."

"Oh, no. But it's easier to hear it, feel it, experience it—whatever the 'it' is—when we're away from our usual routine. It took travel to help me access it, even though I didn't know I was seeking it."

"What about our neighbor's spirituality? Mabel is always wanting to get me in touch with her Holy Spirit."

John laughed, nodded knowingly and said, "She's tried to save me, too. She'll never find true spirituality. Formal religion can be a bridge to spirituality; but she and other fanatics are stuck on the bridge. They'll never make it to the other side until they let go of the rule book and truly get in touch with themselves."

"Tell me more about your 'ah ha' moments."

"There were so many this last trip," he said, squinting as if to recall a particular moment. "For example, the night I stayed with a Quechua family on Taquile Island, and being with the incredible Uros people who live—whole communities—on giant woven rafts. There was a peace there, despite the poverty. They were truly attuned to nature while working hard to survive. I'm not saying I'd trade places with them, but they have a certain serenity that many of us in the so-called advanced civilizations don't have."

"It seems to me that there would be few 'ah ha's' here at The Villa."

"Not true. There are times of peace, well being. I can't really explain."

"I wish you'd let me know when an 'ah ha' hits you," I laughed. "But that's not the way it works, is it?"

"No. It sounds to me like you need to get away from your routine, give yourself a chance to experience the 'ah ha'. Would you come with me sometime?"

"To South America?" I laughed.

"Perhaps a trip to Central Oregon or the coast first." We smiled at each other, then he said, "Thanks for the coffee and conversation."

"Good night, John," I said, escorting him to the door.

He had given me much to think about. Sleep came peacefully as I allowed my mind to wander in search of an 'ah ha.'

CHAPTER THIRTEEN

Returning to The Villa after a month in Seattle, Grace seemed to be recovering well from the broken hip; at least she put on a good act. She shrugged off the episode, saying she might be getting clumsy in her old age. Dee often called me to provide status reports on Grace's physical and mental condition, and to remind me that we'd meet Thursday after dinner to tell stories. I didn't bother to tell Dee that our secret storytelling was now common knowledge throughout The Villa and that we were known as The Scheherazades. As if to capitalize on the tag, Carol purchased matching caftans for the four of us, insisting that we wear them whenever we told our stories. Mine was a deep turquoise; Carol's was ruby. As much as I hated the idea, I'll have to admit that the caftan was beautiful and felt wonderful. I just hadn't worn anything like that before; I left flamboyant clothing to Jesse.

Dressed in our jewel-toned caftans, Carol and I fluttered down the hall to the elevator, descending to the first floor and Grace's apartment. Dee, in an emerald green caftan, greeted us with great enthusiasm; Grace sat regally in a wheelchair, the sapphire silk of her caftan accentuating her blue eyes. Dee squealed with enthusiasm at the sight of Carol and me. "Gorgeous, simply gorgeous! I've never had anything like this in my life."

"You look like a Celtic queen in green, Miss Ryan, " I said. "Grace, welcome back; you are stunning in blue."

"It's good to be home again, but I couldn't have done it without Dee. She's been my savior."

"The management is concerned about Grace," Dee said, bustling about, getting Carol and me settled with tea and pastel mint candies.

"Concerned about what?" Carol asked.

"They get a bit pushy when they think someone is ready for The Haven; they disapprove of the wheelchair," Dee said, sitting next to Grace. "Are you comfortable?"

"I'm fine; now quit fussing."

"Well, how are you, Grace?" I said.

"The doctor told me I'd have to give up smoking, drinking and sex. So I asked him if that would make me live longer. He told me 'no' but it would seem like it!"

Carol and I burst out laughing; Dee frowned, then said, "But you don't smoke. Oh, you're joking, aren't you!" This just made the three of us laugh harder.

"At least you haven't lost your sense of humor," Carol said. "Really, how are you?"

"It was a lucky break; they pinned the hip and I'm doing fine, but I need to use the wheelchair or the walker. The only problem is that sometimes this type of break can—how did the doctor put it?—can 'go south' and it can't be re-pinned. A hip replacement isn't an option either, for several reasons."

I could see she was trying to be light-hearted about her condition, but there was something darker lurking behind her cavalier attitude. "Call on us anytime to help. We won't let anyone ship you off to The Haven." My bravado was hollow; The Villa was for active seniors and the care level very specific. I often wondered if I had a relapse whether I could stay.

Grace said, "Tell me all the news and gossip. Dee's brought me up-to-date on new residents and the menu improvements; I believe we can thank Carol for that. You're chairing a dining committee now?"

"Trying to," Carol laughed. "It's like herding cats. I'll get things started, then turn it over to one of the other committee members. I just want to implement the suggestions from my San Francisco caterer; when I suggested that Jell-O of any color be banned, I was practically stoned to death. What is it with old people and Jell-O?"

"Beats me," Grace said. "I hate the stuff."

Our conversation was like a string of broken pearls, bouncing this way and that, small episodic bits of information with digressions and daily details. Raw facts, randomness and surface details gave insights into the unlinear telling.

Dee said, "I heard something about Val and Carol being called The Scheherazades. Is that true?"

"Well, that's partially true," Carol said. "You and Grace also have that designation."

"But why?" exclaimed Dee.

"Val's friend—John Gurian—dubbed us that."

"What do you mean my friend?" I exclaimed. "If it weren't for your pillow talk with Jim and his big mouth, no one would be the wiser."

"Now, now, girls," Grace laughed. "This sounds very interesting, especially the pillow talk part; let's have the details."

With a coquettish toss of her head, Carol said, "Jim and I've been seeing each other, and John and Val have been having dinner with us. And," she paused, giving me a raised eyebrow, "John gave Val an Alpaca throw."

"How'd you know that?" I asked.

"I saw it on the chair in your living room. It wasn't there the last time I was in your apartment and I know it is from South America. Writers are very observant."

"The great detective strikes again."

Dee and Grace laughed at our verbal sparing, then Dee said, "How do The Scheherazades fit into all this?"

"Let me tell it," I said, hoping to defuse further rumors about any involvement with John. I gave a succinct recap of the conversation, mentioning that it was not unusual for people in many cultures to tell stories for a variety of reasons.

Grace said, "Native Americans are great storytellers, too. I knew quite a few Indians when I lived in Montana. Their stories about Coyote were a way to teach their children how to behave; the stories were object lessons. Traditionally, they only told stories in the winter, never at other times."

"Why just the winter," Dee asked, passing the candy dish around.

"As I recall, they only told them when Snake wasn't around to overhear the stories and tell them to others."

"That's like us; we don't want others to know our stories," Dee said. "Let's be sure Snake doesn't hear us!"

We laughed. Then Carol said, "I imagine that the tribes were too busy during the other seasons with their hunting and gathering to tell stories, waiting until winter to teach their children and to keep the ancient stories alive."

"Shall I get Mr. Snow to watch for Mr. Snake?" Dee asked. We agreed that if Snake decided to join our group, we'd let her bring the cat.

"You know, I like the designation of The Scheherazades," Grace said. "I've been called a lot worse things than that! Now, let's hear a story."

"You tell one," I said.

"No, I'm too tired tonight; next time. It's your turn Val."

"Yes!" said Carol. "She has a secret that I know." Turning to me she said, "You need to share it with Dee and Grace."

"Oh, God," I sighed. "Okay. I had a mastectomy three years ago; I'm in remission and doing well." I started to give some details, but stopped. This was the kind of conversation people slide into when they don't have something better to talk about. "Look. Let's keep our storytelling to something more interesting than past illnesses. I refuse to let cancer be the driving force in my life; after a year of the disease taking precedent, I made up my mind that it can be conquered."

"I agree," Grace said. "I know I'm very tired of my hip!" We laughed and settled more comfortably in our chairs, waiting for someone to pick up the metaphorical 'talking stick.' Finally, Carol spoke.

"Val has another secret." All eye were on me; a flood of anticipation set my skin prickling. Then I realized Carol meant my tattoo, not Jesse.

In a very serious tone, I said, "I'm not sure Dee and Grace can handle my...other secret."

"Oh, please," whispered Dee. "We're friends; we won't be shocked."

"Okay, if you think you can take it." I sighed, furrowed my brow and winked at Carol.

"Oh, do get on with it," Grace said. "Nothing you could tell us would be earthshaking! I'll bet my secret is worse."

"Are we really telling secrets tonight?" Dee asked, with her usual not-quite-getting-it look.

To put Dee out of her misery, Carol said, "Let me tell; it's so great." She paused dramatically, then said, "Val has a tattoo on her butt."

"No!" Dee exclaimed.

Grace wheezed with laughter. "When did you do that? And more important, why?"

"It was a fortieth birthday present to myself, just a whim. It made me feel very daring. My image as a conservative banker needed, no, I needed to prove to myself that I had a less serious side." Again Grace and Carol exploded with laughter, while Dee sat quietly slack-jawed. Finally, she spoke.

"Did it hurt?"

"A bit." Again, all eyes were on me. I felt as if I could read minds. "It's a Talisman rose, about two inches long. Only those individuals who are privileged to see me buck naked get to view it."

The conversation then bounced from tattoos to body piercing. Pros and cons, strongly held opinions, and general curiosity about the reasons for body art soaked up another twenty minutes before a silence settled upon our group. It seemed as if none of us were ready to tell a story this evening. Perhaps we were getting reacquainted; we'd gotten out of the rhythm of meeting and talking. Telling personal stories isn't something to be done on command. The teller and the listeners must be ready; tonight didn't seem like the time. But Carol wasn't about to let me off the hook.

"Tell us about your childhood, Val; there must have been some experience that makes you dislike illness so much."

My childhood. Yes, I could talk about that. It wasn't a bad childhood; stifling, but not bad. "Okay. Just the other day I was thinking about my misspent youth, the days of visiting the sick and needy instead of playing. We were Methodists. My father attended church sporadically, more as a business-contact thing than out of devoutness. He liked to be seen with his family. On the other hand, my mother and grandmother were believers; Mabel would have loved them. My mother was a Lady Bountiful, the wife of a successful man. Traditionally, women were to do good works, to impress the community on their husband's behalf, if nothing else. Visiting the sick and needy was the woman's role in philanthropy, while the men wrote checks more often than not, to impress their peers rather than from a deep belief in a particular cause. It was the women who got down in the trenches."

I paused to take a sip of tea, wishing I had a funny or exciting tale to tell as Carol did, yet glad I didn't have her kind of background. I glanced at my listeners; they seemed to be with me, nodding as women do to encourage the speaker. That's one of the stupid things women do—nod, agreeing with the speaker, even if they don't. I'd worked diligently to avoid that female acquiesce bit of body language.

"Nearly every Saturday after lunch, my mother and grandmother would visit the less fortunate—as they were called—taking them flowers, food, clothing, whatever was needed according to the church records. My brothers got to stay home and play or go sailing with father, but I had to dress up and accompany mother. Her philosophy, as far as I can tell, was that pretty little girls cheer up shut-ins. So, I'd have to put on a fluffy dress and patent leather Mary Jane slippers and go with Lady Bountiful and Grandmother Walters. To make matters worse, I had to sing for some of the shut-ins."

There was a groan of understanding. "How old were you?" Dee asked.

'This went on from the time I was four or five until I was twelve or so, when I stopped being cute and became more intractable." My listeners responded with appropriate mirth. "This was the period of Shirley Temple's early movies. I had dresses just like Shirley's movie clothes. I could sing Animal Crackers in My Soup and The Good Ship Lollypop. I imagine that many little girls did that in those days." I shut my eyes, seeing myself on the porch of some old house, playing alone, trying to be patient until the women were through talking. Boredom and obedience seemed to rule my early years.

"I remember one visit that left a deep, disturbing impression on me. This one sick old woman lived in a dilapidated Cape Cod; the clapboard was cracked and shingles were missing from the steep roof. It was very dark and smelly inside—a musty, unclean odor, as I recall. I always had to go in with my mother and grandmother to present the flowers, while they carried the baskets of food. Then I was allowed to go outside and wait until the visit was over. On this particular visit, I had to go bed side and sing for the woman. She had long, white hair that hung past her shoulders and huge pale eyes— cataracts, probably; she looked like a witch right out of my fairytale books."

I paused, conjuring up the scene, trying to banish the disgust I felt then—and even now. "Anyway, when I finished singing "Jesus Loves Me" she reached out and clutched my arm with her cold, claw-like hand and said 'Amen.' I can still see her long yellow fingernails and wrinkled skin stretching over crippled hands.

"As I recall, mother said she'd been a Flora Dora Girl or some kind of showgirl fallen on hard times, then into a wicked life. Good deeds were always more worthy if performed on sinners."

Murmurs of understanding gave me time to remember the rest of that day. "I was dressed in my Shirley Temple dress; it was white organdy with red dots matching the Shirley Temple doll in my arms. It was one of those toys adults buy for kids but don't want them to play with. It was part of the image my mother wanted for our sick-and-needy visits. When I was finally allowed to go outside, I drew a chalk Hopscotch game on the crumbling sidewalk, found a small stone to use as a marker and began to play. I always took chalk with me so I could amuse myself with a game or just draw on the sidewalk."

"I loved to play Hopscotch," exclaimed Dee. "It's something you can do alone or with friends." Murmurs of memory and the clink of teacups floated around the room. I continued my story.

"A little girl came across the street toward me; she'd been watching for awhile, but I'd ignored her. Without a word, she picked up the doll, cradled it in her arms and rocked it. I don't know what came over me, although I'm sure a psychiatrist could say, but I told the girl she could have the doll. About then, my mother and grandmother came out and saw the little girl running home with the doll. My mother called out something—not quite as bad as 'Stop, Thief!' but close. I told her I gave the girl the doll and mother just came unhinged!"

Carol laughed and said, "So much for the Shirley Temple image."

"Exactly," I said. "She wanted me to get the doll back, but by then I was in tears and the girl had disappeared." I sipped my tea and reflected on the memory. "I suppose that was my first philanthropic act."

Carol said, "I'd rather write a check than work in the trenches. I hate the look, the smell, the sight of sick, old people."

"Well, thank you, Carol," Grace said, only half joking.

"Oh, I don't mean you!"

There was an uncomfortable silence, until Dee spoke.

"I never had any money to give, so I had to take care of people," Dee said.

"Everyone has a way to make their community better," said Grace, with a far away look. It seemed as if she was about to tell us something, then changed her mind. We sat quietly, unsure whether to continue or break up the evening. It was then I remembered an old aunt we often visited.

"We used to visit old relatives, too. One was Aunt Isabel. I think she was my grandfather's sister, a former schoolteacher. My Grandmother told me that Aunt Isabel invented the slide-rule; of course that wasn't true, but she did know how to use one. She lived alone in a dark, old Victorian house that smelled like mothballs. She occupied the kitchen and dining room, sleeping on an old couch next to the wood stove; as I recall, everything else seemed shut up.

"She offered me a candy bar at every visit; I'd always say 'no thank you'—that I didn't want to spoil my dinner, but she'd insist that I take it for later. The thought of eating anything from her house was disgusting; I usually threw it away, but sometimes I'd give it to my brothers when they had done something particularly fun while I was accompanying Mother.

"Well, to make the visits worse, she had an old dog named Tote. Tote had a flatulence problem, or at least Aunt Isabel blamed the dog. Perhaps it was her." Again laughter.

I still hadn't addressed the issue of hating to talk about disease. That reticence came from my mother's illness. "My mother died of breast cancer." Sympathetic sounds rippled through the room. "She was so foolish. Avoided routine physical exams, never admitted to any of us she was ill until it was too late. She had let it go so long, that she had an oozing sore by the time we dragged her to the doctor." I stopped, transported back to the last weeks of her life—in terrible pain, refusing any kind of comfort. It was God's will, she said. Bullshit!

"I guess what I'm trying to convey is that growing old and being sick has never appealed to me. My feelings are really over-the-top; I'll admit it." A pall had settled over the room. "I'm sorry; I shouldn't have gotten so serious. Anyway, I don't plan to get old and sick without a struggle. I intend to live forever; so far, so good."

Carol said, "When I was young, I prayed that I'd look like Elizabeth Taylor; now I pray I won't!"

We needed a laugh, even if it was at an old joke. I was thankful that Carol could get us out of the morass. She said, "I think we understand how you feel and why. Who's going to tell a story the next time we meet?"

Grace said, "I'd like to tell you about my nurses training and how I got to Montana."

We took our cups to the tiny kitchen with Dee saying she'd clean up and see that Grace was tucked into bed. The knock on the door surprised us.

Dee answered the door; Jim was standing there with a concerned looked. "Is Carol here?" Dee opened the door wider and Carol said, "What's happened?"

"You've got an emergency call from San Francisco. I just happened to be in the lobby and the Director asked if I knew where you were."

"It must be about Kenneth," Carol said. "Thanks for finding me; good night, ladies. I'll talk to you tomorrow." Jim and Carol hurried towards the lobby. I said good night to Grace and Dee, returning to my apartment feeling uneasy for no particular reason.

The next day, Carol was on her way to San Francisco. Kenneth had indeed taken a turn for the worse. His son and daughter-in-law had taken an earlier flight south, leaving Carol to fend for herself; however, she didn't seem concerned. Ten days later, Carol was back—a widow, wearing a chic black suit and talking about returning to California. But talk was all she did. I'm guessing that she was still afraid to be out on her own.

So, for a while longer, the Scheherazades would work their magic, increasing our allotted time on earth. Surprisingly, I was looking forward to hearing Grace's story. Now in her late-nineties, she must have seen and experienced many things that would seem very strange to the rest of us. Dee, in her early eighties, probably could relate to Grace's interpretation of life more than Carol and I as the 'youngsters' of the group.

CHAPTER FOURTEEN

During the time Carol was gone, Dee enlisted me in her plan to get Grace on her feet and keep her out of the Villa management's view, thus out of the Haven. We fixed simple meals in Grace's tiny kitchen, spirited her hither and thither to the Bridge table or craft room, putting her wheelchair out of sight. I knew we weren't fooling anyone, but Dee kept the illusion of Grace's imminent full recovery at the fore, even though I knew this was the beginning of a downward spiral. Grace didn't say anything to me, but she'd give me a look or a small smile when Dee would go on about getting things back to normal. I had seen The Villa's letter to Grace suggesting that it was time to "take advantage of the extra care The Haven could provide."

After nearly a week of this, I gratefully escaped for a few days at the Oregon Coast with Kara and Callie who flew from Boston to Portland; renting a car we drove west for a mini-vacation.

"Why is the ocean so cold?" Callie asked, teeth chattering, her lips blue from an abbreviated plunge into the Pacific.

Handing her a towel and sweatshirt, I mumbled something about the Japanese Current, then said, "Let's go to Moe's for clam chowder and then to the factory outlet mall." Callie honored me with a high-five and a kiss on the cheek. So far, I was batting a thousand with my granddaughter. Within the hour we were dry, warm, and swept up in the crowd at the huge shopping complex. Turning Callie loose with a pocketful of cash and a designated hour and place to meet, Kara and I staked out a corner table at Starbucks for a latte.

Kara said, "I think the trip's been a great success. You never know how teenage girls are going to respond to a suggestion that's not their own. Callie is much more difficult to raise than the boys were."

"Hmmm," I agreed, licking the milk foam from my lip. "That's what I've heard; I wish you'd come sooner."

Kara looked thoughtful, then spoke in a tentative voice. "I was uncomfortable bringing Callie here when Jesse..." She paused, seemingly at a loss how to say what I knew was on her mind. She began picking at her cuticle.

"Jesse was no threat to you or the kids. Your generation should have a more generous view of such relationships."

"We do," Kara said, "but not when it's in the family. Does that make me sound..."

"Old Fashioned? Judgmental? Yes, but I understand. Surely you knew I'd never have compromised...

"I know you wouldn't," she said with emphasis on the 'you.'" She paused, then continued. "But I didn't know Jesse."

"And that's your loss," I said, as gently as I could.

A chill passed over our table. I wondered if it were the coastal air, or mother and daughter at odds again. Kara spoke first.

"I wish I had met her; she must have been very talented, respected in her field."

At last Kara had opened the door I'd left ajar to my relationship with Jesse. Would Kara enter? I said, "Yes. She was well known for her camera art and was in high demand for magazine layouts. She also had work in a prestigious journal of contemporary photography; two of her photographs are available in platinum."

Kara frowned, looking puzzled. "How could pictures be in platinum; you mean like recordings?"

"No," I smiled. "Exceptional work is offered in a limited number of original signed prints. The photographs are printed in platinum on 100% rag paper; they're very expensive to buy, some increasing in value over the years."

"I've probably seen her work in Vanity Fair, but didn't realize it."

"I'm sure you have. Her last layout was in the April issue two years ago. She was on her way to a GQ shoot when the plane crashed." It was still difficult to talk about Jesse's death, but nothing would stop me now that Kara had broached the subject. I stirred my latte, putting my thoughts in order. "I'm not sure I'd still be alive if it weren't for Jesse. When I considered not fighting the cancer, she took over, making decisions for me until I was able to face the situation intelligently."

"Is that why you didn't include me?

I watched Kara gnaw on the hangnail as I carefully chose my words. "It wasn't fair of me to shut you out at a time like that; Jesse was always urging me to call you, share with you the decisions, the prognosis; yet, I knew she was as afraid of you as you were of her."

"Afraid of me?" She lifted her eyebrows in disbelief.

"She didn't want to lose me to anyone or anything." A great silence settled over us. Even the noisy shoppers, the traffic, the ocean waves seemed muffled.

After what seemed like dead air for an inordinate time, Kara took a deep breath and asked, "How did you meet?" She gave me a small, encouraging smile that seemed more artful than genuine.

Blood sang in my ears; its pressure increasing as it did when I was in a tense situation. While giving Kara the basic information, my memory replayed the scene in slow motion. It was a Friday evening and Burckhardt Gallery was crowded with patrons—wineglasses in hand, compliments on their lips, and checkbooks at the ready to honor the emerging artist. This was Jesse's first one-woman show. Free-lance photography of weddings, bar mitzvahs, and an occasional assignment for local newspapers and public relations firms had previously funded her art. This show proved to be the breakthrough for doing the kind of work she loved.

Mitch, the gallery manage, invited me as a personal friend and, also, as a corporate buyer. While none of the photographs were suitable for the bank, I purchased the photograph that hangs in my apartment. It looks like undulating sand dunes, but in reality it's a close-up section of two nudes. The soft sepia tones and exquisite lighting are an excellent example of her early work.

Of course Mitch insisted that I meet Jesse. The touch of her hand at our introduction was nothing less than strange fire. I couldn't tear my eyes from hers; she was looking into my soul. Nothing like this had ever happened before; she could have pealed me like a grape right there. I attempted to bolt, but she reached out, laying her hand on my arm. That's all it took. She saw. She knew.

After the reception, she took me to her studio. The exotic nature of the situation and her casual acceptance of carnality fascinated me. It took patience for her to break down my resistance after a lifetime of Victorian upbringing, social attitudes, and the fear of ruining my career. But this beautiful, talented young woman found something in me that no one else had ever fathomed. She was patient, but determined.

I said to Kara, "Our friendship started that evening, slowly growing to a deep, committed relationship that lasted nearly twenty years."

"You must have been circumspect since it didn't seem to affect your career," Kara said, a bit stiffly, I thought. Still, it seemed to me, that she was willing to continue her quest for understanding.

"True. We kept separate apartments, but were able to vacation, spend weekends together. If we both hadn't had demanding careers, it would have been more difficult to stay apart. But that's what kept us together, our single-mindedness when it came to our careers. Later, when I retired from the bank, we began making plans to buy a home together. But before we could make it happen, I became ill and, then, she was killed." I paused to collect my thoughts, trying to ease her homophobia. "Being part of a couple creates a safety zone, as you know in your relationship with Duncan. I needed that, too. I didn't have that with your father; it took me years of resisting my nature. When Jesse came into my life, I felt complete."

Seeing Callie coming towards us loaded down with shopping bags was just what we needed at the moment. "Look at that face," I said, laughing. "Teenage consumer triumph, if I ever saw it." Kara agreed and turned back to me for a moment, placing her hand on mine, and truly looked at me. I could have wept with happiness.

Two days later we were back at The Villa, sharing lunch with Grace and Dee in the small, private dining room off the lobby. I'd arranged for this special luncheon so my two "families" could meet. Dee and Grace were as charmed with Callie as she was with them. Kara and I were amazed and amused at the instant bonding of the three. I stifled tears of pride and joy at the scene. After too long, I had my daughter back, if not completely, at least it was a beginning. When they flew back to Boston late that afternoon, I sunk into an unexplainable melancholy.

The next day, as I checked on Grace while Dee was with her crafts group, our general conversation turned personal. It was as if she could see how low I felt with Kara and Callie gone, of settling back into The Villa routine.

"Tell me," Grace said.

"What?"

"Whatever it is that has you down. I've never seen you like this."

"I should be happy; I think I have my daughter back now after too many years of hostility, misunderstanding."

"Want to talk about the problem?"

I looked at her, wondering if I could tell her, if she would be offended, if I would lose her friendship. Perhaps it was worth a try as Grace and I seemed to have forged a strong, but unspoken link.

"It can't be that bad," Grace said with a smile. "In my ninety-seven years, I've seen and heard everything. That's one of the problems of living so long."

A buzzing in my head was either a warning signal or the unlocking of my reserve. I took a deep breath and plunged in. "I'm a lesbian; my daughter would never acknowledge that."

Grace remained quiet, her face impassive. I straighten my back and continued. "I didn't even acknowledge my true nature for many years; no wonder my marriage ended. I put all my energy into my career. It wasn't until I met Jesse that I could admit who and what I was. Even then, I guarded my secret so not to upset my family, my position in the community, my career." Again I paused, studying Grace, to see how she was taking this revelation. Her faced was calm, her eyes thoughtful. "Anyway, while we were at the beach, Kara finally asked about Jesse and I was able to tell her of our relationship, our love, how she cared for me when I was going through chemo. When Jesse died, I felt I had to hold my grief in check, to not show too much emotion, to again deny our relationship. That was hurtful to me and unfair to Jesse. I'm still in the process of forgiving myself for not being honest." I waited quietly, examining my aging hands, rubbing the blue veins that tracked between bony knuckles.

Finally she spoke. "Well, I'll be damned!" A wheeze of laughter filled the room.

I looked up to see her smiling. "I've never met a lesbian before, or at least not that I know of. I'll be damned." A broad smile crinkled the wrinkles around her eyes.

I nodded and smiled at her response, saying, "People picture us as coarse women with crew cuts and bad taste in clothes. But we come in all sizes, shapes, colors, attitudes and from very diverse backgrounds. I'll have to admit there are some that even scare me." Grace's chuckle made me grin.

She said, "Kara has accepted this now?"

"Beginning to. I think she knew or suspected for longer than she realized. Charlie, her father, became aware after our divorce. When I saw him in the hospital, he said he was glad I had someone special in my life. I think that's why he wanted to see me so that he could tell me he finally understood why I wasn't the perfect wife."

Grace was quiet and thoughtful, then taking my hand said, "You don't belong here; leave." I jerked away, stung by her words.

"No, no," she laughed, reaching for me again. "The Villa. The Villa's no place for you. Take a trip, move closer to your daughter and her family. Don't settle for this yet."

"I don't understand…"

"Look. You're too young to be here. Most of us are eighty or more. You're not even seventy yet. You'll age too quickly here. You'll experience our old age before you're ready to undergo your own old age. You're a young-old; Dee and I are old-olds. The Villa is for the old-olds."

The tears that had plagued my days since Kara left erupted again, running silently down my face; I knew Grace was right. My pattern of negative thinking had returned and I wanted out. Even though I knew my perception of reality was inaccurate, I seemed stuck. Grace continued to talk softly, squeezing and patting my hand as elderly women often do.

"Go on a trip. Travel shakes you up, gives you lots to do so you can't think of sad things. That's why I took a trip when Enes died. Later, I got caught up in the challenge of travel, new places, new people, new foods, not the mindless escorted tours, although I eventually had to go on those as I got less steady on my feet." Her blue eyes searched my face, reading me as if she could see deep inside. "Everything that looked black at first changed. There's so much to discover; if you stay here, you'll get old before your time."

"Sorry I'm such a mess today," I said, blowing my nose and taking a deep breath. "Funny you should suggest travel; John said I needed to get away, too, but you're saying move away, aren't you?"

"Yes. This isn't the place for you. Why did you ever come here in the first place?"

"It was early in my battle with cancer when Jesse died in the plane crash. And, at that time, my daughter and I weren't close. I just wanted to crawl in a corner and die. It made sense then, but now…"

"There, you see? Go. You can always settle down later, here or someplace closer to your family."

"I traveled quite a bit before," I said, warming to the suggestion. "Most of it was on business—Japan, Hong Kong, Australia. And I've flown into most major American cities. But I've never really seen America."

"Well, then. Go on the road."

"Should I buy a motorcycle?"

"They're too dangerous."

"Hop freight trains?"

"You're not the type." Grace said, trying to keep up the banter, but she looked tired, in pain.

"I've taken up too much of your time."

"No, no. Your story made me forget my pain, for that I thank you."

"Thank you for getting me out of my funk. Is there anything I can do for you?"

"Perhaps I'll take a nap. Help me to bed."

I wheeled her into the bedroom and allowed her to use me for support as she carefully stood, then sat on the edge of the bed. I gently lifted her feet and legs. Stretching out, she motioned for me to pull the hand-knit afghan over her legs. "A little water and that prescription bottle…there," she said pointing, her thin hand trembling. "I am hurting a bit. Thank you."

I blurted out, "I don't want to share this story with the others."

"Of course. I'm sure Dee would be…confused. And Carol, well, who knows?"

After I had Grace settled, I sat for a few minutes to make sure she was comfortable; when her eyes closed, I slipped quietly out of the apartment. She'd given me some things to think about. Traveling is like existing in a different stratosphere, a kind of therapy. Jesse and I often used mini-vacations to recover from demanding career pressures. Stepping out of the roles we played in public; we became girls again—ice cream cones, kites, giggling—even a pillow fight once that was sexually charged; we experienced the openings and closing of life, the breaking in and the breaking out that kept us whole.

A rush of emotions brightened my mood as I returned to my apartment. Intrigued at the thought of travel, or even moving, I remembered how I'd always loved driving; selling my car before coming here was the hardest, and dumbest, thing I'd done. I thumbed through magazines, reading car advertisements, visualizing myself behind the wheel of each glossy vehicle—SUVs, vans, luxury sedans, sexy sports cars. Pulling out an old road Atlas, I traced highways with my finger, taking secondary roads, seeing myself freewheeling in North Dakota, Pennsylvania, Georgia, Texas, New Mexico. There's so much to discover away from home, especially this home, I thought. I'm not yet a finished person; there's still time to grow, to do the things Jesse and I talked about. Dear Grace, that wise old woman, was right: I should do something productive with the time I had left.

CHAPTER FIFTEEN

As Grace waited for the drug to take her pain, she thought of the story she'd tell the Scheherazades after dinner. Still clear in her mind are the trip, her days as a student nurse and her life in Montana. A stab of pain slammed into her back; Grace talked to the codeine—"come on, come on, take hold; I've got to think about my story for tonight." Finally, the drug began to dull the vicious disease insinuating itself into her fragile bones. Dreams came.

Grace is young, excited, boarding the train to California. Her hat, wide-brimmed in pink and black velvet, is pinned securely to her intricately twisted knot of coppery brown hair. She is on the train from Portland to Los Angeles; sitting on the red plush seats, feet and knees together, hands clutching a new black purse, this is her first trip alone.

There is a long sidewalk, swept with wind and dust; she holds her hat to her head with one hand, the other hand dragging a heavy suitcase. The sidewalk seems endless, then abruptly becomes a large kitchen where mounds of carrots and cabbage need peeling and chopping. Forgotten faces swim before her as she struggles to prepare the vegetables; her mother's face presses close, scowling, thin lips saying "the wedding first."

Grace moves restlessly in her drugged sleep. Her neck damp, hair escaping from the pins in her thin knot of white hair. Thirst enters her dream; she walks to the loggia and bends over a white porcelain fountain for a drink. Tennis courts shimmer like the water in the fountain. Grace runs to return a serve, sweating, while courtside, girls in white dresses sip lemonade. Half-waking, Grace fumbles for a tissue on the bedside table, dabbing at her damp face, swallowing hard, her throat sticking upon itself. She tries to recite the lesson on diathermy. Sinusoidal and galvanic currents. What are they? She can't remember.

Surfacing slowly from her nap, mind dull, body lethargic, Grace turns her face to the nightstand where she keeps a photograph of Enes looking strong and young, hands on hips, legs wide-spread, a broad-brimmed hat set square on his head. She smiles at him, saying she'll soon join him.

Later that evening, we gathered in Grace's apartment like a bouquet of exotic butterflies, our jewel-toned silk caftans shimmering in the lamp light. There is an undercurrent of anticipation that has not enveloped us before; the other Scheherazades seem as eager as I to hear Grace's story. Perhaps we were finally hitting our stride as storytellers.

Dee fluttered about with the teapot and a plate of cookies. "My neeth Mary Alith broth these today," Dee lisped, passing the plate to Carol. "She made them herselth," Dee said with obvious pride. "I wasn't sure she'd ever learn to cook—or even try."

"What's the matter with you?" Carol asked, taking a cookie."

"Blither; new teeth," Dee said.

"Did you put soda on the spot?" Graced asked.

"Yeth. I have an appointment with the dentith tomorrow to get the darn thing fist."

I joined in the laugher, glad I still had my own teeth. Grace and Dee were always battling their dental bridges and plates. I didn't know if Carol's teeth were hers or not, but I assumed she still had her own, which looked beautifully capped. For a group of old broads with various health problems, we were in a good mood, although Carol was an emotional yo-yo; she had been like that since Kenneth died. One moment she was in tears, berating herself for being such a bad wife; the next minute she was excited about being single again and moving back to the Bay area. Grace, Dee and I didn't have a clue what more to do or say to her; we'd run out of assurances that she had been a fine wife, even though we didn't really know what we were talking about. I suppose only Grace could really understand what it meant to be widowed, although I felt as if I'd gone through it too when Jesse died.

We each took a cookie and, after tasting it, praised Mary Alice's talent, although it was questionable as far as I was concerned. Dee beamed, saying, "I hope they'll come again thoon. Maybe I'll give a lunthon like you did, Val, to meet your granddaughter."

"What luncheon?" Carol said, looking piqued.

"Oh, it was no big deal," I said. "Kara and Callie came for a few days while you were in San Francisco. We had a great mini-vacation at the coast and then Dee and Grace had lunch with us one day."

Carol looked mollified, yet agitated, abruptly changing the subject. "Well. Let's hear your story Grace." The room became still except for a whisper of fabric or clink of cup on saucer.

"I can't remember a time when I didn't want to be a nurse," Grace began. "My doll's arms and legs were always splinted, or their faces spotted with some dire disease I'd put there with crayon or pen; the cats and the dog ran whenever they saw me with scissors and strips of rag; have you ever tried to bandage a cat?" Grace was rewarded with chuckles and smiles.

Grace frowned, either in concentration or from pain; I couldn't tell. "Perhaps it was my great uncle who gave me the idea of becoming a nurse. He fought in the Crimean War and told stories about Florence Nightingale, the nurse who first practiced medical hygiene. Anyway, I didn't mind when I had to drop out of school to care for my mother and other family members when the great flu epidemic hit in 1918. I played nurse for real.

"After that, I got an after school job at a dentist's office—washing instruments, sweeping the floor, general clean-up. Dr. Stratton urged me to become a nurse. We belonged to the Seventh-Day Adventist Church at that time and they had a school of nursing in California, so I wrote for information. I was seventeen when I left home. A high school dropout, tall and skinny, ugly as sin, and in the way at home. My sister, Hope, was two years older and beautiful. She could play the piano, sing, dance. She had a raft of suitors in high school; she was engaged to be married that summer. Mother was busy sewing the trousseau, embroidering linens, planning the wedding. She said I could leave as soon as the wedding was over; I guess they needed my help. But everything I said or did seemed to annoy the family that summer." Grace sighed, a bitter smile flickered for a moment before she continued.

"My father worked for the Union Pacific Railroad; he was able to get rail passes. When I told him I'd applied for nursing school and needed to get to Glendale, he asked how soon I wanted to go. It seemed as if he didn't care I was leaving home. I suppose my feelings shouldn't have been hurt, but they were."

There was an audible gasp from Dee. She looked as if she would cry. "I know, I know," she whispered.

"Yes," Grace said with a wry smile. "I wasn't valued at home, at least compared to Hope. But I loved Hope very much. Everyone loved Hope." Grace looked far away as if seeing her family projected upon the opposite wall.

Dee all but exploded. "Families can be so cruel. Why is it the oldest always seem to get what they want and the rest of us..." She stopped and looked around, shame-faced. "Well, never mind; sorry I interrupted."

Grace gave Dee a loving smile. "That's all right. We can be angry about things—clear the air, so to speak." Carol nodded her head in agreement and I poured more tea. When I sat down, Grace continued her story.

"Let's see; where was I? Oh, yes. The trip. It was so exciting! I'd not been away from home by myself before."

"When was this?" I asked.

"1923. I can still remember what I wore. I had a navy blue suit and a white blouse I made. The jacket was long, like a three-quarter length coat. Over that I had a brown topcoat and a black and pink velvet hat with a stand-up crown and a wide brim. It took three hatpins to keep it on. My hair was very long and thick; I wore it in a big double knot at the back of my head. You wouldn't know it now, but my hair was brown then." She touched the diminished knot of white hair she carefully twisted and pinned each morning.

Dee said, "My hair was red and curly. It was thick, too, when I was young."

"I've bleached my hair for so long to keep it blonde, I don't have a clue what the true color is any more!" laughed Carol. "What color was your hair, Val?"

"Kind of dishwater blonde, I guess. Lady Clairol helped me out until I turned gray at an early age," I said. "Go on, Grace. Tell us about your trip." Quite honestly, hair-color talk bores me.

"I can remember sitting on the red velvet seats of the passenger coach, my hands clasping my new purse, my feet and knees together, looking very prim and feeling very grown up. The free pass my father got for me didn't include a sleeping berth, so I sat up for two days and two nights. I must have looked a sight when I got to Los Angeles!" She smiled at us and shook her head. "I took a basket of food with me. Apples, sandwiches, fried chicken, cookies. It had to last until I got there because I didn't have much money. On the last morning, I splurged and ate in the dining car. For thirty-five cents, I had strawberries and toast and coffee. There was a rose on the table in a tiny silver vase, and white linen, and china with the Union Pacific crest in gold on them. It seemed so very elegant."

Carol said, "I can't imagine taking that long to get to LA. We're so spoiled flying there in a few hours; even driving only takes—what? Twelve, fourteen hours?"

"You have to remember that the Golden Gate Bridge hadn't been built yet," Grace said. "They put the railroad cars on the ferry to get us from Oakland to San Francisco, then couple our cars up again to a train that ran between San Francisco and Los Angeles."

Impatiently, Carol refilled our cups this time and sat down as Grace continued. I wondered why she seemed so agitated this evening; it was as if she wanted to pick a fight.

"I was disappointed when I arrived. It was overcast and windy; I was expecting sunshine, tall buildings and movie stars strolling with their Russian Wolfhounds. I imagined it looking like—in the movies. Instead, it was rather ordinary, as I recall. Well, anyway, then I had to catch a trolley car to Glendale, that took another hour or more. I felt so small lugging my suitcase to the Sanitarium."

"Sanitarium?" Carol exclaimed.

"It was next to the hospital, but we started our training at the Sanitarium." Grace explained. "You see, the Sanitarium and its School of Nursing were established in 1906. It was a primitive school then; there were no modern conveniences like elevators, hot and cold water in the rooms, or even central heating. Water, supplies and instruments were sterilized on the kitchen stove and boxes were nailed together and painted white to serve as supply cupboards. By the time I got there in 1923 things were modern for that time. True, the student nurses still worked long hours; sometimes we'd be on duty as long as 24 hours at a time. We were paid six cents an hour and out of that we had to pay tuition, buy uniforms, books, and our meal tickets. We also had to tithe ten percent to the church.

"I can't imagine." Carol exclaimed, shaking her head. "And you stayed there? Finished?"

Grace gave her wry chuckle and nodded. " Oh, yes. Our days were a blur with classroom study, chapel, kitchen work, cleaning rooms, and serving patients in the dining room. I hated serving, but didn't mind working in the kitchen. I must have peeled a carload of carrots and chopped a mountain of cabbage for Cole slaw," she laughed. In the kitchen we wore long green aprons over our blue and white striped student nurse uniforms. The rest of the time we had white aprons over our uniforms.

Carol rustled her caftan and clanked her bracelets impatiently. What is her problem? I wondered. There was a glitter to her eyes, a hardness that I'd not seen before. It flashed across my mind that she might be drinking again. I rejected that notion as unfair and returned my attention to Grace.

"We were strictly chaperoned, too; our teachers lived with us in small cottages on the Sanitarium grounds. But there was fun, too. Picnics, croquet, tennis, and wonderful places to visit—the Griffith Planetarium, the Hollywood Bowl and the San Gabriel Mission."

Grace's eyes sparkled and her pale face developed a lovely glow; her memories, somehow, made me feel young and alive again, too.

Grace took a sip of tea before continuing. "Health care at the Sanitarium was up-to-date, offering the famous Battle Creek Treatment, which emphasized physical therapy, a vegetarian diet, exercise and rest. For the convenience of Sanitarium guests, there was a beauty parlor, a barber shop and a gift shop; it was an elegant facility."

"Elegant?" Carol snorted. "Sounds more like a workhouse to me."

"No, really. It was lovely. Originally, the sanitarium building was a Victorian hotel built in late 1800's. As I recall, a depression kept it from opening and it sat empty until the church bought it and established the Sanitarium.'

Carol rattled her bangle bracelets again, asking "Who used the sanitarium? Were they mental patients?"

"Oh, no, not the clinically disturbed. This was quite exclusive. In fact, advanced reservations were necessary as many Hollywood stars came to be cured of syphilis, exhaustion, drug and alcohol addiction.'

"Movie stars?" Dee interjected. "Anyone we might have seen?"

"Oh, yes. And they would entertain each other, too. Sometimes we could hear what was going on in the parlor, or even be there, if we had been assigned to a patient in a wheelchair."

Dee nearly clapped her hands in excitement. I found her reaction as much fun as Grace's story. "Well, tell us the gossip," I said.

"The patients, or guests as they were called, often gathered in the parlor for musicals, travelogues and talks by prominent lecturers. Perhaps guests might be treated to a violin concert by Jules Lepsi of the Philadelphia Philharmonic, who was spending the winter at the Sanitarium, the first year I was there. Once, comedian Ben Turpin got up and put on an impromptu skit. Clara Bow and other stars could be seen wandering the grounds or entertaining friends in the covered loggia. Oh, it was heady stuff for us."

Carol laughed, saying, "You could have been a reporter for the National Inquirer; earned a nice bit of change telling tales about the stars."

Grace shook her head, dismissing the suggestion as if it were unworthy. Dee said, "Were you homesick, since this was your first time away by yourself?"

"Oh, yes. What I missed the very most was coffee, and mother's pot roast. Even though we belonged to the church, we weren't strict vegetarians at home. No pork or shellfish, of course, but we did eat other meat and drank coffee, which we weren't allowed at school."

"What did the Sanitarium serve?" Dee asked.

Grace pondered a moment and said, "Soybean patties and kidney bean casseroles are what I remember most. That got pretty boring after awhile." Grace rested her head on the back of her chair, looking up and smiling. "I made lots of good friends there; we were very close. In fact, for over fifty years we stayed in touch by mail. We wrote letters and forwarded them to the next name on the list. It would take months for the package to get back to you. You'd take out your old letter and put a new one in the shoebox and mail it to the next person. I'm the last one left." Grace sighed and went on with her story.

"I got into a lot of trouble when I nearly flunked Bible Study, but they never found out about my greatest sin." We shifted in our chairs, eager to hear of Grace's misdeed.

"Well, each month when I had my period, I'd walk to a nearby diner and spend fifteen cents for a waffle and coffee. My classmates could always tell when I'd had coffee, but they kept my secret." This revelation was greeted with much laughter and a request for more of her rebel antics.

"Lois, my best friend, bobbed her hair and they were going to expel her, but I got all the other girls to agree we'd bob our hair, too, if they made Lois leave. They let her stay, but she had to wear a switch, a hairpiece, until her hair grew out again."

I said, "You rebel, you!"

"Oh, I wasn't that much of a rebel. I wanted to graduate." She grinned, then nodded as if remembering more. "One time after a picnic, I sent some lemonade to the lab for urine analysis. There was a lot of excitement when they thought the patient's label had been lost and that a diabetic was in trouble."

It seemed impossible that all this happened before I was born, that young women were as mischievous then as now, only in different ways. My respect, even love, for Grace deepened.

Carol asked, "What about boy friends?"

Grace nodded and smiled. "I had a crush on a handsome intern, but my best friend, Lois, had her cap set for him. He and I were tennis partners. No one could beat us at doubles. Lois was pretty, but unathletic. They married, but it wasn't a happy union. I was lucky that he introduced me to his older brother, Enes."

"Now we're getting to the good part," Carol exclaimed. "Tell us your love story."

"Well, it was a love story, not a marriage of convenience or a match pushed upon us by family or friends. Enes was very shy, but I knew he loved me. His letters were lovely; I still have them. We had a long-distance courtship while I finished nurses training and he established his veterinarian practice in Billings. With him in Montana and me in California, it helped us finish what we each had started on our own." Grace sighed and shifted in her chair. It seemed to me that she was hurting. I wondered if I should offer to get her pain pills.

"As soon as I graduated, I returned to Portland and began planning my wedding. We had it at home; I made my own wedding dress and the cake, too."

"What was your dress like," Dee asked in a dreamy voice.

"It was...let's see; it was ecru chiffon with satin trim around the cap sleeves and at the drop-waist. It had handkerchief points at the hem and, oh, I can't remember..."

"Where did you honeymoon?" Carol asked.

"Yellowstone Park on our way to Billings. We had a Model T Ford; Enes taught me to drive on our wedding trip." Grace chuckled, coughed repeatedly, and rested her head on the back of her chair. I could tell she was tiring.

"You okay, Grace?" I asked, offering her the glass of water next to her chair. "Need a pain pill?"

"No. I'm fine. Just tired of talking." She coughed again, then said, "Dee, tell us your story."

CHAPTER SIXTEEN

We looked at Dee in anticipation. She seemed surprised at Grace's request. I said, "Wasn't this storytelling your idea to begin with? We haven't heard a thing from you."

Dee flushed and fluttered her hands in her lap, then said, "Well, I don't know what you'd like to hear."

Carol said, "Tell us about your first love."

Dee lowered her eyes and slowly shook her head. The room was so quiet that I gave a start when Grace's Cuckoo Clock tolled the half hour. This seemed to help Dee make up her mind. "I guess I could tell you about Tito." She paused, as if waiting for our approval; we urged her to continue.

She smiled shyly and said, "His name was Tito Baldavino and we met when we were sixteen years old." She stopped again, her head tilted to the side as if listening for repercussions by naming her love. "He worked for my family, shoveling snow, raking leaves, spading the garden. My father was not well; he had a weak heart. Tito lived in a poor part of town not far from our house, but across the bridge. He and his family went to the same church we did."

I could tell she was warming to her story, enjoying the spotlight, something I imagined she didn't have too often. Carol filled Dee's teacup again, and urged to her go on.

"He used to bring me wild flowers and pretty stones. It was during the Depression and no one had much money. He asked me for one of my curls. I tied a blue ribbon around it and gave it to him at church one day. My parents didn't like him because he was foreign. His parents didn't speak English and they had lots and lots of children;

but we had a large family, too. One day he went away to seek his fortune and said he'd come back for me at Christmas, but he didn't."

We waited for her to continue, but she just sat there, looking sad. "Don't stop now," Carol said. "What happened next?"

"Sometimes I'd get a postcard from him—New York or New Jersey; we lived in Chicago at the time. He always said he loved me and would come back. My parents said he'd never come back, that he was foreign trash and not someone I could see. During the two years I waited for him, I finished high school while helping Mother take care of the little ones. Father was always sick, but he managed to keep Mother expecting." Dee's face flushed; she waved her hand as if to erase what she had revealed. She cleared her throat and said, "My older sister Agnes, became a nun and my older brother, Michael, a priest. Father and Mother were so proud of them. But with so many little ones, Mother really relied upon me."

"As the second Christmas came around, I was sure Tito would come back for me. I imagined him walking up our street and what I'd say and what he'd say and...But Father and Mother told me to forget about him. Even Agnes was on their side." Then Dee sat up a bit straighter and gave us a bright smile. "It was two days after Christmas that this big black Packard drove up and parked in front of our house. I was in the kitchen cleaning up after supper and the little ones began hollering that a man was coming up our walk. Father went to the door; we didn't know anyone with a big car like that. In fact, we didn't even own a car; we always took the trolley." She paused, preparing us for Tito's resurrection. "It was Tito!" Again she paused, looking at each of us as if she had just revealed her greatest secret.

"He had a bag of oranges and a beautifully wrapped package with red ribbons and holly. The little ones were jumping up-and-down reaching for the oranges; father just stood there, looking at Tito and then at the Packard, then back to Tito. Tito was very polite, wishing Father a Merry Christmas and asked to see me. By then I was standing in the hall, all a twitter." Dee pressed her hands to her bosom, her cheeks were as pink as they must have been sixty-five years ago. "I rushed to accept the oranges and gave them to Sean, who was ten, thanking Tito and wondering why Father was being so rude, not inviting our guest in. Mother had left her knitting and was in the hall now, too. Well, I just pushed past everyone and went out on the porch and closed the door."

"You go, girl!" Carol said, laughing. We joined in her laughter and urged Dee on.

"Well, he proposed to me, right then, right on the porch. It was cold and snowy, but I didn't feel it at all! I said I'd marry him and he handed me the pretty box and then...kissed me." A cheer went up from the Scheherazades.

Dee flushed a deeper pink, smiling broadly. "Well, Tito drove off, saying he'd see me the next day and ask Father for my hand in marriage. But when he did, Father said 'no'"

We responded with appropriate indignation, but Dee waved our comments away. "Father thought Tito was a gangster because he was Italian and had a big car and fancy clothes. Mother said she needed me to help her, that I couldn't leave because she was expecting again." Dee stopped the telling, just looking at us, as if we were strangers and she had made a faux pas of some kind.

"You can't stop now," exclaimed Carol. "What happened?"

Dee licked her lips, nodded as if convincing herself that she could tell us. Her words rushed out in short bursts. "I was heart-broken. I ran away with Tito. He said we'd be married in New York, but..." Again Dee stopped as if unsure she should tell.

"But, but what?" Carol asked impatiently. I put my hand on her arm; Dee couldn't be rushed. I was guessing that she'd never told another person this story.

"We lied about being married and got a room at a hotel run by someone he knew. He kept saying we'd marry, but he always had some work to do, errands to run for somebody. I knew I'd made a mistake, yet, I loved him. I worried about Mother, her confinement hadn't been going well. I felt I had to tell her where I was so she wouldn't worry, and that I was well and happy. So I wrote to her; two weeks later I got a letter back saying that Father was dying; he'd had a heart attack and she needed me. She blamed me for his death." Dee shook her head and sighed. "Of course she said all kinds of other unkind things, too, but I could understand that. She needed me because Agnes was in the convent and Michael was in seminary and there was no one but me to help her."

Carol said, "Damn, I wish I'd heard your story years ago! It'd make a good novel."

"Oh, you can't write about it or tell anyone, please!"

I said, "No one is going to let this story go out of the room, Dee; I'll see to that." I gave Carol a hard look; she shrugged and settled back in her chair. "Go on, Dee."

She nodded, hurrying on as if glad to get it out. "I told Tito that I had to go home, at least for a while. He said if I left, not to come back. But come back to what? A dingy hotel room? We had a terrible row. It finally dawned on me that we'd never marry. Yet, I loved him." Tears filled Dee's pale blue eyes and her nose turned red and began to drip. She dabbed and sniffled, then continued her story. "He bought me a railroad ticket and I went home and never saw or heard from him again. Mother said I was a fallen woman, soiled goods, that no man would every want me."

"Oh, Dee, how awful," I said.

Grace said, "But that's the way it was in those days. It seems utterly wrong, even silly now, but that was our generation."

Dee nodded, then rushed on with her story. "To make things worse, I was pregnant, but miscarried soon after I got home. I was hauling buckets of water for the wash and, well, it doesn't matter now. It was a terrible year with Father's death and Mother's difficult delivery; she had twin boys. The only thing that made it bearable were the babies, even though Donnon was flawed; Brennan, the one you've met, was fine. They were like my babies; helped me not miss the one I'd lost."

We sat stunned. This was not the bubbled-headed spinster I'd envisioned. I'd sold Dee short, never giving her credit for anything but a superficial, meandering life. Instead, Dee had grown up quickly, facing the judgmental world and raising twin baby brothers, several younger siblings and caring for a sick mother. Compared to her life, mine was easy. I was hoping that Carol would remain quiet while Dee dealt with her feelings in telling her secret. How brave she was to share her story. Was I brave enough to share mine? No. Grace was holding Dee's hand, as if to give her what strength she could spare. I was startled when Carol spoke.

"I had a baby when I was seventeen; I only saw him once, for just a minute. Usually, they didn't let unwed mothers see our babies before the adoptive parents took them away. But there was a problem with mine."

That stopped us in our tracks. Carol sat quietly, examining her French manicure; I held my breath. It was Dee who saved the moment from becoming more awkward; she timidly touched Carol's hand, saying, "I'm so sorry you lost your baby. Would you like to tell us?"

Carol shrugged on her what-the-hell attitude, smiled and said, "Sure. We said we'd tell our stories; this one's not been told, not even bits and pieces of it in any of my novels."

Teacups forgotten, we turned our attention to Carol.

"As you recall, I dropped out of the traveling burlesque troupe when I was in Portland. I really didn't have a choice because I was pregnant; fortunately, one of the older strippers had a sister in Portland who knew someone, who knew someone else, who could solve my problem. But an abortion was out of the question; I was too far along. In those days it was all back alley stuff. Anyway, this woman knew someone—it was all very complicated and hush-hush—knew another woman who worked at a home for unwed mothers. Usually, the home only took girls from so-called 'better' families because they wanted quality babies for their adoptive clients, at least that's what I was told. They interviewed me and asked if I had a picture of the father. I did, or thought I did. My high school sweetheart, Buddy, was as blonde and blue-eyed as I. Guess the matron thought she had a good breeder." Carol gave a short bark of laughter, then took a deep breath and continued.

"There were about ten girls at the home in various stages of pregnancy. We were in our mid-teens to early twenties, most knocked-up by brief encounters with servicemen or family members. We did light housework, helped in the kitchen, and got a bit of schooling each day. I don't think the women who came in were real teachers, just do-gooder volunteers, church ladies—you know the kind, but one was really nice and she helped me appreciate books and reading. I hated the typing class, but was glad I knew how when I got to Hollywood. The point was that once we delivered, we had to leave, get out and get a job.

"My pregnancy went well and there were adoptive parents waiting for me to deliver; guess they thought they were going to get the ideal blonde, blue-eyed baby. Well, I surprised them, and myself." Carol stopped as if to make sure she had our undivided attention. Again, Dee gently urged her on, not that Carol needed it by my way of thinking.

"After delivery, I was pretty groggy. The Matron had a bundle in her arms and said something like, "What is this?" I was so tired. Confused. She held the child out to me, pulling the blanket away from its face. I looked at it, still not connecting it with me because it had thick, wet, black hair. I asked what it was. She said it was a boy. Then I said something like, 'He's not mine.'"

Carol seemed very cavalier in her attitude and telling of what I thought was pretty heavy stuff. Dee oozed sympathy; I thought she was going to take Carol in her arms to comfort her, but Carol didn't look like she needed or wanted any comforting. It was as if she was trying to top Dee's love story. I was feeling very nervous, as if I had a precognition that things were going to go very wrong.

I looked at Grace, wondering what she was thinking. I could tell by her face that there was something going on in her mind about these revelations; I had faith she'd say or do something to heal whatever pain or emotional stress Dee and Carol were experiencing at the moment. But Grace remained quiet, almost distant. Finally, Carol began to speak again, softly at first, then with confidence; it seemed overly dramatic to me.

"But he was mine, just not the blue-eyed blonde we'd all expected. His father was Texas Washington, a black shipmate of Buddy's."

Oops, I thought, struggling to keep from smiling. That's the last thing I expected. How naïve could I be? I saw Dee blinking her eyes as if trying to absorb this twist in the story.

"The couple who was to adopt my baby changed their minds when they saw the dark hair and skin color, although he wasn't black, just different, and his nose, but then all babies have smashed noses. I didn't realize it at the time but my baby was a problem for the home; how to find another adoptive couple, quickly, was a big problem. Fortunately, during that time, many blacks had moved to Portland to work in the Kaiser shipyards where Victory ships were being turned out for the war. When I left the home two weeks later the matron told me she'd made arrangements for a Negro family to take him.

"Oh, good," sighed Dee. "I'm sure he had a very nice home."

"I convinced myself that he did and went on with my life, but sometimes, I'd wonder where he was and what he looked like when he grew up. Once I even thought about trying to find him, but the records were sealed, of course."

I'll always regret what I said next; basically I killed the Scheherazades when I opened my mouth before putting my brain in gear.

CHAPTER SEVENTEEN

With Oregon's new Open Birth Records Act, I suppose he could find you, if he wanted to."

"Wouldn't that be exciting?" Dee gushed.

"I could look now, couldn't I?" Carol said, her face animated, a dramatic aura enveloping her whole being. "Yes. I'll contact the County Records office tomorrow. What fun!"

I tried to be the voice of reason, especially since I'd unintentionally put the idea into her head. "I'm not sure 'fun' is the reason to take such a step after all these years. What would he be now? Fifty or so? He might not appreciate…"

Carol interrupted. "I wouldn't just barge in on his life. Just find out where he is, see how he turned out, what he's doing now. We could meet, if he wanted to."

I inwardly groaned, looking to Grace to say something wise and wonderful. She simply looked at me, as if saying 'Now you've done it.'

"I didn't mean to put ideas into your head," I stammered.

"Oh, you didn't," Carol responded in a most condescending way. "I've often wondered what happened to him. Of course these sentimental thoughts usually surfaced when I was three sheets to the wind." She gave a self-deprecating laugh. "Let's see. I could hire an investigator to help me. Once we found him, we'd set up a meeting. I'd tell him who his father is and let him know about me."

"Dee said, "Oh, yes. How exciting. You could find him, I know you could. You could tell him you wanted a better home for him than you could give him at the time." She seemed to want closure to the story; reuniting mother and child was a tidy conclusion for Dee.

"Now, Dee. I don't think Carol should make any decisions tonight." I turned back to Carol, saying "What could you possibly say to him? If he were interested, he'd have found you by now." This train was going too fast to God knew where. I looked at Grace for support; her frown said it all. I continued. "He probably doesn't even know he's adopted; maybe he wasn't adopted, just given to a family to care for. How do you think he'd feel now? Finding out his mother is white? Leave well enough alone."

Carol stood up quickly, whirled towards me and said, "What do you know? You've got your daughter and grandchildren; I could never have any more children; I don't have any family left."

"Think of the man, not the baby. This isn't one of your novels where you can manipulate the ending," I said, probably with more heat than necessary.

"Don't bullshit me! You don't know what real life is." Her voice was loud and shrill. "You never had to make your own way in the world. Just a nice cushy bank job; you didn't have to live by your wits or...or...on the whims of agents, publishers and editors. Your one divorce was nothing; I've had three and dead a husband. I doubt you've lost anyone you loved.

That was a low blow; fortunately, I kept my mouth shut, rather than responding. She wouldn't have heard me anyway; she was on a roll.

She sat again, making sure she had our attention, which she did. "Kenneth's death was a terrible blow to me. We had eleven wonderful years together. He understood me. He gave me what my other husband's couldn't—kindness, financial security, social position. We had a wonderful group of friends, although I was disappointed in them when he became sick. They drifted away, leaving me alone to cope."

I was relieved that she was talking about her husbands now; perhaps she'd lost interest in finding her child.

"My first husband was a struggling actor; we were both very young. A group of us went to Tijuana one day, had too much sun and tequila and four of us got married, more or less, on a dare. But his ego and determination to be a star killed the marriage in less than a year. Fortunately, a Mexican divorce was as easy to get as a marriage. He was never a star; he just disappeared from the Hollywood scene.

"Next, I married an older man who helped me get my first book published. We used each other. I needed doors opened for my writing career and he needed, what do they say now? Oh, yes. 'Arm Candy.' I was very pretty then and looked well in the clothes he bought me. He was no good in bed and had a cocaine habit that was draining his bank account, so I got out; I heard that he over-dosed several years later."

Dee was sitting there with her mouth open; Grace looked as if she'd fallen asleep. To me, Carol's soliloquy sounded half made up as she went along.

"Then I married my agent. That was fine as long as my books sold, but the first time one was a bomb, he left."

She stood, slowly, regally and walked to the window. I wondered what she could see other than her reflection; maybe that's what drew her there.

Softly, she said, "I need to find my child, to see if I've done anything right in my life."

For the first time, she sounded sincere; I could see her point. Perhaps all the other stuff was simply anger she'd held in for years, not that I could imagine her ever keeping secrets like Dee and I had for so many years.

Turning to face us, she began to speak, softly at first, increasing her volume and delivery speed as if she were in a one-woman play.

She had center stage, reveling in it, making up a story as if plotting her next cheap novel. She took a pace or two left, then paced right, spun and struck a pose, bangles spinning on her outstretched arm. "The drama of the search; the joy of discovery; the tension of the meeting; there would be the darkest moment, of course, then fulfillment. Finally, the denouement."

"What the hell are you talking about?" I asked.

She giggled. "Writer's speak."

Was this how she developed her novels—verbalizing the story, acting out the parts? Her voice became more dramatic, the trials and tribulations mounting; she embellished each; at least that's what it sounded like to me. She kept taking cheap shots at me. How'd I get mixed up in her soon-to-be-published potboiler? Finally, I'd had enough. "If you'll excuse me, ladies, storytelling is over as far as I'm concerned." I walked out the door, her voice following me.

"Typical. Just typical, walking out on life."

I closed the door firmly, but softly, my mother's voice echoing in my head: "Don't make a scene." Cheeks burning, I ran up the back stairs, embarrassed I'd mentioned the damned Open Records law, angry that I didn't respond in kind, even though that's not my style. I should have told her she didn't know anything about me, that I'd lost the love of my life, that she shouldn't have interrupted Dee's story, taking away her moment in the spotlight. I should have told her that she was an egotistical bitch, that we didn't give a rats ass about her youthful indiscretions, that she was screwed up, shallow, and selfish."

As I reached my apartment, my thoughts turned to Dee and Grace. I knew Dee would put Grace to bed, but I worried that the scene had upset them. "Damn!" I said to my dark, empty apartment, fumbling for the light switch. How could Carol steal Dee's thunder? For once Dee was in the spotlight, sharing her deepest secret, then Carol jumps in with her bombshell, ignoring Dee and her revelation. Selfish bitch! Poor Dee. What a mess!

I pulled the silk caftan over my head and threw it on the floor as if it were Carol. I'll be damned if I'll wear that stupid thing again. This is the end of the Scheherazades, I told myself stepping into the shower to wash away Carol's words, my bitter thoughts. I continued to mumble to myself until I turned out the bedside lamp. Forced intimacy always ends badly, I thought.

CHAPTER EIGHTEEN

The day dawned hot and muggy, a bloody sun reluctantly struggling over the distant hills. I wanted to get my walk done before the day became unbearable, so I put on shorts and a tank top, fleeing my apartment before others, meaning Carol, would be up. I knew I couldn't avoid her forever, but I wanted to choose the time and place. There was a girl in high school who loved to bait me, to criticize my good grades, my clothes, and my disdain of the cheerleaders. She said—and I believed her—that the only reason I hated the cheerleaders was because I could never be one. The girl knew no more about me than Carol did now. Why is it difficult to shake unkind words when, intellectually, you know they are spoken without benefit of fact, yet return to haunt us in one form or another at the oddest moments.

After thirty minutes, I stopped in the shade of a giant oak near the 15th green to catch my breath; I'd been alternately jogging and walking, which probably wasn't very smart on this polluted day. A foursome was putting; I listened to their friendly banter and laughter as the men made side bets, talking about the next "skin" and what it would be worth. At the moment, their golf game seemed to make a lot more sense that sitting around telling stories. Grace is right; I need to leave The Villa. Today I'd begin car shopping, give The Villa my notice and start to pack. Suddenly, I felt very young and light, as if I could skip all the way back to my apartment. I took several tentative hippity-hop steps to see if I still could do it, then sedately resumed my morning walk.

I wasn't surprised to have a phone message waiting for me: it was Dee asking—no, begging me—to call her as soon as I was back. Of

142

course I did, apologizing for walking out last night, and asking about Grace.

"Oh, she's fine," Dee said. "We just wanted to make sure you are okay; you seemed so upset last night."

"I'm fine. Carol made me angry. No, that's not right. I let myself become angry over her misspoken words. I know better than that."

"You never get mad at anyone. It surprised me and Grace."

"Just let it go. I'm fine. What can I do for you?"

"Grace wants you to have lunch with us today in her room."

"I though you said she was okay."

"Well, she is, as far as she can be with her hip and The Villa saying she must go to The Haven. I don't think they should make her move."

"I know, but maybe we can break the rules, at least try to reason with the Management." I knew talking to the manager about policy was pointless, but it made Dee feel better when I said things like that.

"Do you think I should ask my brother to say something? He's a stockholder and a director on The Villa board."

"Good idea, Dee. I'll go with him, unless you'd rather; one of us should tell them Grace's side, that her mind is fine, that it's just her body that's going."

"You go; you're better at that kind of thing. I get too nervous."

"Okay. You call your brother and set up a time, if he's willing to get in the middle of this. But don't be surprised if he says 'no'. This is a very delicate situation; he may not want to get in the middle of it."

"Well, I'll think about asking him."

"Okay. See you for lunch; eleven-thirty?"

"Yes. I'm really worried about Grace."

"Me, too. Goodbye"

After my shower, I logged on to the Internet, answered e-mail from one of my grandsons and a couple of long-time friends, and then priced cars. I wouldn't know what I wanted until I test-drove several. God, it felt good to think of something besides assisted-living politics and nasty neighbors. Would I leave for good or just a few months? That depended upon the proverbial 'bottom line.' Perhaps John would have some idea about closing my apartment.

I rapped lightly on John's door, wondering if Mabel were watching me through her peephole. He greeted me with a bright smile and ushered me into his cluttered apartment.

"Morning, John. May I borrow a cup of information?"

"Of course. I have a room full, as you can see. Here, let me clear off a chair; I get more careless each day. Too much stuff!" There were maps covering a dining table and piles of books on every chair; file cabinets lined one wall of the living area.

"Nice decorating touch, those files," I laughed. If House Beautiful gets wind of that, they'll steal your idea."

"Yeah. I'm afraid this room looks more and more like my office at the University. The roll-top desk has been in the family for decades, and I have to have a computer desk; well, you know how it goes. Please sit down. Coffee? It's still hot."

"No, thank you. I just want to pick your brain. I'm going away. Whether it will be forever or just a few months, I haven't decided. My dilemma is whether to sell out or just close my apartment for several months as you do. How does closing it up work when you are on extended trips?"

He told me how he arranged to be away; we discussed the pros and cons of selling compared to closing. If I sold, the $30,000 buy-in would be lost; closing the apartment made more sense because the monthly cost dropped one-third, reflecting the cost of food, cleaning and laundry. I could always sell later.

"I'm glad you're going to travel; perhaps you'll find your 'ah ha'," John said. "When do you leave and where are you going?"

"I don't know," Val replied. "I need to buy a car and get some financial affairs in order before I leave the area. My target date is October first, but I'm flexible. Tentative plans include driving to the East Coast after I attend the PTI board meeting in Denver in mid-October. I'll probably spend the holidays with my daughter and her family, perhaps heading south and west after the first of the year to find some sun. I need to be back in Portland for an appointment in June." We talked of things to see and do on the trip; he burrowed in a file drawer for brochures that showed archeological sites in New Mexico and Arizona he felt I'd find interesting. I welcomed his suggestions.

"It's almost lunch time," John said. "Shall we sit together and continue talking?"

"Sorry, I'm having lunch with Dee and Grace in her room. Grace isn't doing well and The Villa management wants her to transfer to The Haven. None of us like that idea, particularly Grace."

John murmured his sympathy as he escorted me to the door. Mabel was standing in the middle of the hall with a very guilty look on her face. "What the hell are you doing, Mabel?" I snapped at her. "I'm getting very tired of your nosiness!"

She flushed deeply, mumbling something, quickly returning to her apartment. "Well, that was rude of me," I said to John. "But, damn it, she's one of the reasons I'm leaving."

John simply smiled and nodded. "I think she's more interested in Carol than you."

"You're saying that I'm boring?"

"Hardly. Let me know your plans; I may have more suggestions for things to do and see."

"Thanks, John." I hurried down the hall to meet Dee and Grace, thinking of my rudeness to Mabel. Yes, I was getting snappish and irritable. There's nothing like alienating Carol and Mabel in less than a day. Yet, it felt good to be a bit feisty.

Dee had lunch on the table when I arrived at Grace's door. Mr. Snow was prowling around, checking to see if anything was different from the last time Dee had brought her cat to Grace's. "Hi, Dee. Is Mr. Snow searching for Snake in case he's listening to our stories?" I said, giving Grace a hug. "How ya' doin'?"

"I'm okay. I just didn't feel up to the dining room today. I seem to be the hot topic for the day. But I can understand it; there are others who are close to being sent to The Haven, too. The quarterly evaluation makes everyone nervous."

"That's for sure," I said, pushing Grace's wheelchair up to the table. "Even I get jumpy when they start asking questions about additional care I might require. I realize that all assisted-living places must evaluate residents periodically, but it's probably just a way to increase the monthly fees," I said, feeling more cynical than usual.

Grace said, "I'll know when I need more care; then I'll take things into my own hands. No one is going to put me on morphine drip in The Haven."

"To hell with them!" I said. Grace and I laughed, but Dee remained serious.

"Don't joke about things like that," Dee said. Sick people need lots and lots of good care. My mother had incredible pain in her final year of life. I wished I'd had someone to help me; maybe then I wouldn't have…"

Grace and I waited for Dee to finish her thought; instead, she urged us to eat before the quiche got cold. We ate silently for a moment, then Grace asked Dee, "How long did you care for your mother at home."

"We'd always lived together. Have I told you about moving from Chicago to Portland?"

We murmured 'no', either because she hadn't or because we wanted her to talk. Quite honestly, I can't remember if she told us anything about her life except the ill-fated love affair.

"Mother, my three younger brothers and the twins and I took the train from Chicago to Portland soon after Father died. We had no means of support; what money we had in the bank wouldn't last very long. We sold the house and furniture, taking only what we could pack in three large trunks. Mother was weak and not well after giving birth to the twins; Agnes and my oldest brother were taking their vows in the church and couldn't help us. She needed me to help her, especially with three active boys and the two babies.

"Mother's cousin Minnie had a boarding house in the northwest area of Portland. She invited us to live with her; of course we worked for our keep. I cooked and cleaned; the boys chopped wood, swept the walk and ran errands. Mother didn't do much, couldn't do much, but she did the mending, made quilts and knit sweaters and caps for the boys. I took on most of the heavy chores like the cleaning and laundry. When Cousin Minnie got sick, I ran the boarding house and cared for her, too. When Minnie died, she left the house to Mother; I just kept taking in boarders and that's how we kept a roof over our heads. By now, the boys had finished high school and went into the army. During the war, I worked at Wilcox Memorial, a birthing hospital; it was part of Good Samaritan Hospital. The boarding house was just a few blocks from there; I could walk to work. I worked there until Mother got too ill to keep the boarding house going while I was at work. So I quit and spent the next ten years nursing her. As for the twins, Donnon died from the measles when he was three, but Brennan grew up strong and went to college. He takes care of me now. He's the one on The Villa board." She smiled, blinking back tears of pride.

"After so many years together, I guess I just got used to living with my mother and caring for her. She was never quite right after having the twins and Father's death. I'm surprised she lived as long as she did, but I think she enjoyed life. She had friends in for cards; they played Whist. I used to play with them sometimes."

"Where did you learn to play Bridge?" I asked.

"One of our boarders. He lived with us for many years, until he became ill and his family took him away. Mr. Moore was his name. A nice man. He'd get a game together several times a week in the living room of the boarding house. He was very patient with me, but Bridge wasn't that hard after playing Whist. They're similar in some ways."

Dee paused. Lost in memories. Finally, she said, "Will this story count toward the one-thousand-and-one nights?"

"Don't see why not," Grace said.

"But Carol isn't here."

I said, "It doesn't matter that we don't stick to a solid foursome; you may have a story just for Grace's ears. Carol may have one just for me, not that I can imagine that happening now."

Grace asked us to help her to bed and finish the story there. "My old back is killing me. Stretching out will help and I'll enjoy your story more, Dee." I cleaned up the luncheon debris, while Dee helped Grace. Once again, we settled in to hear more about Dee's life.

"I couldn't send my mother away, to a nursing home, after so many years of caring for her. Anyway, nursing homes were really terrible in those days; not nice like this or The Haven. We didn't have the money, either.

"Mother had very definite ideas how things should be done and wasn't shy about telling me. It was a 24-hour-a-day job, but I didn't mind. I'd always cared for her, but it was a lot of work later when…" Dee sighed and looked pathetically sad. "The doctor showed me how to give her shots when the pills didn't help her pain. I wish he hadn't."

We waited for Dee to continue. Instead, she began to cry. "Dee," I said, putting my arm around her shoulders. "What?"

"I killed my mother."

CHAPTER NINETEEN

No, no. You took good care of her," I said.

"No. I was so tired and she was in such pain. I wanted it to end. Month after month. Year after year. She was whimpering in pain. I gave her an extra pill; it didn't help. I gave her another and another. I had to crush them up and put them in a spoon of applesauce. She could hardly swallow, but I forced the medicine down her. Her moans were heartbreaking. Then I gave her the shot of morphine."

I looked at Grace. Her eyes were closed and she was shaking her head slowly from side-to-side.

"Then I gave her another shot."

"Dee, that was a long time ago. I'm sure you handled everything well. You mustn't second-guess yourself."

"She told me that if I hadn't ruined myself, I could have married and afforded a private nurse for her."

I said, "She didn't mean that; she wasn't herself."

"She did mean it; I was never good enough for her."

"I took her life. I was glad when she was dead."

"Hush, now," I said, rocking her like an injured child. "You aren't capable of that. You did the best you could at a difficult time." I felt her shudder and reach for her handkerchief.

Grace's stern voice broke through Dee's wailing. "Stop that right now, Dee. Val's right. You aren't the kind to hurt anyone. You were trying to make her comfortable. It was her time to die. We all have a time."

Dee sniveled and nodded, wanting to believe Grace and me. What a burden to carry all these years, I thought. Dee picked up Mr. Snow, cradling him, seeking comfort from the warmth of big cat. "Maybe you're right. That was a long time ago; my mind isn't what it used to be. I always felt guilty about killing her because it was a relief to have her gone; she could be very difficult at times. I hate feeling guilty."

"Am I going to have to give you my lecture on giving up guilt? I gave it to my daughter on my last visit. I told her that I gave up guilt at forty and she should, too."

Grace said, "Val's right. You have to let this guilt go; there's nothing you can do now. You did the best you could at a very difficult time."

"But I killed…"

"No, you didn't," Grace said sternly. "You helped her through her pain during her last allotted days. All of us should have someone as caring as you to help us through our last days."

Dee seemed calmer now, as if a great burden had been lifted. She listened carefully to Grace, then said, "I hope you're right. We should think of the living, not the dead. Like Carol thinking of her baby, of finding her son."

"There'll be hell to pay if Carol finds him," Grace said with a snort.

I said, "That's the truth! She seemed out of control last night. Maybe she's changed her mind by now."

Dee said, "I don't think so. I heard that she's looking for a detective right now. Millie told me about something called the International Soundex Reunion Registry that's made just for finding people."

"How does that kind of stuff get around?" I asked angrily. "The gossip mongers in this place!"

Grace removed her glasses, holding them out for me to take; I placed them on her nightstand. She said, "We can worry all we want about Carol and it won't do any good."

I said, "Yeah, you're right; Carol will do what she wants."

"I guess I wasn't surprised that Carol had a baby," Grace said. "Lots of babies were born to young women during World War II; babies often come at the wrong time in one's life."

"You mentioned opening a birthing clinic in Montana; guess you have first-hand knowledge about that," I said encouragingly, in hopes of distracting Dee as much as anything else.

Grace slowly smiled and nodded. "During our first year of marriage, I fixed up the house and gave birth to Bill, our first son. It was during that time I realized that giving birth in Billings was not ideal. Before I became a mother, I'd made several house calls with the local doctor on difficult obstetrical cases; even the local midwife called me occasionally. Enes was often gone for days at a time birthing calves and foals on isolated ranches; I told him I needed to use my training just as he used his.

"I had an easy pregnancy and an easy birth, but I knew that anything complicated could end badly. I convinced Enes that women needed as good as care as the animals he helped. Finally, he agreed with me that expectant mothers needed a place to stay, particularly those living miles from town.

"Our home and veterinarian clinic were on the edge of Billings— just off Main Street which is nearly the middle of town now. We had a big old farmhouse; the barn and corrals were about a quarter of a mile past, down the lane. We borrowed $12,000—that was a lot of money in those days—to remodel the house and add on a surgery, diet kitchen and rooms for laying-in. I think the reason the banker was so agreeable about the loan was that his wife had just lost a baby, nearly lost her life, too, so it made sense to him in a very personal way.

"We opened in June, 1930; the local paper even wrote a story about the Bonner Maternity Hospital. We had room for ten patients. We lived upstairs while below everything from amputations to pneumonia and maternity cases were treated. Even though I meant to just have maternity care, the facility was used as overflow from the Billings hospital."

Grace began coughing; I handed her a glass of water from the carafe on the nightstand; she sipped carefully. "Confinement was a lot longer then than now, wasn't it?" I said as an encouragement for her to continue.

"Oh, yes. New mothers weren't allowed to get up, comb their hair or exert themselves in any way. We charged $50 a week for room and board, and that included the pre-and-post natal care. Women from outlying areas would come to the hospital two weeks before their babies were due and live with us. I remember one time we stopped in the middle of dinner for a birth. I delivered two or three generations of babies and had five children of my own during those years. It was a happy, if hectic, life."

"Who used your facility besides ranch women? I asked.

"The women always listed their occupation as 'housewife' and the fathers put down rancher, farmer, truck driver; we had the families from shopkeepers to common laborers. It wasn't unusual to see the newborn be the third, seventh or tenth child born to the family, particularly the poorer ones."

"When did you finally quit?" I asked.

"We were in business for over 25 years, although I did less and less towards the end; by then Billings had grown and we were doing mostly repeat customers; the newcomers used the new hospital."

Grace gave a deep sigh; whether in remembrance or fatigue, I couldn't tell. She looked so frail; maybe it was right for her to go to The Haven. Would Dee's brother and I be meddling?

Dee was chattering away about caring for her twin brothers when they were babies, how she loved the feel and smell of children after their bath. "Donnon was retarded; people pretty much gave up on them in those days, but he was so sweet and loving. He died of measles when he was three. My mother believed that Brennan took all the strength and brains from Donnon when she was pregnant. I never believed that; babies are what they are. I missed Donnon even though he took lots of extra care while I was looking after the other little ones, mother, and working for Cousin Minnie. I guess that's why I enjoyed working at the maternity hospital during the War."

Grace moved slightly, as if drawn to this part of Dee's story. "What did you do?"

Dee thought for a moment before answering. "Scrubbed instruments, washed rubber gloves, then powdered them when they were dry. I'd make up surgical bundles with gloves, instruments, pads and other things, then sterilize them in the autoclave. But I developed a terrible rash from the liquid green soap use for cleaning. My hands and arms peeled clean up to the elbows. So they let me help in the nursery—change diapers, rock fussy babies, and feed the ones who weren't nursing. I loved that."

We talked late into the afternoon. Occasionally, Grace would nod off and I'd start to leave, but the minute I stood up, she asked me to stay awhile more. Strange. It was as if she and Dee were drawing strength from me; I could almost feel it being sucked away, yet felt enriched by their need to have me there. Thoughts of buying a car and leaving evaporated. This crone circle of master teachers and healers was finally working as it should; we took what we needed from sharing bits of our lives with each other. There was no tension, no requirement to tell a story by Carol's design. It felt good, yet, smacked of childish exclusion, junior high school stuff, ousting a member who no longer fit the changing criteria of our crone circle.

About half-pass four, I left to dress for dinner; Mitch was picking me up at six o'clock for a wine-tasting party at the home of mutual friends. The day would have been perfect if I hadn't returned Kara's phone call.

CHAPTER TWENTY

The telephone message button semaphored my attention. Kara's voice was broken and muffled as she relayed her message: Charlie was dead; cardiac arrest. I returned her call; the gist of it was that a memorial service would be held at the medical center; his ashes would be sprinkled at sea, his final voyage on his beloved sailboat.

Somehow I said the wrong thing. I don't know what it was that made her come unglued, although in hindsight I guess linking his heart attack and his final trip on the Cardiac Arrest, was rather tacky, if not prophetic. Immediately we were into it again. All my hopes for a loving relationship with Kara were dashed by one remark, whatever it was.

"Fine. Don't come," she snapped at me. "You aren't wanted anyway."

"Kara. I just said I'd come if it would help you, but that I'd stay away if it would be awkward for you and Charlie's second family."

"You have no idea how much Beth helped when you weren't there for me." She took a deep breath and launched into her recitation of wrongs I had done and what a wonderful woman her stepmother was. "I was alone, rejected. Being from a divorced family in those days was terrible. I..."

I tuned her "I" recital out, as usual; it was old ground, trod to dust. It seemed as if neither one of us could get by this reoccurring argument. Finally, I got a word in. "Can we just stop? I'll call back later."

"No. You've said enough."

"Let me talk to Duncan."

"He's not here."

That didn't ring true; there was a deep silence. "Kara," I said as softly and patiently as I could, "I'm truly sorry you've lost your father. I'm glad that he and I were able to forgive each other before he died. I'm glad you and Beth had a good relationship. If there's anything I can do to make things easier for you, Duncan, and the kids, I will. I'll fly out as soon as I can or I'll stay here. Think it over and let me know."

Still no response, just vague long-distance phone noises. "Okay?" I asked.

"Fine." The dial tone hummed in my ear. Now what do I do? E-mail Duncan; that would work. Immediately I logged on to my son-in-law. Maybe he could tell me what would be best for Kara and the family.

I swore softly as I quickly changed for the party. What did that girl want of me? Well, I raised her, so I can't blame anyone but myself. Muddled thoughts banged around in my head; thank God I had something to take my mind off the situation for a few hours. Later, I'd be clear.

But before I was able to think about Kara and Charlie again, I ran into a delicate situation on my return to The Villa later that evening. As usual, I walked up the back stairs to my apartment. Just before entering the hallway I heard Carol's voice—loud, strident, tearful. I skulked in the stairwell, feeling like a voyeur. As far as I could tell, Carol was reaming Jim out; he kept shushing her. She wouldn't be shushed. No doubt Mabel was lurking behind her door, listening, too. Now there's a pretty picture: Mabel and me staining to hear something that didn't concern either one of us. That imagine was so objectionable, I ran down a half-dozen steps, then ran up again, singing loudly the first thing than came to mind. "I get no kick from champagne, I get no..." By the time I rounded the corner, Jim and Carol had stopped talking. Silently acknowledging me, Jim said to Carol, "I'll call you tomorrow. Okay? Good night." He gave me a small nod and walked briskly down the hall as if he would burst into a run. Carol started to close her apartment door, then stopped as if she would say something to me. I mumbled some kind of greeting and fumbled with my key in the lock.

"Come in for a minute." Carol said.

Oh, God, I thought. Do I really want to deal with last night's spitting contest now? Oh, well. Better to get the air cleared. "Okay, but just for a moment. It's late."

Carol looked like hell—mascara flaking, eyes puffy, face drawn and pale. She flopped down on the sofa, her negligée gapping open, exposing crepe-skinned cleavage. Not a pretty sight. No wonder Jim ran, I though to myself wickedly.

"Jim's gone."

I thought we were going to talk about last night's outburst against me; obviously, she'd forgotten it. "I beg your pardon? He's moving?"

"No. He just doesn't want...I don't think I'll see him again." She sighed and rested her head on the back of the sofa.

"Why?" I was lost; was there something I should know and didn't?

Then her demeanor instantly changed; a hard smile turned her face grotesque. "No big deal. It seemed to me we should take our relationship to the next level, but he panicked when I suggested getting married. It was insulting! You'd think I was asking him to support me or something. I could buy and sell him. I don't need him. Typical man. He's glad to sleep with me, but doesn't want commitment."

This was a lot more than I cared to know; who's sleeping with whom can be burdensome information. Then I noticed the bottle of Scotch and two glasses on the coffee table. Carol splashed tawny liquor into a glass and held the bottle out to me. I demurred, wondering if she expected me to take a swig out of the bottle or use the glass of melting ice cubes that must have been Jim's. So, she was drinking again.

"Don't give me that look," she said. "I can handle my liquor. Now that the stress of Kenneth's illness is gone, I can take it or leave it. But that damn Jim..."

Yeah, right, I thought, wishing I hadn't acquiesced to her late-night chat invitation, especially when she went into details about their affair.

"...so then I told him, we could move into the vacant corner unit on the third floor, knock out the wall to the single unit next to it, and have a really nice place—around 2,000 square-feet. Well, you should have seen the look on his face! Hah!" She poured herself another drink. "I said I'd pay for it, but he got really snotty and then I threw him out. Or something." She began to cry.

Just what I need: a crying drunk. I stood and moved to the door. "Carol. It's late. Go to bed." Cliches filled my mind, but not my mouth: You'll feel better in the morning; no she won't. Jim will reconsider; I doubt it. Get some sleep and you'll find a way to work it out; in a pig's eye.

Was it only a couple of months ago that I was standing at the door ready to run out in the middle of her "I don't-want-to-be-here monologue? Once again, I was trying to escape, yet moved by her distress. As I turned the doorknob to leave, the fire alarm sounded; I jerked my hand away as if I'd set it off. Adrenaline surged; knees became fluid. Carol lounged on the sofa, saluted me with the glass of Scotch and downed it in one gulp. I jerked open the door and came face-to-face with Mabel in the center of the hall looking wild-eyed and carrying her bible and a birdcage. It was right out of a Hollywood comedy, pink sponge rollers bobbing, Chenille robe awry, panicky bird sounds coming from the covered cage. The sight of her made me want to burst out laughing. By then, John came out of his apartment dressed in pajama top and jeans, carrying his laptop.

"Come on, ladies, let's go downstairs," he said, taking Mabel's elbow and giving me a wink. "Carol coming?"

"Sure," I said, returning to her apartment and pulling her off the sofa. Now she was a giggling drunk. Shit. As we entered the lobby a fire truck pulled into the circular front driveway, firemen running through the door, one shouting evacuation instructions, the rest scattering throughout the building; I headed for Grace's room; Dee was there, clutching Mr. Snow.

"I'll get Grace; you put the cat in its cage and go outside. I'll take Grace out through her patio."

By the time I got Grace into her wheelchair and wrapped in a blanket, it was all over. False alarm. Residents were milling about the lobby, some laughing, some complaining, some distraught. Earl suggested that the management open the bar; Carol invited him to her place for a drink. Dee decided that she and I should stay with Grace in her apartment. Grace said she didn't need two women and a cat as overnight guests. We got Grace settled again and I walked Dee and Mr. Snow "home." The alarm went off again. Dee screamed, I ran back to Grace's room. Shouts of false alarm echoed through the hall. The firemen assured us that it was a system malfunction and that one fire unit would stay at The Villa until morning. By the time I got Grace and Dee settled and wandered back upstairs, talking to others on the way, Carol was holding court in her room with Earl and several other residents I knew by sight, but not by name. She motioned me to join them as I walked by her door. I gave some sort of declining motion; they laughed. October first couldn't come fast enough for me.

CHAPTER TWENTY-ONE

Of course the false alarm was the main topic the following day; I was stopped two or three times on my way out for my morning walk by residents who wanted to know where I was, what I did, how I felt when the alarm sounded, but in truth, they just wanted to tell me of their experience. I listened with patience and amusement, feeling like an obedient daughter listening to an aging parent. How quickly I was separating myself from "them" now that I'd taken the first step to leave.

By the time I returned from my walk, the management had posted a sign inviting everyone to gather in the Great Room that afternoon at three o'clock for refreshments and an update on The Villa's fire and security system. I went more in support of Dee and Grace than for my own need. We sat to one side of the crowded room, sipping pink lemonade and enjoying the vitality in the room now that the seniors had something to expound upon besides their own aches and pains. Grace, Dee and I exchanged our take on the evening; they were particularly interested in Carol. Her behavior last night made for good "chewing"; soon, I was beginning to believe my embellishments of the evening's events, although I skirted around Carol and Jim's sleeping arrangements and just said that Carol had proposed to Jim and that he had turned her down.

Dee was shocked at Carol's boldness in proposing; Grace was amused, but concerned about the drinking. "She says she can handle it, but alcoholics can't, you know." Dee and I nodded in agreement, as if we knew anything about alcoholism. "The Villa looks the other way if the drinkers are quiet, but they don't put up with rowdiness;

Carol better be careful. When I first moved in, the management evicted a married couple who drank and got into loud arguments."

"Speaking of leaving, I've decided to do some traveling this fall; October first I'm gone."

Dee gasped, "Oh, no! Well, yes, travel, but you'll come back?"

"I'm not sure. I don't know what I want to do, but I need to stretch my wings while I have my health."

"Good for you," Grace said, looking like a skinny Buddha, if there is such a thing. "Fall is a perfect time to see the world. Where are you going?"

"I have a meeting in Denver mid-October; then I'll drive east to see my daughter and family. If they invite me, I'll spend the holidays with them. Oh, I forgot to tell you that Charlie died."

"Oh, my." Dee said. "I'm so sorry." She took my hand and looked sorrowfully at me. Grace murmured her sympathy.

"Thank you." I said, accepting their condolences. "But, it wasn't unexpected. He told me he wasn't as well as he looked when I saw him. Kara is very upset, of course. I don't think I'll go to the memorial service. It's best if I leave it to Kara and his second family; they're still close even after the divorce."

"He divorced his second wife, too?"

"Oh, yes. My guess is that she divorced him. Huge egos are hard to live with." We watched the room fill with residents, Dee smiling and waving at some, many, in fact. She seemed to know most of the women.

"Look, look. See that couple just coming in?"

I did as bade, seeing an elegantly suited, white-haired gentleman and on his arm, a tiny woman dressed in a mink coat, velvet hat, leather gloves and carrying a black satin purse. "What in the world?" Grace said.

Dee explained. "They moved in two days ago and at dinner she comes dressed to-the-nines, as if they were going out to a fancy restaurant. I heard that she never goes out of their apartment without him. Some say she has dementia, but I don't think they allow that in The Villa."

"I think we all have a touch of dementia," I said with a laugh.

Grace smiled in agreement. "Does she keep her coat on? She'll die of heatstroke in here, if she does."

"Just wait until you see what she's wearing over her dress when she takes her coat off."

We stared in anticipation. "I don't see anything," Grace said.

I looked closely; then I saw it—an old elastic Kotex belt. "Thank God she hasn't got a sanitary pad hooked to it. I didn't know you could still get things like that." It made me sad to see someone being the center of ridicule; yet, her husband was kindly solicitous, either unaware of the inappropriate item, or taking it in stride, keeping her self-esteem in place. I preferred to think of him doing that, ignoring those of us who might find it amusing.

The conversation returned to my proposed departure.

Dee said, "My, oh, my. Mr. Snow and I will miss you."

"Thank you, Dee. I'll miss you two wise women. And even Mr. Snow."

They laughed, knowing that cats weren't high on my list.

"Well, look who's here," Carol said, sweeping down upon us with Earl in tow. "You look like conspirators. What's cooking?"

"Carol, Earl. Join us?" I was trying to be polite, observing that Dee and Grace were giving them the once-over, twice.

"No time now. We're going to the casino; the bus leaves in a few minutes."

Earl said, "The Management is just going to blow smoke this afternoon. There's nothing new for them to tell. At least the false alarm got the blood stirred up." He laughed loudly and swatted Carol on her rump. "Come on, let's go."

Carol giggled. "Okay. I don't want to sit in the back of the bus."

"Why not? We could make out there like a couple of teenagers." More laughter. Ugh, I thought.

I watched Grace and Dee as they watched Carol and Earl leave. Grace said, "Maybe The Haven would be a good place to go; at least I could avoid that."

We returned to speculating about the people we knew and those we didn't until the management put on their dog-and-pony show complete with slides, flip charts and the fire chief. In all, it was a fine afternoon, if you liked that sort of thing. I think I held up my end of the conversation, but my mind was miles away—literally. Mental lists of places to see and things to do ran like software, sorting and storing, editing and inserting, formatting and filing.

After the program, Dee and I took Grace to her room. As we helped her to bed for a nap, she said, "Remember when we first talked about telling stories? How we'd use our extra thousand-and-one-nights?" She searched our faces for confirmation, then continued. "I said I'd throw myself a 100th birthday party. I'm going to do that now, soon; I don't think I'll see my face on Willard's TV show."

Dee said, "Oh, of course you will; I've already got the address of the Today Show so I can send in your photo."

I didn't detect any confidence in that statement. "Great idea, Grace. None of us should wait to do anything we want."

Grace scowled at Dee. "Don't you dare send my picture to Willard. I'm going to celebrate my 97th birthday here in the next week or so. Will you help me with some of the details?"

"Sure we will. I'm a great fetch-and-carry person. Tell me what you need and it shall be done." I gave her a sweeping bow.

"Should I reserve the private dining room? It should be big enough to hold your family," Dee said.

"No. No family. We did that two years ago. It was nice, but boring. No. It will just be us, the Scheherazades."

"Carol, too?" Dee asked.

"I can't leave her out." Grace thought for a moment. "I know. I'll invite everyone. We'll have it in the Great Room; champagne, cake, balloons. No presents. Don't want them. There's nothing I need anymore. Maybe I'll give the presents. What was it you said you would do with a thousand-and-one nights, Dee?"

"Oh, I can't remember…"

"She said she'd do something exciting like taking a balloon ride." I said.

"That's right," Grace said with a slow smile.

"Oh, I was just joking." Dee looked flustered.

"And what did you want?" Grace's eyes bored into mine.

"There's nothing I want except health, some more years to feel good, do things."

Piously, Dee said, "That's up to God. Only he knows the number of our days."

Grace raised her eyebrows at me.

+ + +

The Labor Day holiday was a non-event at the Villa. The weather was muggy; I was restless. Perhaps that's why I accepted John's invitation to take a trip with him to Eastern Oregon. In one way, I'm glad I did; in another, I wish I hadn't. What began as a mini-escape from The Villa became a pivotal point in my life. I guess I should start at the beginning in my attempt to explain this.

Earlier in the week, Duncan and I agreed that there was no reason for me to attend Charlie's memorial service. Kara, with her Stepmother's help, had arranged everything; it would revolve around his colleagues and immediate family. Needless to say, I was relieved. I talked to Kara and she sounded fine, as if our earlier phone conversation hadn't taken place. Her attitude relieved me of the burden I'd carried around when we'd first talked of Charlie's death. I guess it was this happiness that gave me the impetus to accept John's invitation with hardly a thought.

He said he'd like to show me several of his favorite Oregon out-of-the-way places, spots where an "ah ha" was guaranteed. I laughed at that, but he was right.

"This is strictly a jeans and boots affair," John said. "I'll make all the arrangements.

"Fine," I replied, "But I'll pay my own expenses and share the cost of gas."

"You bet you will; seems like women have most of the money in the world now a days," he laughed,

"We do and we know how to use it. When do we leave?"

"How about Thursday?"

"Fine."

"Aren't you going to ask where we're going?"

"Nope. Just don't make the sleeping arrangement too primitive; I like my creature comforts."

I'd come to respect and enjoy his thoughtful approach to life. I'd even told him about Jesse, although I didn't elaborate on our personal relationship, simply saying we were best friends and that I was still grieving over her death. His patient listening and introspective observations helped me get past the shyness of crying in front of people. He helped me to see that grief was nothing to be ashamed of.

It was after my "Jesse revelation" that he invited me on the High Desert excursion in his old Toyota camper-thing with nearly 100,000 miles on it. It was stocked with an extra can of gasoline, as well as water, an ice chest, camp stove, and other survival gear, even though he promised exquisite accommodations along the way.

We left Thursday soon after breakfast and drove east along the Columbia River, stopping at historical sites and viewpoints. It had been years since I'd done this; it made me even more eager to start my own trip East. "This is a great dry-run for my trip," I said, carefully pouring him a cup of coffee from his battered Thermos bottle as we eased back into Interstate highway traffic from a photo opportunity stop. "I can see that I'll need to do more than just throw my suitcase in the trunk."

"I like to be prepared for any road emergency, but more than that, I like the option of not keeping to a schedule. You never know when you'll find something special and want to stay where there may not be facilities."

"The 'ah ha'?"

"Definitely, but more than that. It was serendipity when I found the hotel in Condon. I had no idea there was anything like it in wheat country. Of course I should have guessed, because the town was once a booming agriculture center. Most small towns like that disappear as the economy changes, but all it takes is one person with a vision. You'll see what I mean when we get there."

"Where in the world in Condon? It's not on I-84," I said refolding the map I'd been scanning.

"Find the Biggs junction, then follow highway 206 to the southeast."

"Ah, ha," I laughed, finding the town. "There, I've had the 'ah ha' you promised."

"We can do better than that."

We drove in silence, absorbing the landscape of brown velvet hills of Washington across the wide Columbia River; huge barges pushed by small, powerful tugboats, moved at a stately pace up and down the center of the channel. They were loaded with goods from Portland and would return with tons of wheat grown in eastern Oregon and Washington.

Sagebrush and rocks framed the interstate highway, its multiple lanes hosting double-trailer freight trucks, motor homes, business and vacation passenger cars, pickup trucks and an assortment of motley campers like John's. After taking a rest stop at Biggs Junction, we drove southeast through rolling hills of golden wheat stubble and newly plowed fields ready for planting winter wheat. The narrow, two-lane road dipped and curved through hills covered with dry grass and volcanic rock. I watched for coyotes and magpies, asking John if this was rattlesnake country. He assured me it was. We picnicked on peanut butter and jam sandwiches by the side of the road; looking west, we could see the Cascade Mountain Range, its snow-capped peaks diminished by the hot summer. To the east, fields of gold and brown and green became nature's plaid blanket.

It was late afternoon when we arrived at the Condon Hotel, which had been restored to its former glory; once again it was the centerpiece of this tiny wheat-growing community. After settling into our rooms, we wandered the main street, stopping at the General Store and an art gallery, finally relaxing in the second-floor atrium of the hotel for a drink. "What do you think?" John asked me as he sipped his bourbon and water.

"Perfect," I said, nibbling on my martini olive. "They even have data ports in the rooms, but that doesn't take away from the historical feel; they've done a splendid job of restoring it while catering to the needs of the modern traveler." We sat in companionable silence, then I asked, "I'm ready to hear about our itinerary; will you tell me now?"

"Of course. You've been more patient than most women would be. I've enjoyed that."

"It felt good to let someone else take charge for a bit; however, I doubt if I could go much longer without knowing," I laughed. "I'm big on being in charge, but this has been a nice change."

"The John Day Fossil Beds are about twenty miles farther on. We'll see them early tomorrow, then explore the country around the town of John Day; after that, I can't promise you anything but adventure."

CHAPTER TWENTY-TWO

The crisp, blue September morning was made for our trip to the fossil beds. The road rambled through the tiny communities of Mayville and Fossil, next skimming over the 3,000-foot Butte Creek Summit, and winding down to the John Day River, where we stopped to enjoy the cool shade of the canyon wall. We sat on a smooth boulder enjoying coffee and granola bars from John's well-stocked camper. Only the sound of water and an array of birds calling out their territorial boundaries disturbed the quiet morning. I breathed deeply the scent of juniper and sage, slowly filling my lungs, holding my breath before returning it to the open sky. Whether it was a true "ah ha" or not, I couldn't tell; I only know that I felt an internal peace that was so strangely powerful that it unnerved me.

"Are you okay?" John asked.

Tears I could not hold back wet my cheeks. "I am more than okay," I said softly. "Thank you for bringing me here."

"We haven't begun to see the things I want to share with you. Come on. You'll like the next stop."

The visitor's center of the John Day Fossil Beds was located on a ranch dating from 1918. The large white home that must have been a haven for weary travelers in the early 20th Century now held beautifully detailed fossils of extinct flora and fauna. We walked trails that looped through amazing terrain, reading markers pointing out a specific feature; John seemed to know something about each and enjoyed expanding the information for me.

I was enthused about gathering new story material for the Scheherazades. Looking back was fine, but I was eager for the now, the future. I knew Dee and Grace would love to hear about the things we saw like the pet bear at the miniscule town of Mitchell, and Picture Gorge where ancient pictographs mark the rock wall along the river. How could I begin to tell them of this sixteen million-year-old formation? John said that Native American trade routes between Canada, Mexico and the Great Plains intersected there. Closing my eyes, I tried to see the gathering, hear the tumult of horse's hooves and the babble of multi-tribal greetings and trade.

That evening when we were settled in John Day, one of the larger small towns in the area, I called Kara from my motel room. "I've gone Country Western," I told her and Callie, who was listening on the kitchen extension. "We've driven through miles and miles of wheat fields and now we're in cattle country; there's logging, too. Oh, I'd love to share all this with you."

"Next summer we'll come again," Callie said, "Can't we Mom?"

"Perhaps. Maybe we can get the whole family together for a trip to Oregon; Duncan's mentioned more than once that he'd like to see the Pacific Northwest."

"I'd love to see all of you next summer; in the meantime, if you don't have plans for the holidays this year, what would you think if I came for a few days?"

"Cool, Grandma," exclaimed Callie.

"Yes. That would be nice," Kara said. "It's been a long time since we shared a holiday with you."

I told them of my plan to drive east and why I wanted to get away for a while. We agreed to talk again after my Central Oregon trip.

The following day, John and I rambled across the Painted Hills, and had a latte in Prairie City, which once was a major shipping point for cattle and an important post for the late-1800's military, then returned to John Day for a tour of the Kam Wah Chung Museum, a former Chinese store, religious shrine and meeting place from 1885.

Sharing a pitcher of beer that evening while we waited for our pizza, I confessed that I was exhausted, but exhilarated. He teased me about sleeping under the stars. "Would that be so bad?"

I thought a moment, saying, "I've never done that. As long as a rattler doesn't share my sleeping bag, I'll give it a try."

"Good, although I don't have any plans for that this trip. Maybe next time."

"What's our agenda for tomorrow?"

"We'll travel south," he said, tracing our route on the map, "then northwest to Bend, but before Bend, I promise you a dinner you won't forget."

"The food or the setting?"

"Perhaps both, but I think it's the setting and your fellow diners that make it special; people come from all over the world to experience the meal."

"Where is this place?"

"Silver Lake area." He pointed to the map again. "There's a sixty-five year-old line shack that was once home to a cowboy from the nearby million-acre ZYX Ranch. Now it's call the Cowboy Dinner Tree Restaurant; I hope you like steak."

I said, "Yes", and then asked him to show me again where we'd go next, which he did, the names rolling lovingly off his tongue: Burns, Riley, Wagontire, the Abert Rim, Paisley, Summer Lake, Christmas Valley and Fort Rock. Our relationship of being casual neighbors turned to friendship on this trip. We started each morning at first light and were comfortable driving for hours with hardly a word spoken. I might have a question about the area or a distant rock formation; he answered knowledgably and fully, each of us enjoying the silences between. The country south of Burns was beautifully desolate with its textured terrain in subtle earth tones spiked with sage and chamois and sepia shadows. I imagine the bluffs and hills changing colors as the sun shifted, its rays filtered by clouds and dust storms.

We picnicked along the way, stopping often to wander a few hundred yards off the road, stretching and complaining how our backs were getting too old for sitting so long. We'd scramble over a rock formation and sit for a while, absorbing the panorama, pleased at our agility to reach such a prized viewpoint.

"How could I have lived in Oregon for so many years and not traveled this area?" I said.

"It doesn't look like much is here when you look at the map, but it's filled with wildlife, spring flowers, working ranches, and small communities. Oh, look! Antelope." He pointed to my left. I saw nothing. "There." He lined my head against his arm.

"Oh, yes! I see its white rump." As suddenly as it was there, it was gone.

"Farther south, there's an alkali lake that's harvested for brine shrimp, which is frozen and sold for tropical fish food."

"How do you know all this stuff?" I laughed.

"My head is full of useless information. You should know that by now." In companionable silence, we returned to the camper and continued our trip. It was early evening when we stopped for dinner outside of Silver Lake.

The Cowboy Dinner Tree was truly a shack, a place the uninformed would pass by as quickly as possible. Yet, two dozen or more cars, pickups and campers were parked on the dusty lot. The natural landscaping of rocks, junipers and sagebrush punctuated by slashes of rimrock looked like a Hollywood movie set right down to the 7,000-foot Hagar Mountain which loomed over the scene. In a bit of whimsy, a rustic birdhouse perched on a pole near the entrance to the restaurant, which was accessed by a wooden walkway.

We found our table on one of the side porches hung with cow-country memorabilia—bits, bridles, branding irons and items that made no sense to me. John said, "You won't find cuisine here, just good old American chow." He was right. By the time I finished my salad and bean soup, there was no hope of doing justice to the slab of grilled beef, the fragrant pan rolls, baked potato, and the sourdough chocolate cake. We boxed up our leftovers and packed them in the ice chest before starting our two-and-one-half hour drive to Bend, our final stop before returning to The Villa. Dusty and tired from our day in the desert, I was looking forward to a long, hot shower and a soft bed.

The sun had set by the time we started our drive west, but a full moon rising behind us illuminated the fenced alfalfa fields lining the two-lane road. At first, I thought cattle were in the fields. As my eyes adjusted to the dark, I could see the animals were deer, huge herds, fifty—perhaps one hundred—browsing, moving slowly en masse. Suddenly, several decided the grass was truly greener on the other side, clearing the fence onto the road in front of us. John braked and swerved; I could see their rumps as they gracefully jumped the fence of the opposite field.

"That got my adrenaline going!" I said to John. "They sure have big ears."

"That's why they're called mule deer." He said, peering into the dusk. "This may be a slower drive than I anticipated; I haven't seen such large herds before. They must know it's bow-hunting season." We drove in silence, straining our eyes for impetuous deer. The fields ended as we climbed into Ponderosa Pine country, then down to High Desert grasslands; road signs pointed to Christmas Valley and Fort Rock. The next thing I remember was the "whomp, whomp" of a helicopter.

CHAPTER TWENTY-THREE

The voice seemed far away; vibration and whine encapsulated my body. The voice came again. "You're doing fine," it assured me. I fought to open my eyes. "Can you tell me your name?"

"Val."

"Good. Tell me again."

"Val Kenyon."

"Are you in pain?"

"No. I don't think so. Where's John?"

"Right next to you."

I tried to turn my head but a collar of some kind prohibited movement. My eyes drifted shut, but the voice said, "Wake up. Talk to me, Val."

"No. I'm fine."

"Yes you are. Can you squeeze my hand?"

I did what I was told, but not with any enthusiasm.

"Now squeeze with this hand. Good. Can you wiggle your toes?"

I must have drifted off again, because the next thing I remember was a huge fish tank, ceiling high with strange colorful creatures suspended over the heads of people engaged in random choreography. What seemed strange then made sense to me later. John and I had been transported by Air Life to St. Charles Medical Center in Bend. Doctors and nurses efficiently went about their business cutting off my dirty clothes, inserting IV needles, drawing blood, rolling my gurney down the hall for x-rays, then back to the ER. The fish tank was a glass-enclosed office in the center of the ER; it hung with plush sea creatures and other whimsical aquatic life. It gave me comfort that the professionals working on me had a sense of humor.

I continued to ask about John; their responses were ambiguous to say the least. Worry set in; I prepared myself for the worst. It was confirmed when the hospital chaplain introduced himself. "Is there family we can contact for you?" he asked.

I had a sense of disconnectedness. "Not now. If I'm okay, I'll call them later. What about John?"

"I sorry to tell you that he died in route to the hospital." He waited patiently for my response, taking my hand.

Don't touch me I thought. I need to process something. What was it? Oh. John is dead. It seemed as if I knew he was dead before the airlift, but how? Hot tears welled in my eyes; it felt as if a heavy weight had been placed on my chest. There was a sound of someone's grief, a deep moan; I felt it in my throat. I wanted to cover my mouth, to stop the sounds, but one arm was taped, heavy with needles and plastic tubes; the chaplain held my other hand. I pulled it away and hid my face as best I could. "Go away," I said.

"All right, but I'll be nearby. Would you like the nurse?"

"No."

A flood of tears came; I clutched the flannel sheet to my face, hiding as best as I could the torrent of grief. I cried for Jesse, for Charlie, for John, for myself. Someone was fiddling with the IV tree; I could hear the squeak of soft-soled shoes. My arm with the needle taped to it was repositioned. Chills sent my body quivering; someone carefully removed the sheet I was clutching and covered me with a fresh, warm blanket. I drifted away.

Sometime later, I had no idea whether it was ten minutes or ten hours, a doctor came in. Young. Kind. Gentle. "Hello, Val. I'm Doctor Solomon. How are you feeling?"

I struggled to surface, to respond, to be co-operative. "I don't know; you tell me."

"You have a concussion and some superficial cuts on your hands and face. We took a couple of stitches on your hands, around the knuckles; the butterfly strips on your face should hold just fine. Nothing broken according to the x-rays." He began checking me out again, from head to toe. "Does this hurt?" "Can you bend this or that?" He spent a lot of time looking into my eyes, moving the bright light this way and that. He asked about my vision.

"There are swirls of black ink in my left eye. What does that mean?"

"Perhaps a retinal problem; can't say for sure. Sounds like an ophthalmologist should see you." He finished his examination, then said, "I think you're ready to go up stairs. We'll keep you a day or so. Is there family we can call for you?"

"Not now."

"Fine. I'll send in the nurse."

The next morning, after a restless, dream-filled night, I was bathed, re-examined, re-bandaged, and taken by wheelchair to an examination room where an ophthalmologist did a comprehensive exam, informing me that I had a torn retina and that he needed to do laser surgery immediately, which meant as soon as the equipment was free. I was stiff and sore; the cuts on my hands throbbed and stung. The black swirls in my eye continued to fascinate and frighten me. Would blindness be my fate? While I waited for surgery, a State Police officer questioned me, as well as telling me what they knew about the accident. A nurse's aide retrieved my wallet, lipstick and comb from the pocket in my cargo pants, which were in shreds from being cut off. Another chaplain stopped by to see if I needed a prayer. A light breakfast came. I questioned the food, saying I was to have surgery; the LPN brought the nurse, who explained laser surgery wasn't affected by a light meal. I managed to drink the coffee and apple juice. I slept.

On waking, I again was asked about John's family. It surprised me how little I knew about him. "He has a daughter in Portland; I don't know her married name. I suggest you call The Villa; they can give you the information you need." I could tell them that he was a good, kind person who was trying to help me experience an "ah ha." But if I said that, they'd send in the mental health team. Finally, I agreed to call "my people" as they so gently put it. Kara offered to fly out; I assured her I was fine. Next I called Dee because she liked to be the one to carry messages. Finally, I called Mitch, who agreed to drive to Bend and take me back to Portland the next day. There was nothing I could do about John, except talk with his family when they were ready.

The loss of friends and family weighed heavily. The need to leave The Villa was stronger now; there was an urgency to see my family, tell them I loved them. And, there was Grace and Dee. It seemed as if I could hear their age-clocks ticking, ticking, and far away, my clock was running down, too.

A week after the accident, the Scheherazades gathered for afternoon tea in Dee's apartment. By now, my blackened eyes were fading to pale greens and yellows; the stitches on my hands would come out next week and the butterfly tapes had fallen off my face, revealing cuts from flying glass on my temple and cheeks; the wounds are small and healing quickly. However, the ache in my chest is the same kind which plagued me when Jesse died. The term "broken heart" must have come from this heavy, dull ache that lingers just under the breastbone when grief sets in. I hadn't cried since the torrent released in the ER when I heard about John and mourned for all those who had left me—Charlie, Jesse, my parents, several friends. It feels as if pressure is building up again, but I did not want to "lose it" in front of my fellow storytellers.

I greeted Dee and Carol, and kissed Grace on her cheek, saying it's good to see her. She'd aged more than I expected in the time I'd been gone. We settled in our usual places, teacups in hand. Dee passed around a box of Godiva chocolates one of her extended family had given her. "My family is so good to me," she said, when quizzed about the expensive candy. "They're always giving me lovely things for no reason at all."

"There's a reason," I said. "They love you because you are such a nice person." She blushed, pleased and embarrassed at the compliment.

As usual, it's Carol who demands the storytelling begin as if she had no use for sentimental chitchat. "Val, tell us everything."

What is "everything"? The trip? I didn't feel like giving them a travelogue, and it seemed inappropriate to speak of John as nothing more than a tour guide. The accident? I don't remember. The information I have is a second-hand reconstruction done by the State Police. A passing motorist found us trapped in the crushed vehicle, upside down in the ditch with three dead deer. The motorist called 911 and the Christmas Valley EMTs responded, calling in Air Life from Bend because of the seriousness of the situation. Why I survived with minor injuries and John died is unfathomable. Is there something unfinished in my life? Am I required to be available for some unknown scheme in life? Finally, I spoke.

"I'd like to talk about John. He is—was—one of the most kind, intelligent, generous men I have ever known. Why we became friends, I don't know; but I do know we enjoyed each other's company. We could drive for miles without talking, yet, talk for hours about a wide variety of things. He was very knowledgeable; when I asked about a landform or the background of a small town, he was generous sharing his knowledge. He had always wanted to be an archeologist, but his mother insisted he become an English teacher, to follow in her footsteps. After retirement, he was able to follow his dream. He found inner peace in his travels; he wanted to share that with me, to help me find my inner peace when mind, body and spirit come together. He called it an "ah ha." He wanted to help me find my "ah ha.""

"Did you?" Carol asked.

"There were wonderful moments of tranquility, of joy being isolated in some of nature's most beautiful, desolate landscape, of almost stepping back in time in the small communities we explored, of meeting people who worked the land, moved cattle, fell timber, made lattes and pizza in the middle of nowhere. Yes, I supposed I did have an "ah ha" but not some epiphany as you might expect—as I thought I might have. It was more a feeling of well-being, of happiness, of tension draining away.

Dee said, "I'm glad John was able to follow his dream before…" She stopped unable to say the obvious.

"Isn't that why we've been sharing our personal stories? Carol said. "Telling how we followed our dreams? Grace became a nurse; Val became a banker; I became a writer."

"I became nothing," Dee said softly.

"Not true," Grace said. "You don't have to be a profession. You're an exceptional person; that's more than most people can say."

"I agree," I said. "Dee, you are a humanitarian. It might not be possible to say that was your dream, but you've reached a much higher calling than, say, a bank president." I'm not sure they understood my self-deprecation, but Dee seemed pleased. I continued. "Not everyone has a dream they can articulate, but there's an inner compass that takes us there, wherever "there" is. At least I hope so. John and I talked about following our dreams, as he did for the second half of life. I reached my ultimate business goal, being CEO with the bank early in my career, but I don't have a clue about the second half of life."

I motioned with my hand that I still wanted to speak, but the thoughts weren't coming together as quickly or clearly as I wanted. Finally, I said, "I'm not sure how to express this, but I don't understand why my life was spared. I'm ordinary, not one to consider myself as a contributor to some cosmic scheme. I don't understand why John had to die. I want to understand, so it will hurt less."

It was as if I'd dumped something distasteful in the middle of the floor, like the proverbial "Elephant in the Living Room" that no one wants to acknowledge. Walk around it? Ignore it? Eat it one bite at a time? Leave it to Carol to get things moving again, if on a tangent.

"I'm sure you had a dream, Dee. What was it?"

Dee examined her lap for a moment; looking up with a slight smile, she said, "I wanted to design hats. I'd draw pictures, painting them with watercolors; I must have had dozens of sketches hidden in the bottom of my handkerchief drawer. My sister Agnes said it was a waste of time, frivolous foolishness." She giggled. "I'd spend hours in front of the mirror, decorating my plain Sunday hat with ribbons and scarves and flowers. When we'd go downtown, which wasn't often, I'd spend most of my time looking into the hat shop windows. Once, I even went in to a very exclusive hat shop and tried on several. I'm sure they knew I wasn't going to buy one; they were expensive and not for, well, me."

Grace said, "Remember Lilly Dasche' hats?"

"Oh, yes! All the society people and movie stars wore her designs. They were gorgeous. I don't see why hats had to go out of style," Dee said.

"We're too casual now; no one has time to dress up," Grace said.

Carol said, "Women in black churches wear very elaborate hats. Some have dozens of fancy hats; they consider it a way of praising God."

"I used to like hats; we had to wear them to church, too," I said. "My favorite one when I was a young woman was a brown felt derby with a long pheasant feather that stuck out in front. The last hat I wore was a baseball cap to keep my head warm when I was in chemo."

After a few minutes more, we'd pretty much exhausted the hat topic, but the pile I'd dumped in the middle of the floor was still there. Grace took us back to why some people live and some people die and how it affects our lives.

"Val, I think you're still with us because you have things to do—not that John didn't have more to contribute; he gave us great pleasure with his slide shows. Perhaps you're still with us for some reason that isn't apparent to you now."

I shook my head in disbelief, studying the floor. Carol spoke again. "Don't you remember anything about the accident?"

She was not to be denied an account of my great adventure. Fine. I'd tell what I knew just to get past it. "We had dinner at a quaint restaurant that once served as a line shack for a cowboy who worked on a million acre ranch that's still running cattle and producing alfalfa. It truly is a shack, but people come from all over to experience it. The food is—as John explained—chow, not cuisine. Our fellow diners that night came from Portland and Seattle, as well as some local ranchers and farmers; it was also the third visit by a Canadian couple. They were charming; we sat with them that night. The owner told us that one customer flies in from Alaska every year and trades her a fresh salmon for his steak dinner.

"I couldn't eat all my dinner, so we packed it up in the ice chest that John had in his camper. He was prepared for any emergency or whim that would take him away from civilization. We had a three-hour drive to Bend where we planned to spend the night. The sun had set by the time we finished dinner, but a full moon made it seem almost as bright as day. There's a stretch of the road that goes through miles of fenced alfalfa fields, which were filled with huge herds of deer. We had to watch carefully because they would jump the fences and dash across the road. John was a good driver; he knew when to be wary of wildlife. It seemed as if we were past the main migration or whatever it was, and I relaxed—was looking out the side window. The next thing I was aware of was the sound of a helicopter."

Dee emitted little gasps and squeaks of concern; Grace listened with her eyes closed. Carol urged me on. "When I came-to in the helicopter, my neck was in a brace and I was pretty fuzzy; whether it was the concussion or they had given me something, I don't know. The flight nurse, a young man, talked to me, asking questions; I assume this was part of checking my vital signs. He and another nurse—a woman, I think—spent most of their time working on John. And that's about it."

I didn't want to talk about it any more. I think Grace understood this, because she asked about the eye surgery.

"Oh, that," I laughed. "You would have loved the technology. It was amazing. The doctor explained what he was going to do and I asked him how the laser beam could go through the cornea without damaging it. I still don't understand, but he said the beam doesn't affect any tissue that isn't being aimed at. It was like tacking the tear in my retina with the laser beam. The beam was a bright, evil green— rather chartreuse in color. There was a thumping in my eye, but no pain. He circled the tear with two rows of 'stitches' or 'welds'. My own ophthalmologist checked it yesterday and says it looks great. I still have a few floaters—tiny black dots—but they will eventually go away."

"Yes, I'd love to be in the medical field now with all the diagnostic tools and medical advances," Grace sighed. "On second thought, I wouldn't; there's not enough time to give to patients. We used to know our patients well because we bathed them, turned them, tucked them into bed at night. We even gave them massages. Of course the doctors treated us like dirt; but I think doctors give nurses more respect now. At least I hope so. How was your care at the hospital in Bend?"

"Wonderful. St. Charles is one of the top ten medical centers in the nation. Would you believe they have room service? You can eat anytime, day or night, by phoning the kitchen and ordering off the menu."

Carol sniffed. "I find that hard to believe."

"No. Really. I ordered a chocolate milkshake at midnight just to test the system."

Dee wanted to know if it was a good one. That made us laugh, but we still hadn't dealt with the Elephant in the Living Room.

Carol said, "You seem so depressed. That's not like you. I have some Prozac, if you want."

"I'm on enough drugs with my cancer; I don't need any more. I guess I don't handle grief very well."

"That's why you need a pill. I got these when Kenneth died. They really helped."

I just shook my head 'no'. Grace said, "I don't trust all the new pills they have now. The side effects are worse than the cure."

Dee jumped in with a recitation about arthritis drugs she and others are, or had, taken, and the side effects. We agreed that the fancy drugs advertised on television were part of our culture now, the computer-generated names as familiar at Coca Cola and Pepsi.

To my mind, the conversation was deteriorating; I wanted to leave, yet, there was that damned Elephant. "How do you handle grief? We've all lost loved ones. What's the proper way?"

Carol said, "I don't think there is a proper way. Everyone handles it differently. Some keen and wail; others internalize it. I knew Kenneth was dying for a long time, so it wasn't a shock; all the final arrangements had been made, so it was simple."

"Simple?" Grace said. "No death is simple." We waited for her to continue, but she sat quietly with her eyes closed.

"Dee timidly said, "Funerals always help. The minister's message, the music, the gathering afterwards."

"Yes, sharing helps," Grace murmured.

In an exasperated tone, Carol said, "This evening is a downer. I have better things to do that talk about death. See you later. Okay?" She left. The three of use exchanged glances. I could almost hear a collective sigh of relief. Carol may not have wanted to talk about grieving, but Grace and Dee did. I waited for one of them to set the tone.

CHAPTER TWENTY-FOUR

Grace spoke. "Val, would it help to talk about your grief?" I nodded and drained the last cold sip of tea from my cup. "I guess I don't deal with grief very well. When I was told of Jesse's death, I was very calm; there were arrangements to be made, people to call, sympathy to receive. I was a cool cucumber, shedding but a few tears in the privacy of my apartment. Twenty-four hours later, I went into shock—-nausea, chills, complete prostration.

"I was driving home when it hit; rather than drive any farther than necessary, I stopped at a friend's house. He nursed me through it. It was a hot, summer afternoon—-in the 90's; to have a major case of the chills, shaking uncontrollably, was very strange. He settled me on his couch, covered me with blankets and gave me hot tea. My teeth were chattering; I was shivering so hard that my body was sore the next day. He's a wonderful cook, but I couldn't eat. When we went out to breakfast the next day, he parked several blocks away from the restaurant and made me walk; I didn't think I could do it, but of course it was just what I needed to do to get my strength back.

"As for John, I feel a great sadness, but nothing as traumatic as I did with Jesse. I suppose that's because Jesse and I had been friends for more than twenty years; John and I were just getting acquainted. Guess I'll never understand the "why" of any sudden death, but I hate to put it down as nothing more than an unfortunate accident. No death should be diminished by a simplistic cliché."

Grace said, "We always want to know the reason for things, especially unreasonable events, and the ripples they cause. Like a rock thrown in a pond."

I don't think Grace meant that death was nothing more than a chucked rock, but suddenly I felt too exhausted to continue the philosophical exploration of grief and elephants. I retreated to my apartment.

After returning to The Villa, most of my time and energy was spent on preparing to leave. There were financial details to complete, a car to purchase, AAA maps and motel information to gather, and arrangements to close the apartment for six months. I'd leave about ten days later than planned, but the only commitment I had was the mid-October PTI Board meeting in Denver. When I heard the knock on my door, I'd just logged off after sending Kara e-mail about my proposed itinerary. The knock came again, urgently. It was Carol, hushed and flushed at the same time. Her color was high, her voice lower than normal. My intuition of impending disaster kicked in.

"I have some news," she hissed, pushing past me into the living room. "I hired a private detective and he's found my baby!"

"Well, how about that?" I said lamely. There was nothing to do but to play hostess since she was already in. "Coffee?" Making coffee was a great delaying tactic; I used it often.

"Please." She plopped down on the sofa, arms stretched out, her head resting back. "You just won't believe this!" She waited until I had the coffee maker going and sat across from her. When she was sure she had my complete attention, she began.

"It was rather difficult because of the age of the records, but the maternity home still had the information. It was boxed up and stored elsewhere, but they found materials. Once the detective found the basic information, he used various computer databases and traced my son to Los Angeles. His name is Leveret Flowers and he works in the main post office." She paused dramatically as if waiting for congratulations.

"Amazing, to find him, after all these years. You're sure he's the right one?"

"Oh, Val. You are such a skeptic. You don't trust anything or anyone."

"Guess that's the lot of a banker," I laughed. "Are you going to see him?"

"I plan to. The next step is to write to him; I think a phone call might be too much. Don't you? I'm sure he'll want to meet, but I'd like to give him the option. I'm working on the letter now; I'll get it in the mail today or tomorrow."

"Well. Good."

"You don't seem very happy for me."

"Of course I'm happy for you; I'm not sure I'd be willing to take the risk."

"Risk of what?" Carol demanded.

"He may not want to see you."

"Of course he will. I have information that's important for him—-his father's name, which will be the key to military records, which will allow him to find his lineage."

I couldn't hold my "pan of cold water" any longer. "Not everyone is a genealogy freak. Leave him alone. For fifty years he's been Leveret Flowers; you could be opening a bag of snakes for him."

"Pooh!"

"If you want to do something for him, put him in your will." As soon as I said that, I knew I'd gone too far.

"Damn you! You have no feeling, no romance, no sense of adventure."

I hadn't been "damned" for a long time, if ever. It sounded strange, archaic, almost humorous, but Carol's dramatic flare-up required a response. I took the easy way out. "Coffee's ready; still want some?"

"Hell, yes. You're not going to cheat me out of coffee as well as the joy of finding my son." Her mood swung from one extreme to the other. The glitter in her eyes, her manic animation unnerved me.

Taking the offered cup, she said, "You just don't understand how things were then, when he was conceived. You probably think of me as a stupid tramp. I wasn't. It was the liquor and my youth. Didn't you ever have a youthful indiscretion?"

My youthful indiscretions ranged from reading my brother's Hardy Boys books, to smoking in the girl's restroom at high school. I had no response to her "stupid tramp" remark. Denial wouldn't be believed. The alternative of saying I didn't care, seemed more cruel, so I said, "Tell me about it."

She sipped her coffee, considering my request. "I guess I can, since we're contemporaries. Dee and Grace would be appalled."

Carol crossed her legs, took a deep breath and began her story. "It happened while I was working for Kate McGinty, before I went on the road with the burlesque company. My high school boyfriend Buddy and his shipmate, Texas Washington, came into the bar when they were on Shore Leave. We were shocked to see each other, but it made me very happy. I agreed to meet him when I got off work. Kate warned me not to; they were pretty drunk. But I needed Buddy, to be held, to remember the good times we had before the war turned everything upside down. I don't remember much of the date, but I do remember waking up the next morning.

"Have you ever been so hung over that you didn't know if the retching sound you hear is you or someone else?"

I shook my head 'no' and sat quietly, waiting for her to continue.

"I heard the toilet flush and managed to get one eye open. There was Buddy coming out of the bathroom, naked, scratching his butt with one hand and rubbing his eyes with the other." She laughed, as if her story was nothing more than a narration of one of her novels. Buddy said something like 'Get up, Texas, we gotta get back to the ship.' It was then I felt a hot, heavy body next to me. I turned my head and there was this black back right in my face." She remained quiet. She seemed to be playing the scene in her head.

"I played possum, not wanting to see or hear what was happening. When Texas sat up in bed it bounced so hard I thought I'd vomit. They got dressed and left. I knew I never wanted to see Buddy or his friend, Texas, ever again. It would have been too embarrassing. We were so drunk that night; I really don't remember what happened, but I sure remember the morning after. Sick? I've never been so sick. The bed was spinning; I put one foot on the floor to stop it. Finally I just crawled to the bathroom and threw up. Of course I had to clean up the mess. I found three empty rum bottles; never liked rum since.

"After I cleaned up the mess, I took a bath; I had to go to work that afternoon. That old bathtub was so stained I could never get it looking clean. And the water just trickled out in a brownish stream." She shuddered. "You can see why I love going to the spa. I always feel so clean afterwards." She gave me a bright smile. "Well, you don't care about all that. It's funny that the black seed took hold and the white one didn't. I always thought that he'd grow up to be a famous scientist or something special, that there was a reason for Texas' baby, not

Buddy's to take hold. So what do I get? A postal worker. Isn't that ironic?"

Her laugh was inappropriate, down right weird. She continued her monologue. "Maybe I would have kept the baby, if it had been Buddy's. No. I wouldn't have. How could I have raised it?"

"You did the right thing."

"Didn't I though."

The flat statement filled the uncomfortable silence of the room. There wasn't much I could say or do for her. I'd said more than enough; the rest was up to her. "More coffee?"

"No. Thanks. Guess I'd better finish my letter to him. What a strange name: Leveret Flowers. He still has kin living in North Portland. The woman who took him worked in the Kaiser Shipyards during the war. Lots of blacks came west during World War II for those jobs. Women built the Victory ships—that's what they were called, Victory ships, for the war. She had a large family; guess she felt one more wouldn't hurt. In extended families, they took care of each other."

"Was he legally adopted or just given to the family"

"I'm not sure; no legal papers were found, just the birth record and the name and address of the Flowers family. The detective followed that line of information. One of the Flowers in North Portland remember something about a baby being taken by her Aunt; that's how we found his name, Leveret."

I took her cup and escorted her to the door. "Good luck, Carol."

"Luck has nothing to do with it." She quickly retreated her to apartment.

I wanted to give her one more warning, but it would have fallen on deaf ears. She was right about one thing. I never took risks, not until Jesse came along. Some risks are worth it. Maybe Carol's search would turn out well.

I returned to my task of getting things ready to leave. My mind drifted to the evening John and I sat in the Condon Hotel atrium and talked about life. We engaged in a philosophical game, taking turns to answer two questions. The first one was "What is currently in my life that I would like not to be there?" That was easy for me to answer. Illness and age was all around me; I didn't want anything to do with it. Yet, that was something I had to learn to accept. John agreed, but he wanted us to get past the obvious, to explore deeper issues. I'm not sure either one of us answered the question to our satisfaction, but it was the journey, not the conclusion that was intriguing.

The following day as we sat atop one of the Painted Hills watching the light change the colors of the rock formations, we explored the second question of our game:

"What is currently not in my life that I'd like to be there?" Again, we quickly got by the obvious answers of our dead friends and family, perfect health, our former positions of power. If I had posed the question to Carol at this time, the obvious answer would be her son.

Mentally, I continued exploring the question as I packed a suitcase with winter things and one with summer weight clothes. Perhaps what is missing from my life at this moment is feeling useful. I need to do something that will make a difference to at least one person, preferably many people. Just writing a check to a favorite charity is not enough. I need to find my niche helping others in a more direct way. What? How?

The pounding on my apartment door set me running to answer the summons. Jerking it open, Carol rushed in, sobbing and pushing me out of her way. "God damn it! I blew it! I shouldn't have called him at work."

"Carol, what's happened?" I shut the door quietly, as if to set an example for her behavior. She stormed around the apartment, loosing a string of profanity as good as any you'd hear on the wharf.

"I knew better. I should have just sent the letter, but I couldn't wait."

"Oh, oh."

"Yeah. Oh, oh." She flopped down on the sofa. "She hid her face in her hands; tears and verbal self-recrimination leaked between her fingers. I handed her a box of Kleenex. "Thanks." She mopped her eyes, blew her nose and took several more tissues, then sat back as if waiting for my verbal abuse. "Well? Aren't you going to say, 'I told you so'?"

I sat across from her. "Why did you change your mind about sending the letter you were working on?"

"In a hurry, I guess. Patience isn't one of my virtues, as if I had any."

"You're being way to hard on yourself. Tell me what happened."

"I got the LA Main Post Office number, called there, asked for Leveret Flowers, and, wouldn't you know it, they put me through. Any other time you make a call to the post office you get someone who doesn't speak English and can't operate a telephone. But, no, there he is, saying 'Leveret Flowers' just like, like...Shit."

"What did you say then?"

"At least I had the good sense not to say, 'This is your mother'!" She laughed derisively. "At first, I could hardly speak, hearing his voice. Then he said 'hello' or something because I didn't answer right away. I told him my name and said that I had information about his adoption. He said that I must have the wrong person because he wasn't adopted. By then, I'd come to my senses and pretended that I did have the wrong number."

"Well, then. No harm done."

"But what will he think when he gets my letter?"

"You're still going to send it?"

"Of course." She gave me a look that said my IQ was below 80. "I've gone too far to stop now. Anyway, detectives are expensive."

"That's a stupid reason to continue. Isn't this a wake-up call that you should give up the idea?"

She rose quickly and went to the small kitchen. "Do you have anything to drink?" She began to open cupboards.

I followed her into the kitchenette. "Carol. Stop right there. A drink is the last thing you need now. Think about what you're doing to yourself and to a man who has lived without knowing his birth circumstances, if, indeed, this is the right person."

She whirled on me, eyes bright, hands raised, as if she'd like to claw my face. All I could see were her rigid, curled fingers tipped in crimson enamel. I backed away. She dropped her pose, turned abruptly and left, slamming the door. I almost went after her, but my knees wouldn't cooperate.

CHAPTER TWENTY-FIVE

I t was all down hill for Carol from that day on. She made a point of avoiding the Scheherazades, particularly me, as if I'd wronged her. I assumed she was just embarrassed that she had shared her mistakes with me, as I couldn't imagine what I had done to make her anger so personal. There was no doubt now she had not only fallen off the wagon, but was being dragged by the horses.

I refused to listen to any of the gossip as the busybody network ramped up its communication stream throughout The Villa. I half expected to hear drums and see smoke signals in the hall. Since Dee was privy to several aspects of the rumor mill, she brought Grace and me various stories, opinions, guesses and suppositions. From those varied sources and speculations, we formed our own theory based on our intimate, if brief, association with Carol. We kept our council and hoped that she'd come to us for clarification and comfort, which we were eager to offer.

While all this was going on, The Villa management lowered the hammer on Grace, informing her that she would need to transfer to The Haven or other suitable facility by October 1. This action more-or-less accelerated Grace's plan to throw herself an early birthday party; it would be a farewell party as well. Dee and I made the arrangements as Grace envisioned the event. It would be in the Great Hall right after Sunday Brunch; there would be champagne, sparkling apple juice and a magnificent cake. The cake was to be "spectacular" according to Grace's instruction. "I don't want one of those grocery store bakeshop sheet cakes," she said with derision. So, I checked out several bakers who specialized in upscale wedding cakes, which cost a small fortune. Grace loved the idea, saying she couldn't take her money with her so she might as well spend it on the party.

In addition to the refreshments, Grace had me hire a hot air balloonist to take Dee for a ride. We agreed that it would be a tethered flight from the center of the circular driveway, with the option of a true flight, weather and Dee permitting. I let Mary Alice nee Ginger in on the secret and she jumped at the chance to fly with "Aunt Deidre".

The Villa management was extremely cooperative, handling facility logistics and communicating the invitation to all residents. Dee and I weren't shy about laying the guilt card on them for shoving Grace out the door and into The Haven. Whatever works to get things done right was our motto.

Planning the party and packing for my escape the following week lifted my spirits to the point where I almost felt as good as I did before Jesse died. I suppose part of my "high" came from addressing my grief, sharing it with friends, as well as having something positive and creative to do. It seemed as if planning the party was the first thing I'd done for someone else in a long time; I'd been much too self-absorbed the past year.

As for Carol, she was either highly visible in the bar, on the casino bus, or taking the manager to task for some real or imagined offense; at other times, she'd disappear into her room for days at a time. Once I saw her daughter-in-law leaving Carol's apartment; the look on her face did not bode well. The tale-bearers speculated that Carol had been asked to leave The Villa. Twice I tried to contact her by phone; I left a message suggesting that she come over for coffee. She did not return my calls.

The day of the party dawned clear and brisk, perfect flying weather, the balloonist informed me. Watching him and his assistant assemble the contraption was the hit of the morning for Villa residents. Some bundled up in warm coats to watch, while others crowded near the lobby windows or observed the activity from their south-side apartment windows and balconies. Dee couldn't believe that Grace had actually arranged for her to fly. "I'm terrified!" she told me. I assured her that it was safe and that Mary Alice would be with her. That seemed to make her feel better, and asked me to fly, too, but it made more sense for me to stay with Grace. "Should I invite Mabel to fly?" she asked. I told her it was a great idea.

Once again Dee's niece Mary Alice provided residents grist for their critique mill. The Goth look passé, she had developed one of her own. As one critic commented, "She looks like a cross between Paul Bunyon and Snoopy." With her green plaid shirt, wide red suspenders, jeans and Doc Martin boots, the new look was definitely Northwest Logger. However, the antique leather helmet and long white silk scarf added a jarring note. I told Grace the girl would probably turn out to be a high fashion designer.

Dee and Mabel weren't far behind making a fashion statement of their own with their flying costumes. Bundled up in layers of their warmest clothes, the result was Doughboy-Russian peasant chic. Dee had a mauve scarf tied securely under her chin, while Mabel sported a black felt cloche pulled low on her head. Spirits were high as the two waddled to the balloon with Mary Alice herding them with the enthusiasm of a cattle dog.

Climbing into the balloon basket wasn't easy for the old women. First, a step-stool was brought from the kitchen. Then Mary Alice had "Aunt Dedre" sit on the edge of the basket and hold onto the wires that attached to the inflated balloon, while she carefully lifted Dee's feet up and over. There was much giggling and a few whoops from Dee during the maneuver. On the other hand, Mabel was wide-eyed and silent. Small, flicking smiles and hands clasped in prayer when she was finally loaded was as animated as she got.

A great cheer went up as the balloon slowly rose to the end of the 300-foot tether. The three women waved and smiled. So far, so good, I thought. Tears filled Grace's eyes, whether from laughter or pain, I couldn't say, but it was as exciting for the earth-bound as it was for the passengers. We could see the balloon pilot pointing out things to the women, probably reassuring them that they were in safe hands. Every time he loosed the flames to heat the air, Dee and Mabel shrieked and laughed. The experience would either clear out sluggish arteries or cause a coronary, I mused.

The question now was to fly free or stay safely tethered. My money was on Mary Alice persuading her elders to "go for it." I won. The tether was released and off they floated to the cheers of the crowd below. Shielding their old eyes, the residents watched as two of their contemporaries floated away. Grace said to me in a low voice, "At least Mabel will be near to her God for awhile." We giggled like a couple of school girls and looked forward to Dee's report of the trip when they landed later this afternoon.

I wheeled Grace into the Great Room to see her spectacular cake. The confection looked like an unsteady stack of beautifully wrapped gifts in various rectangular and square shapes. Each section was wrapped in rolled fondant, complete with edible bows of the same frosting. Tinted in apricot, pistachio, and maple nut, the filling of each cake echoed the flavors; real chrysanthemums in a deep bronze color ringed the bottom tier.

"That is unbelievable!" she said, peering at the creation. "I wondered what I was getting for my $500. A fool and her money..." she laughed.

"It's okay?" I asked.

"Beautiful. Just what I wanted, even though I didn't know anything like that existed." I took several Polaroid photos of the cake and Grace. The manager took a photo of Grace and me with the cake.

An informal receiving line formed, moving past Grace, each wishing her Happy Birthday, and, those who knew, saying they were sorry to see her move to The Haven. While the guests were eager to taste the cake, many said it was a shame to cut it. Even though the blanket invitation to the residents said, "No gifts," many brought birthday cards or get-well card. One woman, who Grace did not know, handed her a chipped figurine that might have been a dog. "This is my good luck piece; I'd like you to have it." Grace was moved by the gesture and, after a mild protest that she shouldn't take it, she re-wrapped the tissue around it and placed it in the basket which was filling with greeting cards. "I didn't think people would do all this," she said. "I wanted to give them something without any..." Grace's voice cracked as she struggled to contain her emotions "Will you see that she gets the figurine back when I'm gone?" At the time, this seemed like a strange request, but I agreed.

I wondered if Carol would come to the party. I'd about given up hope, when she, Earl and several other Villa "party people" stopped by the champagne table before wishing Grace felicitations.

Carol ignored me, but bent down to give Grace a kiss on the cheek. "Happy Birthday, Grace, and many more. You look very pretty today."

"Thank you, Carol," Grace smiled, obviously pleased that all the Scheherazades were now part of the event. "I always feel very nice in this caftan, thanks to you." The group went to the refreshment table to admire the remains of the cake and the Polaroid photo of the creation before it was cut. Grace glanced up at me and smiled. She looked very tired and pale, but happy. Everyone agreed it was the best party ever held at The Villa. Even the management said so.

CHAPTER TWENTY-SIX

H elp me to the bathroom, will you, please?" Grace said, after we had watched the balloon become a dot in the sky. I maneuvered the wheelchair from Grace's patio to the bathroom, giving her privacy until she called me to help again. While waiting for her, I turned back her bedspread, fluffed the pillows, stacked newspapers and magazines. Dee and I had taken turns helping Grace for nearly a month now, stalling the inevitable move to The Haven where she could have more personal care for her deteriorating condition. We'd given up our plan to lobby the management; it was obvious that Grace must move soon; however, we resented Villa management pushing so hard.

As I helped Grace from the wheelchair onto her bed, she said, "This has tired me more than I thought it would. I hope they land safely; I wouldn't want a crash-landing on my conscience."

"I'm sure they'll be fine. Mary Alice can help Dee and Mabel carry out the pilot's instructions when they land. I know I was a bit skittish the first time I flew and felt the basket touch down; it almost tipped on its side."

I watched Grace carefully as I helped her prepare for a nap. It seemed to me she had been in a strange mood all day. Tense and distracted at times, she'd then be the life of the party, directing the cake cutting or the toasts to Dee's first flight. I did my best to reassure Grace that she was not the cause of Carol getting louder and sillier on the champagne with Earl and several other Villa party-people.

As I helped Grace remove the blue silk caftan and change into a clean nightgown, I noticed her thinness. The intimacy between us was unexpected; Dee had been Grace's usual helper when one of the healthcare staff wasn't there. For some strange reason, I felt honored that she would trust me to help her today. Perhaps this is why she asked me to stay rather than fly with Dee when the invitation was extended to join the balloon passengers.

I said, "I'm glad Dee invited Mabel to fly with her. That poor woman needs a friend. I swear she's alienated half the people at The Villa."

Grace's chuckle became a groan as she struggled to lie down in bed; I did what I could to assist, but as a nurse I'm next to useless. She painfully shifted her frail body in an effort to find a more comfortable position; the adult diapers crackled. "How about putting another pillow behind me? Ah, that's better. If you think I'm a nuisance now, wait until I ask you to do a couple of other things for me."

"You name it, I'll do it; anything you want," I said lightly. Later, when it was over, I'd replay the afternoon again and again. I filled her carafe with ice and water, adjusted the blinds and moved a chair bedside. "Shall I read to you or would you like a nap until the fliers come back?"

"First, get a bottle of champagne from the caterer; cake, too if you want more. I've had plenty. Then tell the caterer to clean up, and leave the bill at the front desk. And, over there on my desk, are letters to be mailed."

"Okay. I'll be back in a few minutes. I think everyone had a great time today. They really enjoyed seeing Dee's exciting adventure. I swear everyone here loves her. Take a nap while I'm gone, okay?" I looked closely at her—eyes closed, forehead wrinkled, as if concentrating on a weighty problem. Planning this party had taken a lot out of her, I thought, as I hurried out to run her errands.

Most of the Villa residents were gone from the Great Room where the cake and champagne had been served. The caterers were almost finished cleaning up the plastic champagne glasses, paper plates and other party debris. The balloon lift-off had been staged in the circular front driveway; it, too, was vacant, including the chase cars, which were staying in touch by radio with the balloon captain and passengers. The flight would last at least a couple of hours—probably more—if all went well with the winds. I wondered where Carol was, concerned about her drinking. Her moodiness the last couple of weeks had been disturbing. Perhaps I should have done more for her, but what? First her break-up with Jim, and then her son's refusal to meet her after she had found him, knocked her for a loop. She took two risks and both ended badly; but who am I to judge the action of other people? I take only calculated risks that I can live with.

It took me about twenty minutes to complete the errands and return with the champagne. Entering quietly into Graces apartment, I started to put the champagne in the refrigerator.

"I'm awake," she said, "Bring it in here. There are champagne flutes in the cupboard—left side. We'll have a glass together."

"You're a party-doll." I laughed as I moved things from her night stand to make room for the bottle and stemmed glasses.

"Yeah. I'm a wild gal," she smiled, her eyes still closed. She looked so vulnerable without her eyeglasses. "Hand me my specs, please, and pour us some bubbly."

I peeled the foil from the bottle top, untwisted the wire cage and rocked the cork gently until it popped. "Didn't spill a drop," I said, carefully filling the two glasses and handing her one.

"Sit with me for awhile. I need to tell you some things while Dee is gone."

"This sounds serious for a party day," I said, pulling a smile that didn't want to come naturally. We touched the delicate glasses and sipped the sparkling wine. I waited for Grace to speak.

"You've probably guessed that my hip isn't going to heal. But there's more to it than that," Grace said. "They found suspicious cells when the hip was pinned. After lots of tests, it was confirmed. Bone cancer—a rare kind; I chose not to do anything about it, other than stay as comfortable as possible."

A felt my breath escape with a strange, soft sound. My hand felt incapable of holding the glass, so I placed it on the nightstand. Grace seemed very calm, sipping her champagne with a steady hand, telling me these terrible things in a matter-of-fact voice.

"I've lived a good life, a full life. It's time to go before…things get worse."

I started to protest, but she stopped me with a hard look. "You've been through the cancer thing; you know all the steps—shock, denial, anger, acceptance. I went through all those stages very quickly; at my age, you don't have lots of time for each stage. Anger was the briefest; what do I have to be angry about? I've had a good, long life—a loving husband, good children, fine grandchildren, great-grandchildren. I made a difference in the world. I've had fun—still having fun," she smiled and lifted her empty glass at me.

"More?" I said in a voice that seemed too thin, too far away.

She held out her flute to a refill. "I need you to do something else." She paused, the silence of the room pressing in on me. "...if you will."

The word 'anything' came to mind, but I couldn't say it. I nodded. I sensed where this scene could go. A prickling sensation skimmed my scalp; I felt my blood pressure rise as surely as it did when I played a Bridge hand, doubled and vulnerable.

Grace gave me one of her wise woman looks—the master teacher, the healer. "There's a raspberry yogurt in the fridge." She smiled at me, reading me as much as I her. She continued. "The pills are in the nightstand."

My knees wouldn't lift me from the chair. I tried, really I did.

"I'm not going to ask you to do anything illegal. There's a copy of Oregon's Death With Dignity Act in the drawer. And my will. I have a letter from the doctor dated two months ago that I only had six weeks more."

"Why me?" I breathed.

Grace smiled and nodded. "Fair question." She took another sip of champagne. "I was going to ask Dee when the time came, but since hearing her story about her mother and how she felt about it..."

"I see." I thought back to the evening of Dee's tears, her avowal of wickedness. She'll always feel guilty, even though the odds are that she wasn't responsible for her mother's death.

"Pain, the kind I've been having lately, is..." She paused. "There's a thin line between being comfortable and becoming a Zombie. I want to stay in control..."

"Yes." What more could I say? That I understood? No one can truly know what another person is going through at a time like this. When I was diagnosed with breast cancer, I was afraid of the pain, too, but more than that, I was afraid of losing my dignity. Yet, I felt I needed to help her rethink her decision. "Isn't the law being challenged?"

She snorted, then said, "To hell with them. I'm still legal and so are you. I'd do it for you."

"But what of your family?"

"They'll understand."

"But…" She just looked at me. "Okay." What else could I say? Jesse and I had talked about helping each other die, if it ever came to that.

"I knew you'd understand. Now, get the yogurt before I get too far gone on the champagne," she said, giving me her charming chuckle.

Oh, how I'll miss that wry, wise sound. This time, my knees held me and I went into her tiny kitchen for the yogurt. Tears stung the back of my eyes. Could I do this? I knew Jesse would have done it for me; now I had no one to help me if my cancer came back and I wanted to take things into my own hands. What goes around, comes around; perhaps if I helped Grace, someone would help me if, when, I made the decision. I opened the tiny carton, took a teaspoon from the drawer and returned bedside.

I sat bedside, feeling all thumbs and quivery inside.

"I think raspberry is my favorite. What flavor would you choose?" Grace asked. The question was a complete surprise and I had to laugh. "Oh, let's see. Not yogurt. Ice cream. Chocolate. Or maybe Ben and Jerry's Cherry Garcia."

"Ah. The sophisticated palate," Grace sighed. "Now. If you'd just get the pills and empty the contents of each capsule into the yogurt; my old fingers aren't good for that. I also want to take a Dramamine now. Things go better if you take an anti-emetic first."

I opened the nightstand drawer and took out the pills; a DNR—Do Not Resuscitate—form on heavy, bright pink paper was under the drug bottles. I gave her the anti-nausea pill, watching her swallow it with difficulty. I understood now why the barbiturates had to be put in something easy to get down; they'd probably absorb faster that way, too.

She smiled, motioning to me. "Go ahead. Do it."

My hands were shaking as I set about my task, working slowly, careful not to lose a grain. "How do you know these will…"

"Do the trick? I've talked to my doctor; of course he tried to dissuade me. I didn't want to put him in a difficult situation, so I lied to him about doing it; but I think he knows I will. These little devils will work," she said gesturing towards the pile of capsules. "I've done a lot of reading about the final exit. I'm even a member of Compassionate Choices, so I feel confident about the pills and the process."

"How long will…?"

"A couple of hours; sorry it can't be quicker," She smiled at me.

"But…" I shrugged. "I hope you're right…if you're sure you want to do…this."

"I've never approved of suffering. You can call the doctor in a bit, if he doesn't call first; he checks with me every afternoon. His number is there, by the telephone. Dr. Sweet." She looked far away and was silent while I clumsily attended to my capsule opening, dumping the granules into the healthy treat. "I'll tell you something that may make this easier for you. What if you knew something about me that most people would condemn? Would it be easier if you knew I was a criminal?"

"You could never be a criminal."

"To my mind I wasn't and to the women I helped I wasn't; by law, I was." She watched me until I finished emptying the last capsule and stirred the pale pink potion—this now deadly brew that looked deliciously harmless.

"Tell me," I said, more as a stalling tactic than a great need to know her secret. I put the yogurt container on the nightstand, as far away as possible.

"As you know, I founded a birthing clinic in Billings. I saved the lives of many women and their babies. But as the women came back with the fourth, fifth, eighth, tenth pregnancies, and I saw their exhaustion, heard their pleas for help, for birth control, I could not, would not, turn them away. The first one was the hardest. She was eighteen years old and pregnant with her fifth child; she was a real breeder. When she came in just a few weeks along, worried that she was again pregnant—hoping that she wasn't…" Grace stopped talking for a moment, motioning for me to hand her the yogurt. I obeyed as if I didn't have a choice; she was making the decisions today. Taking a spoonful and savoring the taste, she said, "Bitter, but tolerable." She took another spoonful. I watched, fascinated.

"Her name was Gertrude. Married at fourteen; a life of cooking, washing, chopping wood, feeding the stock, everything ranch women did in those days. The babies came one after another. He regularly blackened her eyes." Grace ate another spoonful, then rested the carton on her chest before continuing.

"I did a pelvic on her, asking how the other children were, listening to her concern about not enough food for the kids, a husband that drank too much; well, you can guess the rest of her story—it's an old one. I thought to myself, 'It would be so simple to abort this fetus; she'd never know, never miss this one child.'" Grace brought the spoon and yogurt carton up to her mouth, and took another bite. "My problem was whether to ask her if she wanted to lose the baby or to keep it—how to ask her. So I said something like, 'Would you feel badly if you weren't pregnant?' She said she'd be happy to have anything else wrong with her than to be pregnant again. So I told her I didn't think she was expecting again, but that I needed to do a little cleaning up from the last baby. It was so simple. And she was so grateful...not to be...Of course she was back a year later, pregnant again; we brought that one to full term."

"She wasn't aware?"

"No. But as time passed and I felt more confident with my skills and in sounding the women out, explaining about birth control and other things that could be done, when they asked. But I never took patients I didn't know or hadn't treated before. That was the only way I could justify being an abortionist, although I had several patients who brought their teenage daughters to me. I know it was a fine line, even in my mind, but it was the best I could do to absolve myself."

"You're preaching to the choir," I said. "I've always been pro-choice. But we're not here to discuss politics this afternoon. Grace, I could call the doctor now and we could stop this."

"No." She ate two more quick bites. "I have no doubts about this. I want to be in control. You ought to understand that. You've told us how you like to be in control all the time."

"What about your daughter?"

"You know she's not been sound since her stroke; doubt if she'll know the difference. There's no one who will know or care all that much; the old are expected to die and when we hang around too long, well, it's as if we're taking more than our share of life."

"But your grandchildren, their kids?

"Not a problem. As I said, they expect the old to die."

"Is there anything I can say or do to change your mind?"

"No."

I nodded soberly. "I'll probably do the same thing when my time comes."

"There, you see?"

Tears that had been threatening, now ran freely down my face. I bowed my head and let them flow, unchecked as I heard her scraping out the last of the lethal concoction.

"Now. Let's have another glass of champagne; tell me about your trip."

"This doesn't seem like the time to…"

"Humor me. Make up a story. Rangoon? Paris? The Amazon? After all, we're the Scheherazades, the master storytellers." She sighed, deeply, raggedly.

"But you won't be able to hear the end of the story."

"That won't matter; I'll be free."

I tensed; my leg cramped. As I shifted in an attempt to release the knot in the calf, she said, "What?" frowning at me over her glasses, which had slipped down her nose.

"Leg cramp. And I have to go to the bathroom." I fled from the room, limping as the calf muscle knotted, the pain shooting down to my arch.

Returning I sat again, saying, "So, you want me to make up a story."

"It might help you to decide your future."

"You are truly a wise women, Grace Bonner."

"Here take my glass—and my glasses; give me your hand. Now dream for me."

I took her thin, cool hand; she returned my squeeze. "Well, let's see. I'll buy a van or SUV—a white one with all the whistles and bells—a tape deck, CD, heated seats, compass, altimeter."

Grace interrupted, saying softly, "A sunroof."

"Yes. A sunroof, too. I'll have them take the backseats out so I can sleep in the van if I want to. Get a thick foam pad, a sleeping bag and an ice chest."

"A lantern and a stove," she whispered.

"Of course. Heat and light." I listened to her breathing; it was slow and shallow. "Shall I call Dr. Sweet?"

"No. Trip. Tell me."

"I'll drive to Boston to see my family, but I'll go the long way, up through the Olympic Peninsula, then east through Idaho and Montana…"

"Stop in Billings. Visit my granddaughter. She knows you're coming. The letter you mailed today."

"The letter?" I hadn't looked at addresses on the stack of letters. Now I wish I had. Grace must have written to those she loved to say goodbye. I swallowed hard and continued. "Okay. I'll stop by to see your granddaughter and she can show me your old stomping grounds."

"Yes." Grace whispered.

"I'll take side roads and visit historical monuments. I'll have coffee in small cafes and talk to the locals. I'll go through national parks, see the bears." Panic began to set in. What if...I eased my hand from hers, and clumsily held my fingertips to her wrist, seeking a pulse.

"I'm still here," she said. "More trip."

I held her hand in both of mine now, letting tears run down my face once again. Speech became difficult. "Chicago. I'll find some great jazz clubs there and eat...whatever they eat in Chicago that's supposed to be good." My mind frantically tried to conger up a US map to get the route right, but couldn't. "Maybe I won't use a map—maybe I'll just keep heading east; my fancy car compass will keep me heading towards Boston and my family." I paused to look at her, to listen, alert for any discomfort. I'd sit here for as long as it took.

When the telephone rang, I leapt up, dropping Grace's hand. Guilt flooded my soul. I answered quickly, softly. "This is Val..."

"Dr. Sweet here. How's Grace?"

"I think you should come..." My voice sounded thin, panicky.

There was a pause. "Is today the day?"

"Yes," I whispered.

"How?

"I put, she asked me to put, the contents of the pills in yogurt."

"Did you put the plastic bag over her head?"

"Oh, God, No! I couldn't, she didn't ask..."

"She may experience convulsions; can you deal with those?"

"I don't know...Please come."

"Of course. I'll be there as soon as I can. You'll notice a change in her breathing; it'll become sonorous." Another pause; I could hear some papers or something rustling. "It'll take me at least thirty minutes. How's her breathing?"

"Okay. Fine. I don't know..."

"Stay with her. Her breath will become irregular until it ceases. Can you handle that?

"I think so. How long will it take?"

"An adequate dose should work in a couple of hours. Stay with her."

"I will."

The dial tone hummed in my ear.

CHAPTER TWENTY-SEVEN

According to Dee, Grace's funeral, which was held in a nearby community church, was perfect, from the flowers and the music, to the text, the eulogy, and family remembrances. Even the food afterwards met Dee's criteria for a fine funeral.

I was still numb from my part in Grace's death. No one questioned the events of that afternoon two weeks ago. After all, the doctor had been there when Grace died; hadn't I seen a change in Grace and called him? At least that's what Dee surmised, spreading the story. I was the hero of the event in others' eyes, but it was going to take me a long time to forgive myself, even though the justification of my act was beginning to soften the pain. I had to keep telling myself that I helped Grace; I did what she wanted. Still…

After my last Villa breakfast, I finished packing the overnight bag; my other suitcases—one full of cold weather gear, the other with things for warmer climes—were already in the car. I heard the snort of the moving van that was preparing to take Carol's belongings to San Francisco. As Dee and I had surmised, The Villa's management had asked her to leave because of complaints from other residents regarding her inappropriate behavior. No doubt Mabel had blown the whistle about the noise on the second floor; other residents were offended by Carol's behavior in the communal areas and on the bus to the casino, which she and Earl frequented. Funny—when men act up—it's simply a boys-will-be-boys thing, but when women don't meet the standards set by a generation, a place, or circumstance, she is unladylike, on the rag, or menopausal.

Dee heard that Carol didn't seem particularly upset about the management's request; it was a big joke to her, one she'd no doubt relay to her Bay Area friends. It seemed as if now that Kenneth was dead, and her son didn't believe he was adopted and had no interest in meeting her, Carol believed she had nothing more to lose. But she did have much to lose; if our friendship wasn't of value, her life certainly was.

Dee and I tried one last time to extend the hand of friendship and concern. Since she wouldn't return my phone calls, I wrote her a note expressing regret that she'd be leaving and wished her nothing but good things in her new venture. I found the torn pieces of the note outside my apartment door.

Even though Dee was sad at what was happening to Carol, she seemed relieved a member of our circle would no longer embarrass the Scheherazades and what we had built over the past six months. We grieved for the loss of what the four of us had for a brief time—companionship, laughter and tears, but I knew Dee would be fine; she was a survivor, continuing to find "lost sheep"—the lonely, the rejected, any needy soul who showed up on Dee's radar. She'd then give them genuine concern and true kindness whether it was listening carefully or giving hands-on support.

Mabel and Dee were often seen together since Grace's death and my announcement that I was going to be away for several months. Well, why not? They had their crafts and a strong sense of spirituality in common. That's more than most people have. Friendships are so tenuous, particularly at this stage of life's game.

Mabel was more than willing to be enfolded into Dee's world of love and understanding. And, perhaps, Mabel would help Dee in some way, although the cynic in me wondered how. It seemed to me that Dee didn't feel worthy of accepting love, only giving love and comfort since her mother's death. Whether her mother's demise was natural, assisted, or premeditated, was moot. Dee's overall goodness was worth more than what she might have done in a period of extreme stress.

I stepped out onto my balcony to see if Carol was there; I'd tried her apartment early in the day, but only the moving crew was there. I saw Carol standing beside The Villa's shuttle bus, which would take her to the airport; shading her eyes, looking up, she scanned the building as if to record a last impression of The Villa. I lifted my hand in farewell to this very sad, lonely woman housed inside the polished shell that encapsulated the once-famous writer. There was no response; I have no idea if she saw me or not.

"God be with you," a voice said from the adjoining balcony. Mabel was gazing down at the scene below, her hands clasped as if in prayer. She looked over to me and said, "And God go with you on your journey."

For some strange reason, a lump filled my throat. I managed to mumble "Thank you" before escaping back into my apartment. Even after all these months, that woman freaked me out.

I zipped up the overnight bag, closed the drapes, gave my apartment one last look and locked the door behind me wondering when, or if, I'd return.

My new Silver Forester—no gas-guzzling SUV or spacious van for camping across America—would be my space capsule for the journey to find myself. I tossed the small overnight bag into the trunk and slammed the lid.

"There you are," puffed Dee, hurrying up to me. "I tried to see Carol before she left, but I was too late. Are you packed?"

"I think so; I have my maps, books-on-tape, music CDs, that's all I need."

"I just knew you'd not remember important things," she said shoving a box lunch into my hands. "The sandwich is turkey, real turkey, not the deli stuff you hate. And chocolate chip cookies, and fruit. Here's a bag of Moose Munch to nibble on, and a Snapple, too."

"Oh, Dee. You are too good to me. Thank you." We'd said good-bye early in the day at breakfast, but I knew she'd find me for one last farewell.

Dee enveloped me in a motherly hug, then dabbed at a tear as I got into my car. "Do you have motel reservations?"

"One for tonight; I'll wing it the rest of the trip."

"Stop and rest often so you don't fall asleep at the wheel." Dee frowned, seemingly going through a mental checklist of safe travel.

"Don't worry about me. I'll take my time."

"You'll tell Grace's granddaughter 'hello' for me when you're there?"

"Of course. I'll probably spend a couple of days in Billings with her, seeing Grace's old stomping grounds."

"Where to then?"

Dee knew my plans, but seemed to want to hold on for a few minutes more. "Denver for a PTI Board meeting. After that, I'll take a leisurely drive east."

"You'll be with Kara and her family for Thanksgiving?"

"Yes. I'll stay until the snow sends me south. This kind of trip is new to me; I'll either love it or hate it."

"You'll drop me a postcard?"

"You bet. Here, let me give you Kara's address so you can drop me a line and tell me what's going on at The Villa." I scribbled the information on the back of one of my old business cards. "I'm having my mail forwarded to Kara's until December 31. Why don't you take the Internet class The Villa offers? We could e-mail each other then."

"I don't know. My mind isn't as sharp as it used to be."

"Your mind is fine. Goodbye, Dee. Thank you for being you."

"You come back, now. It'll be pretty dull here without you."

"I doubt that, but thank you, Dee. Stay well for me so I have a reason to return."

The steering wheel was warm from the pale October sun. In my rearview mirror I could see Dee waving as if I were a daughter going off to college. Well, that's what it felt like at the moment. A rush of freedom, a road trip, adventure, a blowing out of the mind and filling it with new scenes buoyed me. I drove over the narrow bridge spanning a creek on The Villa property; this trickle of water, and many others, would enter the Willamette River a half-mile down stream, then in to the Columbia River and, finally, to the sea. The short span was sheltered by maple trees now festooned in leaves of cinnamon and butterscotch, replacing their vivid summer green. The avenue of gaily-colored trees ended at the red brickwork walls that framed the entrance of The Villa compound. I stopped, as instructed by the red and white sign, waiting for my turn to enter the stream of traffic. The thought of leaving made me giddy, a silly smile spread across my face. If anyone had noticed me, I'm sure they would have thought 'There goes a demented senior citizen.'

My neck and shoulders tightened as I gripped the steering wheel, easing into the line of cars, unsure of my driving skills in heavy traffic after being without a car for nearly a year and my recent accident. But, as they say, it's like riding a bicycle; you never really forget how to drive. Confidence quickly returned as I took the exit north to Interstate 5 with its hell-bent mass of vehicles. The on-ramp swept me up and over another bridge, this one spanning the Willamette River. I thought of the many bridges I'd cross on my trip and decided to count them. I took the pencil stashed in the sun visor and made two hash marks on the cover of the map, which lay beside me on the passenger seat.

An exit to Interstate 205 pointed me north for several miles, then east over the Willamette River again. The span was high and wide, six lanes of steel and concrete arching over the silver river which once served as a major transport route to Oregon City, the true end of the Oregon Trail. Instead of the canoes and pole barges of the early settlers, today the waterway was dotted with small outboard motor boats with fishermen trying their luck for the fall run of Steelhead.

The arch hardly seemed like a true bridge, one with a definite beginning and end; it was simply part of the massive infrastructure that linked one area to another, one great city to another. Did it even have a name? All bridges need a name and a sign acknowledging the stream it crosses, I thought, even if the structure wasn't as impressive as the Golden Gate or quaint as an historic covered bridge. After all, these marvels of man's engineering to ease man's journey are as important as the Ancient's mythological aids of passage from the secular world to the divine, but I-205 could hardly compete with rainbows and the Milky Way as bridges between the terrestrial and the heavenly world. Still elated at my escape, I felt as if I was flying high as the river dropped away and the stream of traffic carried me to my future, whatever it was.

In a way, this interstate is my transition to a new life. This one— congested, but wide and smooth—would be in contrast to the others I'd use to reach my destination, be it career or friendship. At least my passage wouldn't be the sword-edged bridge of Islam, or the Cinvat bridge—no wider than a hair—that the Parsiism dead must cross to reach heaven. My bridges would be crossed one at a time; none would be burned. And, I'd not become spiritually stuck on one before finding my "ah ha."